Return to Effham Falls: Tales of Lost Souls

Moorhead Friends Writing Group

Moorhead Friends Writing Group

Cover Design & Wrap by Tiffany Fier

Edited by Robin Cain

Contents

INTRODUCTION 1
Keith Donohue

EFFHAM FALLS 3
Susette Quinn

THE BATTLE OF EFFHAM FALLS 5
William R. Bartlett

THE PAPER ROUTE FROM HELL 11
Neal Romriell

THE DISAPPEARANCE OF FRANK BALSAM 19
Kaye Maxx

SNICKER AND GIGGLE 29
Matthew R. Clark

HEART'S DESIRE PART TWO 47
T.J. Fier

THE STRANGER 57
Susette Quinn

THE NECROMANCER OF EFFHAM FALLS 77
Michael Pickell

LIGHTS OUT 85
Suzi Wieland

FAMILY SECRETS   101
Robert D. Moore, Jr.

LET ME DREAM IN A QUIET ROOM   107
Alexander Vayle

THE DIRGE   125
Daniel R. Haynes

THE SHOE   139
Chris Stenson

BROKEN WINGS   159
Sarah Adams

TALES FROM A SCHOOL BUS DRIVER   169
Barbara Bustamante

LOOSE CHANGE   175
Dan McKay

UNINVITED GUESTS   185
Sadie Mendenhall

VENGEFUL SOULS   199
Scott Dyson

MIDNIGHT CAFÉ   213
Tristan Belmont

Letter to our Readers   223

INTRODUCTION

Keith Donohue

NOTHING STIRS MY HEART so as the call and response of a pair of loons on a Minnesota lake. Or perhaps the high lonesome sound of a train bound for elsewhere. Or the beautiful music of the first snow falling on last spring's pastures. Anywhere there is that delicious joy of being alone with the natural world. Nature reminds us she is good for the soul.

You won't find such a bucolic pleasure in Effham Falls, thanks to the writing talents of the Moorhead Friends Writing Group. More like Moorhead Fiends, and more like a nightmare version of Northern Minnesota.

In the *Return to Effham Falls*, the small town is divided right down Main Street. On one side, life is good, normal, Minnesota Nice. On the other side, well, things might appear normal but are actually charged with the supernatural. The town itself sits above an abandoned mine, and far below is a maze of tunnels that lead you to the Well of Lost Souls, the place where souls go if they can't find their way home.

In these pages, you will find out what trouble lies just beneath your feet. What happens when you find a lost shoe or come across a ghost in a bookstore? Cryptids roam these pages. Stalkers, with bizarre family secrets. There are thieves and murdered grandparents, a school bus driver who ran off with a cocktail waitress, and a wonderful twist of a wonderful life. Necromancy, a tale of the forgotten Battle of Effham Falls, and a headbanger drummer who keeps time for the Vengeful Souls.

There's no place like a small town for indescribable horror, and apparently, no place like a small town for dedicated writers coming together to share their love of a good story, well told. The return to Effham Falls is like coming home, if home is a secretly twisted place.

If you are dark, twisted, and suitably ice-cold at heart, you'll love this book. If not, you'll just have to scream.

Keith Donohue is the author of six novels, most recently *The Girl in the Bog*.

EFFHAM FALLS

Susette Quinn

Secrets are impossible in a small town, or so we are
told.
But what if said town has skeletons of old?
Boarded up out of fear.
Misremembered and ne'er clear.
Amongst the mundane lives of average folk,
Things seem normal till intuition gives a poke.
The bookstore, the drug store, the cafe on Main
From an outsider's eye, all look rather plain.
Mysterious fables lurk beneath the city
And roam the streets with no pity.
Ghosts, ghouls, and trapped souls of the dead,
Who refuse to leave, even when led.
The stories remain, the people go on.
Silently wondering if they'll be the next one.
You'll ponder what they know, when you're looked
at sideways,
Always guessing and avoiding the gaze.
Effham Falls is a place where everyone knows
The good and the bad, and where everyone goes.
Like every small town its charm brings a smile.
So come for a visit and stay a while.
The extreme, the unknown, and the everyday
norm,
Its availability comes in every form.
Small towns have a way of opening doors,
But make sure you know what your cellar stores.

Born and raised in Wisconsin, SUE QUINN transplanted to North Dakota in the late 80's. She raised her two girls in Fargo and is proud to see them take wing on their own. She is a full-time bookkeeper and part-time bookseller. When not busy with her friends or traveling, she can be found writing or editing. She has published short stories in *Tales Of The Frozen North*, *Welcome To Effham Falls*, and *Tales From The Water's Edge*.

THE BATTLE OF EFFHAM FALLS

William R. Bartlett

SETH DAVIES SAT IN his rocker on the front porch and studied the mist rising from the river as it made its way through the woods. "Damnable fog." He lifted his pipe from the table where he'd left it the night before and pulled a tobacco pouch out of his coat pocket. Filling his pipe with a deft touch, he struck a match and puffed until several clouds of fragrant smoke drifted before his eyes.

The door to the house opened and closed behind him.

"Gram'pa? Ma says breakfast is nigh on to ready."

"Tell her I'll be along directly."

The boy turned, but Davies spoke again before the boy left.

"Wait a minute, Carl Herman. How many kids at school have any grandparents?"

"None I can recollect."

"So, I'm the last one?"

Carl Herman nodded.

"I don't know if I should feel honored or lonely. It's a sad thing to be the last."

"We don't talk much about our elders, but when we do, everybody says I should feel lucky."

"Do you? Feel lucky?"

The boy shrugged. "Sometimes. Others, maybe not so much."

"Ever wonder why I never told you about my time in the 2nd Minnesota, back during the war?"

"Only when the other fellas tell me what their granddads told them. That's one of the times I don't feel so lucky."

The old man smoothed his beard. "Sit down, then. You're ten years old now, and you've seen enough life that you should know what I went through. Maybe you'll feel more lucky when I'm finished."

Carl sat on the porch, his feet dangling off the edge while Davies struck another match.

"See that fog coming in off the river? That's what the smoke's like in battle, only it sinks to the ground where it stays and hides the dirt and short weeds. I guess it's heavier or something, I don't know. It just does."

The old man held the match to the bowl and puffed until the fragrant smoke drifted before his face.

"I was in Company B of the 2nd Minnesota Infantry with Captain Milo Gunderson in command. We had finished half of our breakfast, when he called us into line. The captain didn't do it, of course, just had his drummer boy sound the devil's tattoo, and we all knew what it meant. The company wasn't all that far from Chickamauga Creek, but the water was too muddy to drink.

"Anyway, everybody dropped their breakfast, got their muskets with their gear, and fell in. I was a number two man between Yngve Berger and Albert Tollefson, on the rear rank. Inside of two minutes, we and the rest of the brigade were marching down Reeds Road toward the ford in the creek. Berger even said we had a battery of twelve-pounder Napoleons at our rear, so they must have been expecting some stiff action.

"Turns out, Yngve was right. When Colonel Van Derveer deployed our regiment to the right, he put the battery to our left, between us and the 35th Ohio, on the far left. Some johnny cavalry tried to make us run, but they weren't anything to speak of and got run off by Ector's brigade.

"We hadn't been there long when we saw some men running toward us. By then, our whole brigade was lined up and ready for battle, artillery and all. My mouth got dry 'cause we didn't form unless we were going to see action, but these boys coming at us all wore blue. I reckon the secessionists had broken a brigade line back where we couldn't see it, and the survivors skedaddled toward us and safety."

Carl Herman shifted his position but kept his grandfather's face in view.

"Wasn't but a few minutes later, the johnnies marched up from the creek, already in line of battle. We fired a few volleys at them and forced them back. Everything just happens, you know. You fire, you reload, over and over. Too busy to think."

The youth glanced at the door, then back to his grandfather.

"You worried about getting your ma mad at you?"

"No. Um... Well, maybe a little."

"Never mind about her, boy. This is important, and you've got to listen. If you don't know, nobody will, and it shouldn't just be forgot. I'll make sure she knows you're late for a good reason." The old man coughed and spat. "They marched us to the creek to take the ford, but the secesh was waiting for us on the other side. They hit us with a good volley and the man in front of me went down. I didn't even think. I just stepped forward and took his place. We fired back, but that didn't hurt them. They hit us again and someone fell by my foot. Tollefson. Poor man. He went down without even a chance to call for help. Someone was yelling for Captain Gunderson, but I didn't have time to pay attention to that."

The boy studied the fog rising from the river, then turned his attention back to the old man.

"'Bout that time, something hit me on the side of my knee, and I went down. Hurt like blazes, too, and my kersey blues were getting soaked in a hurry, making my hands sticky. Berger fell right on top of me, the big oaf. I rolled over to give him what for, but half his neck was missing. Yngve never hurt anybody and would have given the shirt off his back before you even had a chance to ask. To see him like that, well, I couldn't help myself. I cried so much, I almost forgot about my knee."

Tears formed in the old man's eyes, but he blinked them away. "The boys retreated, and the johnnies marched over me, but didn't pay me any mind. I heard the Napoleons go off a minute later, most likely with either cannister or grape. Either way, the secesh fell back to the other side of the creek as the regiment came back." The old man fell silent for a moment. "Did you know the regimental musicians acted as stretcher bearers during a battle?"

"No, sir."

"They scooped me into a litter and put me in an ambulance, headed back to Chattanooga." He drew on his pipe, but the tobacco had already burned out, leaving only ash in the bowl. "Go on back inside, Carl Herman. Tell your ma I'll be in as soon as I clean my pipe."

The boy jumped up and disappeared through the door without a word.

Davies retrieved his pocketknife from his vest pocket and worked diligently at the bowl, loosening the hardened ash, but not gouging the wood. His wife had given him this pipe as a welcome home gift after the war. *Too bad she didn't live to see her daughter grow up and bless us with a grandson. They'd have made her proud.*

He put his hands on the rocking chair arms and pushed but couldn't get up. The pain in his chest had come again, burning his left arm and stealing his breath. The old man groaned, but no sound came out. Before he could gather himself for another shove, the stabbing in his chest struck one more time, sharper than ever before. He stared toward the fog, the sharp pain gone as suddenly as it arrived.

A familiar voice spoke in a soft, Norwegian lilt. "Seth, what took you so long?"

An old man no longer, he glanced down at his dark-blue, four-button sack coat and kersey blue trousers, then raised his eyes to the speaker. "Yngve? I've missed you. Haven't seen you since that one day, and not twenty-four hours goes by without some thought of you passing through my head."

Berger laughed. "You'd a seen me sooner if you hadn't dawdled."

The raucous, gravelly voice of Tollefson contrasted with the softness of Berger's. "Better get moving, Davies."

"Albert? You, too?"

"Who else? Anyway, you need to hurry. Captain Gunderson's been waiting for you and, as you well know, he doesn't have much patience."

Davies rose and reached to his right, then to his left. "Where's my musket?"

Tollefson and Berger glanced at one another and laughed, but Yngve spoke first. "In the stack on the company street, genius. Come down off that porch and join the rest of the regiment. Let's go."

With a small whoop, Seth jumped off the decking, landing lightly between his two friends. "Hey, remember that time..."

Their voices faded as the old man slumped, his arms hanging loosely at his sides, eyes open and fixed, staring at where his two friends had stood. The pipe grew colder as it lay on the table beside the rocker.

Born in Kansas City, Missouri, but reared in adjacent Kansas, WILLIAM R. BARTLETT (Bill) has been writing the "Word from Dad" feature in *KC Parent Magazine* for over fifteen years, has published a novel, *Nude, Light Housekeeping*, and has four short stories published in various anthologies. Following his retirement, Bill returned to the city of his birth where he lives with his Fayre and Gracious Wyffe of twenty-eight years, two grown, autistic sons, two dogs, and a rather pompous cat.

THE PAPER ROUTE FROM HELL

Neal Romriell

JEFFREY HATED MOST OF Effham Falls. The aging arcade wasn't too bad, and the antique store downtown was creepy, in a cool way. Everything else, however, was terrible, especially when compared to Tampa.

His parents had moved the family from Florida to Minnesota the previous year, and Jeffrey still hadn't forgiven them. In a big city, you could get away with all kinds of stuff. Nobody would recognize you in the sea of humanity. But here in Small Town, USA, everybody knew your face after about a week.

And they were always watching...

The real salt in the wound, however, was the paper route. His father didn't want him to turn out like the kids on MTV who were listening to Nirvana and smoking weed. Not that weed had ever been one of Jeffrey's vices. He was much more enamored by alcohol, but his father wanted to keep him out of trouble, and a job seemed to be his dad's solution.

Jeffrey had fought hard against it, swearing, and threatening to run away, all of which had worked for him in the past when he didn't want to do something. But not this time. His parents, Chad and Carol uncharacteristically put up a united front, and the only thing he earned from the tantrums was the loss of his Super Nintendo and VCR. After only a few days of being forced to read books or stare at the wall, he'd relented.

Having to deliver the Effham Falls Gazette each day meant Jeffrey needed a bike, so his dad had taken him to a bike shop in the neighboring town of Clover. The electric blue, ten speed that they went with had a lot more bells and whistles than Jeffrey expected, including a mount for his satchel and a push button bell for warning people you approached on the sidewalk.

Early on, the paper route had been a good thing– though not in a learning responsibility and work ethic way like his dad had hoped. No, the job provided Jeffrey with a way to case the houses on his route. And it only took a couple of weeks for it to turn profitable.

Labor Day weekend saw many of the families along his route leave town for the last time before the school year started in earnest. Fully half of the houses on 3rd Street alone were empty Saturday morning, and by Monday morning Jeffrey had broken into all of them.

His time in Tampa had taught him well. He wasn't greedy or stupid. He didn't try and steal TV's or jewelry. Sometimes he didn't steal anything. The thrill of breaking into someone else's safe space and creeping around was nearly as satisfying as finding money, or dirty pictures that couples believed would never be seen by another person. That weekend's take wasn't immense monetarily, but it was enough, and it got him into practice for the larger, more profitable homes that made up the tail end of his route.

The properties on 7th Street were older, nicer and, in the case of 4018, creepier. Jeffrey knew, based on some of the conversations he'd overheard at school, that several of the families who lived on 7th had been in Effham for years. Old families equaled old money, and with a little luck, Jeffrey suspected he could land a once-in-a-lifetime score.

Unfortunately, before he could make much more progress, the weather made a sharp change for the worse. Fourteen years in sunny Florida had not prepared Jeffrey for the early morning chill of fall, and the downright punishing cold when October turned into November.

Eventually, using his bike became impossible, and Jeffrey had to ask his father to get up early to drive him. This forced proximity to his dad became a fresh hell — for both of them, if his father's mood was any indication.

By December, Jeffrey had completely given up on breaking into any more homes until at least April. With his one true source of entertainment put very literally on ice, Jeffrey became grumpy and anxious. His hatred for Effham Falls and his parents festered like a puss-filled wound in his stomach.

Each day, getting up became more difficult. Jeffrey would slink out of bed, haphazardly throw on a couple of layers of clothing, rudely pound on his father's bedroom door until he heard a response, then trudge down the stairs to sit sullenly in wait for his dad.

He tried various methods to bring enjoyment to the route: throwing papers at windows, chucking them far off into a snowbank, hiding them in mailboxes. His sleep-deprived dad never seemed to notice, but all of these gave only small flashes of joy. Rolling down that final stretch of 7th Street was the most painful, especially during Christmas weekend when most of the homes sat dark and empty.

But the approach of the new year brought a surprise rise in temperatures and with it, an opportunity for Jeffrey to roll his bike out of the garage. Many members of the community were still vacationing in sunnier climes, likely oblivious to the warmer weather in Effham, and equally oblivious to the fact their homes were about to be broken into.

Jeffrey chose four homes to be his primary targets, based mostly on the look of the home and the type of car parked alongside or in front of them. He wanted to get them all done on the Saturday and Sunday that would mark the last two days of the year. In case any of the properties proved difficult to access, he chose a pair of less desirable locations as backups.

Electric anticipation coursed through him the night before his planned break-ins. Sleep came in fits as he dreamed of finding something so rare, so impressive, that he'd be able to scratch this particular law-breaking itch and move on to other ventures.

Saturday morning went exactly as planned. Jeffrey picked up his stack of Gazettes at the fire station, raced through his route as quickly as possible, and arrived on 7th Street before the sun had risen. The first house on his list was sparsely furnished, and his hopes for a successful score began to fade when the first floor yielded nothing of value.

The master bedroom on the second floor made up for the rest of the house. A mundane jewelry box stuffed into the back of a lingerie drawer was filled with gold and silver rings. Jeffrey didn't stop to puzzle why someone would have so many wedding bands, but he plucked two out and returned the box, satisfied with the score.

The second house Jeffrey targeted contained a wide selection of goods, forcing him to make some tough choices. In the end, he settled on a pair of diamond studded cufflinks. He wore a broad smile as he lazily peddled up the remainder of 7th, carelessly throwing papers at porches.

He reached into his pack to get the paper for his second to last house, 4018, when he hit a bump, pushing the bike towards the home's wrought iron fence. His front tire jammed in between two of the slats and he lurched forward, coming out of his seat when the bike began tipping. Thankfully, he got his feet down in time, averting a potential fall.

Not wanting to draw attention to himself, he quickly grabbed the paper out of his pack. As he cocked his arm to throw, a pale blue light in a second-story window caught his eye. It was probably a clock or some other electronic device, but for reasons he couldn't explain, the light caused gooseflesh to break out up and down his arms.

Jeffrey had found the home creepy since the first time he'd seen it. The gothic architecture, wildly overgrown rose bushes, and gawking stonework gnomes made the place stand out for all the wrong reasons. Creepy as it was, though, he felt drawn to it, like the proverbial moth to a flame. A house that strange had to have incredible treasures waiting inside.

The blue light winked out suddenly, and Jeffrey released the breath he'd been holding. He threw the paper over the fence and quickly got his bike moving forward. He raced down the street, forgetting to deliver the last paper, and turned towards his house. The sound of his heartbeat pounded in his ears as he struggled to catch his breath.

Jeffrey's nerves calmed once he was back in his own driveway, and he chided himself for getting so worked up. The 4018 house was empty and, despite its appearance, was just like all the other empty homes that weekend.

Sunday morning went completely opposite of the plan. Jeffrey overslept, his front tire was flat and, even after all that, he had to wait twenty minutes for copies of the Gazette to arrive. The headline said the Eagles had beaten the Lions, which didn't really matter to him, but there were plenty of sports nuts on his route, so he'd have to be a bit more careful with his throws.

All of this added up to him arriving on 7th Street as the horizon was turning a mix of orange and red. Breaking into two homes wasn't an option, and if he was only going to get into one, it was going to be 4018. He hastily delivered papers until he reached the mysterious house.

The shadowed faces of the stone gnomes loomed over him as he pedaled his bike around the edge of the fence. The rose bushes of the back lawn were gnarled and dense, and it took a moment to find a suitable spot to slip over the wrought iron. Snow crunched under his feet, making more noise than he would like, but before long he made it to the back door.

As had been the case with many of the homes in Effham, Jeffrey found a key hidden in a fake rock resting conspicuously next to the stoop. He gave the adjoining backyards a quick glance, then slipped the key into the lock and tiptoed inside.

Anticipation of stealing from the house changed to confusion as Jeffrey's eyes adjusted to the darkness. The back door entered directly into the kitchen — an empty kitchen. No stove, no refrigerator, no microwave or dishwasher. There were hookups or outlets for all of them, the appliances were just missing.

Jeffrey pulled out a small flashlight covered with red cloth to provide extra light as he ventured through the kitchen and into a living room. He assumed it was a living room but again, the place was empty of furniture, rugs, and anything else one would expect to find.

Despite a complete lack of evidence, the house felt lived in. Jeffrey couldn't explain it, he just sensed something. A smell perhaps? And regardless of appearances, he knew someone lived in 4018.

On the far side of the living area, a staircase led up to the second floor where, the previous day, Jeffrey had seen the blue light. Something was up there. He walked slowly towards the stairs, his footfalls echoing through the empty parlor.

The steps leading up were clean, like every other surface in the home. He tested the first step, found that it didn't creak, and continued up. His courage solidified as he ascended, the familiar rhythm of stealing returned, and he felt calm when he reached the second floor.

There were several doors, all of them closed, and Jeffrey examined the layout for a moment before choosing the room where he thought he'd seen the blue light. A quick turn of the knob, a gentle push, and the door opened, revealing the first furnished room he'd seen in all of 4018.

A short couch with a small table next to it sat facing the windows on the far side of the room. A tall, well-stocked bookcase took up much of the wall to Jeffrey's left. A pair of cushioned chairs were to his right. A trunk resembling a treasure chest from some pirate movie rested under one of the windows. A big, old antique-looking lock hung unlatched on the front of the trunk.

"Gotcha," Jeffrey said out loud, breaking the smothering silence. He strode confidently over to the chest, excitement building as he pondered the trove that might be stored within.

"It's rude to touch other people's things," someone behind Jeffrey said, the voice cold and low.

Jeffrey pivoted, freezing in fear from what he saw. Someone was sitting on the couch, their head turned away from him. Only a second earlier, when he'd passed by, the seat had been empty. It was as if the man — and Jeffrey somehow knew it was a man — had appeared out of thin air.

"Curious little Jeff, what would Chad and Carol think if they could see their boy now?" A hint of humor clung to the soft-spoken voice.

Jeffrey opened his mouth to answer but choked back the words as the man's head swung around. Where a face should have been there was a glowing blue void. The man stood, his slender frame becoming nearly translucent as the blue light grew brighter.

Panic gripped Jeffrey. He screamed as he ran for the door, praying he could get past the nightmarish entity. Shadowy, clawed fingers reached for Jeffrey. His shoulder went numb as soon as the claws touched him.

Jeffrey crashed through the door and, by some miracle, didn't trip as he went down the stairs two at a time. He sprinted across the empty living room when he heard laughter floating down from the second story. Several long strides later, he sucked in the cold morning air as the laughter grew louder behind him. He jumped the fence with a flawless leap and mounted his bike, feet slipping over the snow and ice as he pushed his way towards 7th Street. Bouncing onto the pavement, Jeffrey peddled hard. He didn't look back, even though the laughter followed him all the way home.

THUMP!

Chad looked up from the television. Anger creased his brow. He rubbed his temple, trying to push down the stress just like Dr. Cullen had taught him. He stood and let out a long, bitter sigh.

"Chad, baby, don't," Carol said, trying hard to mask the frustration in her voice.

"I have to check," he replied. Except he continued to stand while an entire car dealership commercial played out. Finally, he walked to the front door.

Chad's hand hovered over the knob for a long moment.

"Chad, honey, please." Carol's voice was weak now and Chad knew if he turned, he'd see tears running down her cheek. Despite his wife's protest, he opened the door and looked down.

In the fading September sun, a rolled-up copy of the Effham Falls Gazette sat on the porch. Chad could just make out the date, January 1st, 1996. The headline, if he could see it, would read LOCAL PAPERBOY MISSING.

From the direction of the street, Chad heard the ghostly ding of a bike bell, which always accompanied the arrival of the paper. Each and every evening for the last two years.

Chad picked up the paper as tears fell from his eyes and threw it back into the street. He slammed the door and returned to his chair, crying along with his wife as Wheel of Fortune played on the television.

Born and raised in Idaho, NEAL ROMRIELLI now lives with his wife on the East Coast. When he isn't writing, Neal enjoys playing *Dungeons & Dragons* and Co-Hosts the *Bad Movie Cold Cereal Party* on YouTube. Neal's debut novel *Site Alpha* came out in 2022 and has since added three short stories (including this one) to his published works. He's currently working on the sequel to *Site Alpha* as well as a fantasy series based on some of his *Dungeons & Dragons* characters.

THE DISAPPEARANCE OF FRANK BALSAM

Kaye Maxx

2001

ANOTHER FIGHT WITH KATH and here was Franklin "Frank" Balsam Jr. sitting at the bar nursing his now warm beer. His dad, Franklin Balsam Sr., refused to let him take over Balsam Lumber. Instead, he managed the front office, dealing with lumberjacks and truck drivers. Occasionally, he hauled a load of lumber to Superior. It wasn't fair.

"Can I get you a fresh one?" The waitress, Roxy DeLuze, asked. Was it his imagination or was she giving him a come-hither look?

"Sure, why not? Hey, what time do you get off?" he asked.

"With you?"

Frank nodded.

"Anytime you want." She winked at him.

Frank was still the picture of health. Roxy wouldn't be the first affair he had and might not be the last. He'd still be single if his father hadn't insisted he marry Kath after she got knocked up. Maybe his father was punishing him for his misspent youth.

Roxy pushed a cold Michelob in front of him. "We close at one, I'd love to get to know you better."

Frank agreed.

He sat in his Polo Green Metallic Corvette after closing until all the lights went dark in the Rusty Nail.

Roxy approached his car. "You want to follow me to the Wayside Motel. I'm staying there until I get settled in my new place."

"Right behind you." Frank wondered where he could park his flashy car so the whole town wouldn't see it. Luckily, when he arrived one of the pole lights was out in the lot and he parked in the dark recesses of the corner.

Roxy couldn't believe how easy it had been to lure Frank back to her hotel. The Amorous Allure hex bag she received from the old witch, Solveig, worked.

Once she'd met Frank, she wanted more. Frank was the kind of person who stood out in a crowd, not just because of his money but also due to his striking appearance. He was undeniably good-looking, with blond hair that caught the sunlight and dark blue eyes reminding her of the Effham Falls.

Roxy wasn't satisfied with the ten thousand dollars Franklin Sr. had given her to get his son out of town. No. She wanted it all: Frank, his inheritance, and that big house on Nudi Street overlooking the falls. She wondered if Solveig had a spell for that.

At Frank's knock on the door, Roxy checked her red lipstick in the mirror and answered enthusiastically.

Frank was in love! He had already filed for divorce and was going to marry Roxy as soon as possible.

Rox didn't want to rush into anything and said they should wait. Too late! He'd all but shouted his love from the top of Effham Falls. Ever since the night in her hotel room three weeks ago, Frank couldn't get enough of her. Her loon-black hair normally cascaded in loose waves down her back but was often tied up in a messy bun while she was working. Her piercing green eyes, framed by thick lashes, seemed to see right through him as if they knew exactly what he wanted. He once told her that he loved the hint of freckles across her nose. She informed him she had no freckles and then immediately powdered her nose. Yes, he was willing to give up all for gorgeous Roxy DeLuze.

Franklin "Lin" Balsam, Sr. sat behind his desk at Balsam Lumber, everything going according to plan. Roxy had gotten Frank to fall for her somehow, and he was even willing to divorce Kathy and leave town.

Lin needed Frank to leave town because the Contract would come due on June 6th of this year. If Lin Balsam didn't have an heir, the demon Aragorda wouldn't be able to collect his soul. The contract stipulated that Aragorda could only collect if the Balsam heir was willing to inherit at the time the contract was due. Since Frank Jr. knew nothing of the contract, let alone the dealings of Balsam Lumber or the estate, getting him out of town and having him sign away his inheritance to be with Roxy might be the best way to escape the clutches of Aragorda.

It was a loophole long shot but it was the best solution available. The deal had seemed like a good one at twenty-five when he had arranged everything, before he met Martha and before she gave birth to Frank, his only child. For fifty years, Balsam Lumber had prospered, pushing the competition out. Aside from the Widow Effham and a few others, he was the richest man in town. Lin couldn't help but smile.

Roxy pushed open the creaking door of Solveig's Cape Cod. The witch's abode was as eerie as she remembered, with shadows moving and the faint sound of whispering voices that had no source. A shiver ran across her skin. This was no time for fear—she had plans, and Solveig was the key to making them happen.

At a worn wooden table covered with candles, dried herbs, and strange artifacts, Solveig sat, her hunched figure wrapped in layers of tattered fabric. Her eyes, sharp and ancient, flicked up as Roxy entered. The witch smiled. "Back so soon, dearie?

The Hex of Amorous Allure worked perfectly. Ahh, but you're not satisfied."

Roxy walked farther into the room, her heels clicking on the old wooden floor. She glanced around before meeting Solveig's gaze. "It worked. Frank's completely taken with me. But I want more."

Solveig raised a silver eyebrow, her bony fingers tracing the rim of a blackened Dutch oven on her stove. "More, you say? What is it you desire, child?"

Roxy leaned in closer, her voice low and urgent. "I want everything. His fortune, that grand house on Nudi Street, and his name. I want it to be mine."

Solveig chuckled softly. "Ambitious, aren't we? Such desires come at a cost. Are you prepared to pay it?"

Roxy hesitated, her mind racing. But the image of herself living in luxury, with Frank completely in her thrall, was too tempting to resist. "I'll pay. Just tell me what I need to do."

Solveig's icy blue eyes gleamed as she gestured for Roxy to sit at the table. From a dusty shelf, she retrieved a small, black leather-bound book. The pages were yellowed, filled with symbols and words Roxy didn't understand. "There is a spell, but it is powerful—and irreversible. It will bind Frank to you completely. He and his fortune will be yours. But it will also bind you to something...darker. You must be sure, Roxy."

Roxy nodded, her determination unwavering. "I'm sure."

Solveig opened the book, the pages crackling as she turned them. "Very well. You will need to prepare a special hex bag, more powerful than the one I gave you before. This one must be made with a lock of Frank's hair, a drop of his blood, and the ashes of something he holds dear. Combine these with the herbs I will provide and recite the incantation at midnight under a full moon, and you must cast it at the Well of Lost Souls."

"Beneath the town?" Roxy asked.

Solveig nodded. "When the spell is cast, Frank will be yours. Mind, body, and soul."

Roxy took a deep breath, her pulse quickening. She knew there was no turning back now. "When is the next full moon?"

Solveig's smile widened, her eyes gleaming. "June sixth, six days from now. Prepare yourself and remember, this power you seek will come at a price."

Roxy swallowed hard but nodded again. She would pay any amount of money. Frank Balsam's life was about to become hers.

Roxy's heart pounded in her chest as she gathered the final items for the spell: a lock of Frank's hair taken from his comb; a vial containing a single drop of his blood, obtained with a careful prick of his finger while he slept; and a small box of ashes from his mother's urn. Each item was carefully placed into the hex bag Solveig had given her, alongside the enchanted herbs and a slip of parchment with the incantation written in Solveig's spidery handwriting.

The evening of the sixth arrived, cloaking Effham Falls in a thick fog that clung to the town like a shroud. Roxy slipped out of the Wayside Motel. She wore a long, dark cloak to conceal her identity as she made her way through the streets. The journey to Agnes Bagman's house was fraught with an eerie silence, broken only by the distant hoot of an owl.

Agnes's house stood at the edge of town, an old structure leaning precariously toward the forest. The locals whispered that Agnes was as old as the town itself, a witch who dabbled in the occult and had long since lost her mind. But Roxy knew Agnes was the only one who could grant her access to the old abandoned mine leading to the Well of Lost Souls where the spell had to be cast.

Roxy approached the house, her nerves on edge, and knocked on the weathered door. The sound echoed ominously, and after what felt like an eternity, the door creaked open.

Agnes stood there, frail and crooked as the house, her eyes gleaming with a knowing light. "I was told you would come. The path is ready for you. But heed this warning: once you enter the mine, there is no turning back. The Well demands a sacrifice, and you must pay the price."

Roxy swallowed hard. She couldn't back out now. She had come too far. "I understand. I'm ready."

Agnes stepped aside to allow her to pass. The inside of the house was just as unsettling as the outside, filled with strange symbols carved into the walls and the pungent smell of burning sage. Agnes led Roxy downstairs into the basement to the corner of the room. With a creak, she opened a door and then disappeared into darkness. "Follow the tunnel down until you arrive at the Well of Lost Souls. It lies deep within. Perform the ritual exactly as the witch instructed, and you will have everything you desire."

Roxy nodded, steeling herself for what was to come. She descended the stairs, the darkness swallowing her when the door closed behind her. The air grew colder and damper as she ventured deeper into the earth, the weight of the hex bag a constant reminder of what she was about to do.

When she finally reached the end of the tunnel, the Well of Lost Souls loomed before her, a deep, foreboding pit pulsing with an energy all its own. The air was filled with the sound of whispering, each one echoing the despair of the souls trapped within.

Roxy took a deep breath, pulling the parchment from the hex bag. She held the paper close to her face, the dim light barely illuminating the words. Her hands trembled as she recited the incantation, her voice steady despite the fear gnawing at her insides.

When she finished, the well glowed with an eerie light, the whispers growing louder. The bag grew warm in her hand, and she tossed the contents into the well.

The ground beneath her feet trembled. Roxy staggered, struggling to keep her balance as the well glowed once more, but this time the light was a deep, blood-red.

From the depths of the well, a figure slowly emerged. Roxy's heart pounded as she stood transfixed and terrified. The figure stepped into the light, revealing itself to be a woman. Her fiery red hair cascaded down her back like a waterfall of blood. Her eyes blazed with an intensity that burned straight through Roxy's soul. She was dressed in dark, flowing robes that shifted and shimmered like smoke, and her skin was as pale as moonlight. "Behold, I am Aragorda! Why have you disturbed me?"

"I've come to cast a spell," Roxy stammered.

"And you understand the price of your wish is your soul?"

Roxy hadn't been told that, but she nodded anyway.

"What do you desire?"

"I want Frank Balsam, Sr. to die so his son inherits everything."

"Hmm. Your request serves me well. I'm due to collect his soul this very eve. Let's make this simple, shall we?" Aragorda snapped her fingers and Lin Balsam appeared.

"What am I..." Lin shook his head, trying to make sense of what had happened, then his gaze focused on Roxy. "You!"

Aragorda laughed. "It seems as if all benefit from your demise."

No...I'm not ready..." Lin sputtered.

Aragorda waved him off. "Your wish is of no consequence. You and I made a pact."

"What if I gave you my son's soul in addition to my own?"

Roxy wanted to speak up but was frozen. If Frank lost his soul, would she keep her own?

Aragorda looked at her as if the demoness could read her mind. "Do not worry. I can still collect your soul as well."

"What's going on here?"

Dammit. Frank had followed her.

Aragorda smiled a slow, predatory grin, sending a chill down Roxy's spine. "Aah, the soul in question."

Frank grabbed her arm. "Rox, come with me. Let's get out of here."

Roxy shook him off. "No, Frank. Things must be settled."

Lin and Roxy turned to face Aragorda.

"Very well. Let us have a look at this soul you are willing to trade for...what? Thirty-three years?

Lin nodded.

Roxy finally spoke up. "Another thirty-three years with him alive?" She pointed accusingly at Lin Balsam. "That's not fair to me."

"Fair! You were supposed to get my son out of town. You have yet to live up to your bargain," Lin answered.

"Enough!" Aragorda shouted.

Once everyone focused on her again, she waved her hand, and Frank Jr. was suspended above the well. His body glowed an eerie red before a blue light cast him upward.

Aragorda pulled her hand back as if she'd been burned. "What are you trying to do? This soul has been sold already!"

"What?" Roxy and Lin answered in unison.

Aragorda advanced on Lin.

"I didn't know," was all he said.

1975

Martha Balsam sat in the front pew of St. Barbara's Church waiting for Father O'Malley, the new priest.

"Good morning, Mrs. Balsam."

Martha turned around. "Hello, Agnes. I didn't know you worshiped here."

"I don't, but I sensed you needed help." Agnes nodded at the cross in front.

"I'm waiting for Father O'Malley." She wasn't about to involve one of the town's rumored witches.

"The young priest cannot grant your son's soul salvation. It interferes with his plan of free will." Agnes pointed upward.

Martha needed to save Frankie's soul. She knew her husband had made some sort of deal with the devil. "How can you help?"

"I can buy and keep young Frank's soul until he dies. I'll bind it to the object of your choosing," Agnes explained.

"I'm sorry to keep you waiting. How can I help?"

Both women looked up when Father O'Malley approached.

"It's alright, Father. We were just praying," Agnes answered.

Father gave Agnes a quizzical look. "Oh?"

"Yes!" Martha blurted. "Frankie has been sick."

"I'm sure it's nothing serious. There seems to be a cold going around," Father O'Malley said before having a seat and saying a prayer for Frankie's health.

Martha and Agnes left the church together and, outside, Martha handed Agnes her mother's Rosary beads. "Do it."

2001

"Sorry, but a sold soul is null and voids a new contract for you." Aragorda snapped her fingers and in a flash, Lin disappeared.

"Where'd he go?" Roxy asked.

"He's in his office about to have a heart attack in five minutes, precisely 6:06 p.m. I'm a stickler for details." She winked at Roxy.

The cave was silent as they waited.

Aragorda broke the news Roxy longed to hear. "There! He is dead. Now our bargain is complete as well."

Roxy was relieved the following morning when Frank remembered nothing.

The entire town showed up for Frank Balsam, Sr.'s funeral. Whether they came to show respect or ensure the bastard was dead, who knew?

Kathy watched as Frank and Roxy sat in the front pew with her son, Sam. Frank would be taking Sam with them to look at houses in Minnetonka. The divorce would be finalized in a few weeks, and Frank wanted a fresh start. He had even sold his shares in Balsam Lumber, leaving the company's fate in the board's hands. As part of the settlement, Kathy would receive the large house on Nudi Street. She was happy to receive it. Martha had loved that house. Kathy had always liked her mother-in-law and often thought she was the best part of marrying Frank. She wasn't sure what she would do for money, maybe take up writing again. She had an idea for a mystery book.

Kathy was lost in her thoughts as she left St. Barbara's Church.

Agnes Bagman approached, clutching something in her hand. She pressed the object into Kathy's hand. "Here..."

"What?"

"Martha wanted you to have them," Agnes insisted.

Kathy stared at Martha Balsam's rosary beads.

"But I'm not Catholic," Kathy insisted.

"Doesn't matter. They'll be safe with you."

Kathy muttered an awkward "Thanks," but the woman was already gone.

KAYE MAXX is a pseudonym of a seasoned romance author Tina Holland. Kaye delves into the mysterious and magical, weaving tales that combine intrigue, charm, and a touch of the supernatural. To find out more about Tina, check out her website, www.tinaholland.com

SNICKER AND GIGGLE

Matthew R. Clark

I snicker and giggle while he weeps
my voice a riddle that haunts his sleep
I watch over his grave both day and night
Find my name, and share his plight

NATHAN READ THE SCROLL out loud as if trying to conjure its meaning with his words alone. But then the bell rang, breaking the trance the riddle held over him. He tore his gaze away from the laminated piece of paper and locked on to the frail old man gathering each piece of Effham's history in his wrinkly fingers.

With reluctance, Nathan handed over the riddle, feeling a strange sense of dread as he let go of the parchment. "Do you mind if I copy this down, Mr. Hahn?"

"Go right ahead. Just hand it back to me before you leave."

Professor Hahn placed all the papers in his leather case. "I hope you all learned something interesting about our town. Tomorrow, we'll look more into Mr. Cullen and the Cullen mines."

Just as he was about to get up from his desk, Nathan felt a tap on his shoulder, hot breath on his cheek. "Vick wants to know if you're down to hang out tonight. She's willing to pick you up."

He glanced at Harper, her eyebrows arched high, expecting his answer. "Who's all coming?"

Harper shrugged. "Vicky, me, Collin, Brendan, June, and you. She said there's a chance of Camron showing up."

Nathan grunted in disgust. "How are any of you friends with that bum? The dude's an asshole."

She stifled a giggle, cheeks puffing with amusement. "What?"

"He says the same thing about you."

Nathan let out a sigh as he slid his notebook into his backpack. "Sure. I got nothing better to do tonight." He got up, handed the riddle back to Mr. Hahn, and left the classroom.

That night, he waited for Vick on the corner of Serpent's Lane and Thirty-first Street. He sat on a worn-out bench, arms outstretched, when his fingers scratched something on the back of his seat. It was an old metal plaque. He couldn't make out the inscription or the face etched into it, time completely hiding the secrets it held. On the other side of the street loomed an old building, lost and forgotten to time. He had heard it used to be the old location of the Rusty Nail Bar and Grill.

He flipped open his phone, the white light bright in the dark four-way stop. The screen displayed the riddle he had read in class. He read it over and over. He felt as if the solution was on the tip of his tongue, but he had not the slightest idea what the riddle even meant.

He heard footsteps somewhere in the shadows, heels clacking on cement. A buzz came from the lamp that illuminated the corner. It flickered once, twice, then went out.

"Oh, no," someone said from the darkness, followed by a giggle.

Nathan froze, his sweat turning into ice. He took out his lighter and flicked it on. The flame exploded out, engulfing the area in an orange dancing light. He scrambled up, dropping the Zippo on the asphalt. "What the hell?"

The high pitch honking of Vick's car brought him back to reality. The streetlamp was still glowing, but the flames he had seen were gone like a whisper. He scurried to her car, opening the passenger side door in a panic.

Vicky stared at him, her green eyes wide with amusement. "You scared of the dark, Madison?" Her teeth gleamed in the cab light, her fiery red hair eerily like the fires that were on the corner.

Nathan slinked into the seat and buckled up. "No, I just thought I saw something."

Her vehicle made a high pitch squeal as they drove down the road. "Harper said you seemed pissed off in class. Are you alright?"

"I'm fine." The riddle replayed in his thoughts. "Snicker and giggle." His mouth formed around the words as if they were a chant to unlock some great mystery.

"Nathan?"

He looked at Vicky but didn't see her, his thoughts a whirlwind of questions without an answer in sight. "Yeah, I'm good. I just have this riddle stuck in my head."

"What riddle?" she asked.

"The snicker and giggle one. Did you take regional history?"

"No. I took enough AP classes in high school. I didn't need extra electives. What's the riddle?"

Nathan opened his phone and recited the line. "'I snicker and giggle while he weeps. My voice a riddle that haunts his sleep. I watch over his grave both day and night. Find my name and share his plight.'"

"Spooky," she said with a sigh. "That's a riddle? What was the question?"

"I think the writer's name. Whoever wrote it wants us to find out who they are."

"Who gives a shit what their name is? The person sounds unhinged."

"Yeah. It seems weird but, I don't know, I'm just fascinated by it."

"Why?"

"When I was a kid, my mom would always give me riddles to figure out."

"Are you close with your mom?"

He nodded. "She had to go through a lot trying to raise me. After my dad died, she had to hold down two jobs. She would work all day and night. I didn't see her much, but whatever she was doing, she made enough for us to get by."

"She never told you what she was doing for work?"

Nathan shifted in his seat. "No. She didn't like to talk about it. I have a rough idea, though."

Vicky raised an eyebrow, on her lips a knowing frown. "People have to do what they can to get by."

He didn't like to think about it. He looked out the window, watching the streetlights flash by in a rhythmic blur. They turned off Serpents Lane and onto Sixty-Seventh Street when the car decelerated.

"Damn it." Vicky hissed when the car jerked slightly, and steam billowed up from the hood in thick plumes. "Not again." She got out of the car and unlatched the hood, getting engulfed with hot vapor.

Nathan stood beside her, the heat causing his face to sweat. "Do you know someone we can call?"

"No. I'll ring my dad in the morning. He'll get it towed to Mike's or something."

"What are we going to do?"

"You never walked before?"

"Where are we walking?"

"To the old Cullen place." She popped the trunk and shoved bottles into her backpack. Every time she moved he could hear the muffled clinking of the glass bottles in her bag.

The pair walked up the deserted street, their footsteps echoing in the silence. The yellow light of the streetlamps dimly lit their path and cast long shadows along the asphalt, their forms traveling with gawking proportions.

"What are we going to do up there?"

She shook the bookbag from side to side on her back. "You don't hear that sloshing? We're going to party."

"If Harper and them are already up there, why can't she pick us up?"

"Why? Are you sure you're not scared of the dark?" She flashed a smile at him, her teeth gleaming in the street's light lamps. "You got me all to yourself and you want to cut it short?"

"You're so fucking full of yourself." Nathan pulled a cigarette from the pack in his jacket pocket but couldn't find his Zippo. He thought of the flames that had sprouted from it and remembered that he left it on the corner. "You got a light?"

Vicky pulled a clear purple lighter from her jacket.

"Thanks." He lit the cigarette and took a drag, gray smoke shooting from his nostrils. "What year did you graduate from high school?"

"2002." She took back her lighter. "You?"

"Last year. 2004. Did you go to Effham High?"

Vicky tilted her head. "I went to St. Barbara's, the catholic school for girls. Fun times." She leaned into him as they walked. "So, do you like older girls?"

Nathan shook his head. "Nope."

She shoved him, laughing. "Asshole."

After half an hour of talking and flirting, they arrived at the broken gates of Cullen Manor. The grand estate loomed ahead, a grotesque silhouette backdropped by the moonless night. Nathan couldn't make out much, but from what he could see, the mansion was decaying. Window frames filled with jagged glass teeth, patches of collapsed roof exposing rotted wooden beams.

"This is the Cullen Manor?" Nathan asked.

"Yup. In all its faded glory. There are some old pictures of this area. It used to look nice. Someone tried to buy it and restore it, but they ran into some problems. Sold the property to the town and left."

"What problems?"

Vicky grinned while adjusting the bag straps. "The place is haunted. The guy got scared and left after only a few weeks. I heard he sunk a lot of money into it too." She sauntered up the cobble driveway, her thumbs tugging on the buckles of her backpack.

Nathan slowly followed where, up ahead, the reflections of brake lights from two indiscriminately parked cars gave a red glow to a vast overgrown yard. "I guess everyone else is here."

"Looks like it," Vicky replied. She inspected the two cars. "Brendan's and Harper's cars. I assume Camron isn't coming."

"Where are they? Are they inside?"

"Yeah, Harper bought an Ouija board and we're gonna play a drinking game with it. They're probably setting up."

A pang of dread spread across Nathan's chest as they both stepped onto the crumbling staircase. The wrap-around terrace, elegance long gone, was littered with empty beer cans and trash. An old sofa sat on one side of the porch, used condoms and wrappers scattered over it. Graffiti covered the brick walls and rotting banisters; layers of scrawled names, crude art, and messages like, "Hell House," "Call Boone for a good time" and "No Cops Allowed."

Nathan pulled a cigarette from the pack. "You party here a lot?"

"No." Vicky leaned over and lit it for him, the small orange flame illuminating the paint on the walls. "The parties they throw up here turn a little wild. I only like to come with people I know." She smiled at him. "So don't get any ideas about the couch."

"You're joking? That's disgusting."

"Well?" Her red eyebrows raised expectantly. "Aren't you going to open the door for me?"

Nathan scoffed and brushed her aside to get to the entrance. It looked sturdy, even after all this time. Deep gouges and scratches crisscrossed the surface, hundreds of names and 'we wuz here' etched into the wood. When he grabbed the brass handle, he saw something: a familiar pair of words crudely carved into the doorway. "Vick, let me see your lighter."

In the orange light, his eyes focused on the grooves. "Snicker and Giggle." His breath caught in his throat as he ran his fingers along the carving.

Vicky stood beside him, eyeing the markings. "That dumb riddle? Someone carved it into the door?"

"Yeah, but it's worded differently." He turned the little switch on the lighter and the flame grew, orange light illuminating the riddle entirely. "'I snicker and giggle while you sleep, my voice soothing, as your heart beats, I watch over you from afar. Guess my name and we'll explore this thing of ours.'"

"Aw. It's a love poem. That's sweet."

Nathan sighed. "It would make sense that someone else read the riddle and had used it to get laid." He couldn't help but feel a little disappointed, but he couldn't explain why. It was the mystery of it that intrigued him. Who was the person the author was tormenting? Why was the author doing it? What was their name?

Confounded, he opened the front door. The receiving room was vast. The shattered windows allowed the moonlight to flow in, giving the place a haunting atmosphere. He expected to see nothing but dust and cobwebs, but he found trash and beer cans as well. The hardwood floors were rotted and jutting up. Someone had piled blankets and pillows in a corner of the room. Folding chairs sat in a circle. Beside them, plastic bags filled with cups and beer.

Nathan took a drag of his cigarette. "Where is everyone?"

"I don't know. I just got here too, Dumb-Dumb."

A few seconds later, a beam of light followed by grunting noises came from one of the many backrooms of the manor. Nathan and Vicky started for the door when they heard Harper's voice.

"You two suck."

"It's heavy."

A strained voice. Nathan couldn't distinguish if it was Brendan or Collin.

"You lift it then, bitch."

That was Collin, Nathan knew. Collin had no qualms about calling Harper that, even if she was his girlfriend.

"You go to the gym all the time and you can't lift a table?"

"It looks really heavy, Harper," June said in a meek voice.

White light engulfed the room Nathan and Vicky stood in and June's frail silhouette came into view. "About time you two got here."

"What's up, June?" Vick said as she shrugged off her backpack. "Camron didn't want to come out tonight?"

"He said he already had plans with Steph. They're going to see a movie or something."

Harper came running in. "Nathan, get in there and help them move the table."

Collin and Brendan were carrying a seamlessly carved table made from a single stone, black and smooth, coated with a thick layer of dust. It weighed a ton and the three of them could barely move it.

"Where did you find this thing?" Nathan grunted as the three of them dragged the table across the wooden floor and into the receiving room.

"It was in the room in the back. Lots of eerie stuff over there." Brendan wiped sweat from his forehead. "Someone burned the wooden one we were going to use."

June took out a disinfecting wipe from her backpack and wiped down the table. They could now see the glossy finish, reflecting the light of the flashlights like a mirror.

"I wonder if it's worth anything?" Collin asked.

"Anything worth anything is long gone," Vicky replied. "Squatters and thieves probably took most of it."

"True, but it wouldn't hurt to look around." Collin skulked around the house while the rest of them set up the game board and lit a few candles.

After gathering around the large stone table and setting out the Ouija board, the six of them sat and played.

Brendan lightly placed his fingers on the flat piece of wood. "What should we ask first?"

Harper placed her fingers beside his. "How about if somebody is here? Isn't that how this shit works?"

Everyone got into their places around the board and placed hands on the planchet.

"Is anyone here?" June asked, and the pointer moved. It slid up the board and landed on No.

"No?" Vicky laughed. "What the hell? Is someone outside?"

The planchet shifted to Yes, and they all stared at it for a long time.

"Who's outside?" Vicky asked.

The planchet moved to C, then to U, doubling at L.

Vicky let out a chuckle. "Oh, I know."

It moved to E, and finally N.

"Cullen? The guy who built this place?" Harper asked.

"He's outside?" Collin said.

The planchet relocated to Yes.

"Where is he outside?" Brendan asked.

The planchet moved to I, N, G, R, A, V, and finally E.

"In a grave? There's a grave outside?" Harper asked.

Vicky sighed. "Yeah, an old headstone is out there."

Harper laughed. "So, you're the one moving it? I didn't know a cemetery was up here."

Vicky stifled a laugh. "I'm not moving it. It's the ghost. Swear."

"No." Collin wagged his finger. "You got caught. Drink."

Vicky sighed and drank a couple swallows of her vodka. She let out a shiver, and Nathan could see goosebumps appear on her arm. But as the others watched her take another few gulps, Nathan noticed the planchet move on its own. It shifted to N, A, T, H, A, and ultimately N.

"Did you guys see that?" he asked, eyes refusing to leave the board.

"See what?" Harper looked down at it. "What am I supposed to be looking at?"

"It moved. It moved by itself."

"Bullshit, dude," Collin said. "You drink for that."

"What?"

"You got caught moving it. Now you drink."

Nathan held up his hands as if in defense. "I didn't move it."

"Guys." June cut in. "Look."

The group gazed down at the stone table where the Ouija board sat. The planchet moved to S, N, I, C, K, E, and to R.

"What the fuck?" Nathan whispered.

"What does that spell?" Brendan leaned over the board to get a better look, but the pointer moved again.

G, I, G, G again, L, E.

"Snicker? Giggle?" June narrowed her eyes. "What does that mean?"

"It's a riddle. Or a part of one." Nathan flipped open his phone and showed them the riddle he had copied from the scroll in class.

"Who is the man? Is he dead? It says he's in a grave," Brendan said. "Whose name are we trying to guess?"

"I think the writer's identity." Nathan dragged his focus from the board and towards the group.

"Did you do this, Harper?" With one eyebrow raised, Collin studied the blonde girl. "I listened in on your conversation about that riddle. You made a joke about Nathan because he read it aloud in the classroom."

Laughing, she shrugged. "I don't know what you're talking about."

Collin lifted the planchet and dangled it from a thin wire. "Drink."

"Fine," Harper whined. "I was just having some fun."

Nathan sighed and pulled a cigarette from the pack. "Going to get some air." He stepped outside, hands frantically searching for his lighter.

"Need a light?"

He turned around to see Vicky standing behind him, her lighter held out and lit. He leaned over and lit his cigarette. "Thanks."

They stood in silence for a while, the night breeze rustling the dried branches of the surrounding trees.

"You didn't have to come tonight," she said. "You could have stayed home and solved your riddle."

His eyes flickered in her direction, but his thoughts were elsewhere. "'In his grave.' You said there was a burial site here?"

Vicky scoffed. "Yeah, Tanner Cullen's grave is in his garden. At least that's who the headstone says is buried there. It could be empty."

"What do you mean by that?"

"Tanner Cullen went missing. Nobody found his body. Everyone just presumed he packed up and left. But when his mother died, and he didn't show up to the funeral, the town figured something terrible had happened to him." She held out her hand. "Want to see his grave?"

He took her hand, and the pair of them walked through the overgrowth. Brambles caught on Nathan's coat and neck, but Vicky seemed to move through the darkness with ease. "Have you been here before?"

"Plenty of times. There's an epitaph on the headstone I like to read whenever I'm here."

"What does it say?"

"'Tanner Cullen. Here he rests, where the pact was fulfilled. Riches he gained, now he lies still.'"

Vicky led him to a meticulously groomed space inside of the overgrowth, though who had cut it, no one knew.

Nathan followed her until they came upon the gravestone, its epitaph carved by a crooked hand, or as if some animal had etched the message into the stone. Whatever had been engraved on it before had faded a long time ago.

She stood in front of the grave and put a quarter on top of the headstone.

"What's that for?"

"Payment. We use his house to party, don't we?" Vicky smiled back at him. Her hair shone bright red in the moonlight. "There's something I haven't told you about this gravestone."

A chill ran up Nathan's spine. "What?"

Using her finger, she gestured for him to come closer to her. She led him by the hand to the back of the grave. She pulled out her lighter and illuminated the rear of the stone. "I didn't want to freak you out, but I thought you'd be interested in reading this."

Nathan grew rigid as he read a second message carved there.

I snicker and giggle when you speak,
I'm the shadow that haunts your sleep,
I'm always near, no turning back,
say my name to seal our pact.

He couldn't take his eyes off the riddle. He contemplated the version written on the door and how it differed from the original. This one was also different, but it seemed more intimate as if the writer was obsessed with the subject.

Vicky leaned intimately towards him. He could smell the alcohol on her breath. "Tanner Cullen was the son of a whore before he gained his riches."

Nathan swallowed the lump in the back of his mouth, yet he still couldn't speak. It was as if he had fingers wrapped around his throat. Her lips were close to his ear. He could hear the wetness of her mouth.

"Rumor was he made a deal with a demon."

Harper's voice came from the overgrowth. "You two aren't fucking back there, are you?"

Vicky let out an audible snarl. "Trying to. Go away."

"Seriously? By a grave? That's so gross and disrespectful."

"Go away, Harper." Vicky sighed and smiled at Nathan. "I really wish it was just us here tonight."

White light flooded the open area. Harper and Collin stepped into the clearing. He held a flashlight, she held him. "Camron and Steph are here." Harper sighed. "They're inside the house, about to drink all your liquor."

Vicky hissed, "Asshole" and tugged on Nathan's sleeve. "Come on. Let's go save my booze."

Nathan didn't speak or move. His gaze never shifted from the carving.

Vicky stepped in front of him, her gaze locked with his, a knowing smile on her lips. "Come on. We can always come back when it's just the two of us." She pressed her mouth against his.

An electric shock coursed through him, a mix of excitement and dread. Her lips were warm, but that warmth didn't spread throughout his body. What spread was ice and despair.

When they arrived back at the manor, Collin and Harper were the first up the steps. Collin paused in the doorway as Camron stood by the couch, a bottle of Vicky's vodka in his hand, and stared down at the condom wrapper-riddled floor. "Was this you and Harper, Collin?"

"I don't use condoms," Colin answered before Harper slapped his arm.

"He doesn't need to know that, you dick."

"Are you drinking from my bottle?" Vicky shouted.

Camron gave her a boyish smile. "It was almost empty."

"That's my three-hundred-dollar bottle of Slix. I was saving that. Put it back."

Camron turned the bottle upside down to show it was empty. "My bad."

"I'm going to kill you."

"You love me too much." He stepped down to meet her in the yard. He pulled out his wallet and handed her a one-hundred-dollar bill. "Sorry. If I had known, I wouldn't have drunk it. I swear."

Vicky snorted and snatched the cash from him. "I guess I'll forgive you this time."

Camron glanced at Nathan. "How's it going, Madison?" He extended his hand.

Nathan shook it almost on instinct. A sense of cold emptiness engulfed him as if his brain possessed information that eluded his conscious understanding.

Camron gave Vicky a gentle nudge with his elbow. "What's going on with him? He looks like he'd seen a ghost?"

Harper's head peaked out from the doorway. "He and Vicky were trying to get it on by the Cullen grave."

Camron laughed. "That's so wrong. I thought you had more class than that, Vicky."

Vicky smiled and shrugged. "Let's go play with the Ouija board. Is Steph inside? Where's Brendan and June?"

"Yeah, she went inside to piss." Camron set down the empty bottle with a hollow thud. "I didn't see June or Brendan when we got here. Only Collin and Harper."

"Brendan wanted to go upstairs. I think June went with him," Harper said.

Vicky let out a worried groan. "The upper level is rotting. They could fall through the floor. Better call them back downstairs."

The five of them reentered the crumbling mansion, the floorboards heralding their entrance. Everything looked the same, yet Nathan felt a foreboding dread. Something had changed. He just couldn't put his finger on it. The room seemed colder, and he could swear he could see his breath as he walked into the house.

"Guys, I think I want to call it a night. I don't feel so good."

The others stood in the room, their backs towards him, still and silent like statues.

"Guys?" Nathan gave Collin's shoulder a shake, but he didn't move. He didn't acknowledge him. Collin just stared straight ahead, unblinking. Camron and Harper were the same.

"Guys, this isn't funny." Nathan rattled Collin harder, yet his friend stood fast.

It was only then Nathan noticed Vicky was gone. He turned around, thinking she might still be outside, but as he did, the front door slammed shut with a loud crack.

In the dim moonlight, a faint line etched itself into the door. Nathan watched, frozen, as the groove deliberately and methodically sank deeper into the wood as though an unseen hand carved it. His heart sank as the first jagged letters appeared.

I snicker and giggle as they freeze

Nathan's heart pounded as the message carved itself into the door. The words were sharp and jagged.

Bound in silence, never at ease

Ice-cold air entered his lungs, chilling him to the bone.

Bid your soul, end my game

The final line appeared, each letter driving deeper into the wood.

Say my name, release their pain

Nathan stepped back slowly until he backed into an unmoving Harper. She was freezing, her skin a shade of blue.

"Vicky?" he called out, "Vicky, where are you?"

An explosion of splinters erupted at his feet.

Say my name

The message appeared again and again, on the floors, on the walls, on the ceilings. He turned around and watched in horror as his friends had the words engraved into their faces. Blood oozed from the wounds on their flesh, down their arms, then pooled on the floor.

The front door swung open, violently, and Nathan dashed out to the deck, where the wood and brick were all carved with the same message.

Say my name. Say it. Say it. Say my name.

He tried to run down the cobble driveway, but a car plowed into a nearby tree, inches from hitting him. The wrecked vehicle's side door bore another message carved into the metal.

Grave

The word grave appeared everywhere. It was in the trees, in the grass, etched into the rock. A sharp pain in his arm and the word appeared on his wrist as blood oozed to the ground

Reluctantly, Nathan entered the clearing, the moonlight engulfing the grave. Vicky stood there, adorned in a sheer white gown, with golden rings in her fiery hair, a curled smile on her lips, and her green eyes shining like an animal's at night.

Nathan stood, stunned. He had always thought of her as beautiful, but right now, she was something else, otherworldly and horrifying, yet completely mesmerizing. "What's going on, Vicky? What's happening?"

She shrugged, her hand gently caressing the headstone. "I just get bored sometimes." She flashed a smile at him, her teeth as white as moonlight. "I've been making pacts and deals for over two hundred years in this town, but no one could quite pique my interest as much as Tanner did." She stepped towards him. "He was my first, and you never forget your first."

"Are you the writer of the riddle? What was its purpose?"

She stepped closer. The smell of smoke filled the clearing, the air chilling around him. "I am. Think of it as a consent form, a contract. By reading and thinking over it, trying to solve it, you allow me to influence your mind. The more you engage with it, the more I can engage with you. Do you understand?"

Nathan's head swam in confusion. "But... how do you have a family? I've met your dad. You go to college."

Vicky laughed. "Oh, that? I told you I got bored. I'll skip the details. But a doctor owed me a favor and allowed me to take over an infant. I've quite enjoyed the human experience. Until I met you."

Nathan backed away from her. "Why me?"

Her eyes softened, and her lips parted. "You bear a resemblance to him. Even your lives are similar. It's as though he's returned to me after two hundred years."

"Who?" But Nathan knew the answer.

"Tanner Cullen. He was just a boy when he made that deal. Dumb and desperate. I felt sorry for him in the end, and I even came to care for him. But he's in hell now, cursing my name."

Nathan's body shook in fear, his eyes never leaving hers. "What do you want with me?"

Vicky smiled. "Straight to the point. I like that. A trade. Twenty years of your life for forty years of luck."

Nathan stood in silence for a while. The fear slipped away as curiosity took over. "You don't want my soul? You just want twenty years of my life? Why?"

"What I do with those twenty years isn't your concern."

"And what if I say no?"

"Nothing. But I have a way of lingering, of doing things until I get what I want."

Overhead, a crow landed on a tree branch, followed by a second and a third. They cawed at each other as they looked down, their black eyes watching Nathan as if to see what he would do.

"I don't need luck. I don't need money. I can get by on my own. I don't need your help."

"Like your mother did?" Her lips curled into a knowing smile. "But I can see your mind's made up." She backed away from him. "Such a shame. I had such high hopes for you. I really did like you, Nathan."

"I don't like older women, remember?"

She scoffed. "I'll come ask you again three years into your sentence."

He staggered through the overgrowth, his mind reeling, trying to figure out what had just happened. What did Vicky mean? The manor loomed ahead, its silhouette a monstrous shadow.

He walked up the crumbling brick stairs, past the crusty couch, and pushed open the door, the messages carved into it gone. As he crossed the threshold, death was there to greet him. His friends, or what remained of them, lay scattered around the black stone table like pieces of doll-like parts. Someone had dismembered their bodies, severing their heads and twisting their arms and legs at odd angles. Blood pooled on the floor, seeping into the cracks of the wood.

Nathan fell to his knees when he saw the eyes of Vicky fixed on him, the word Aragorda carved into her forehead. His breath came in harsh gasps, his vision tunneling as the answer to the riddle, jagged lines in flesh stared back at him.

Red and blue lights illuminated the manor's interior, and sirens pierced the silence. He heard none of the shouting behind him. His vision faded to black, he thought of nothing but the riddle and the answer.

The prison was a monolith of gray bricks. The cells, small suffocating boxes of concrete and iron bars. The walls bore witness to the ghosts of both the previous occupants and the new. Down a shadowy corridor, there was a cell where Nathan Madison sat curled in the darkest corner. The walls of his cell were not bare but covered in etchings made with a sharpened spoon. Snicker and giggle.

Nathan repeats the phrase as he hugs himself then looks up at the security camera, the white glare mocking him. He covers his ears, but her laughter only grows louder. Her voice is a constant reminder. "Only two years, six months, and four days to go."

MATTHEW R. CLARK is from South Carolina where he resides with his wife and daughters. After reading *The Lord of the Rings*

trilogy in middle school, he dabbled in writing fan fiction of his favorite series. This love of fantasy and writing has followed him since. He is currently working on publishing his debut novel and hopes to have it released by 2024.

HEART'S DESIRE PART TWO

T.J. Fier

THE WITCH HAD ASKED, *What's your heart's deepest desire?*

Addison hadn't meant it. She swore she didn't mean for her little brother, Dougie, to die.

A lash of wind burned her exposed cheeks. She didn't care. After what she had done, she deserved to feel as much discomfort as possible.

Did her brother feel pain as he died? Her father said he passed peacefully in his sleep. Addison didn't believe him. Images of her brother choking, gasping, fingers uselessly clawing at his neck as his lips turned blue pushed Addison forward down the darkening streets of Effham Falls.

That morning, she awoke from a restless sleep after casting a frightening spell the evening before with her witch friend Solveig. Why hadn't Solveig told her the truth about what they had cast? Had Solveig known what would happen?

"My fault. My fault." Tears fell, leaving raw trails down her chafed cheeks.

Of course, it was her fault. The spell was meant to give Addison her heart's desire. Who was Solveig to know that Addison's desires were such black, deadly things? A good person would never wish their sick brother dead. He was only eight. He was born with his chronic illness and couldn't help it. He had deserved to live as long of a life as possible.

Addison rounded the corner of 7th Street and Orange. Only one window glowed—Solveig's bedroom. Thank goodness the ancient woman hadn't yet settled in for the night. She wasn't too late. There might still be time to set things right.

The day had been too full of tears, hugs, and phone calls for Addison to make her escape earlier. After her father told her Dougie had died at the hospital the night before, he had wept against her shoulder for what seemed like hours. Addison hadn't said a word as her bear of a father soaked her t-shirt with tears. She had been too shocked to cry.

Her mother returned late in the morning, all color drained from her face except for her red-rimmed and swollen eyelids. She joined the two of them still at the kitchen table without a word.

Pulling himself together, her father blew his nose, swallowed his tears, and said, "Who do you want me to call first?"

Addison had paced between the living room and the kitchen while her parents made call after call. Her father continued to weep during and between phone calls, but her mother was stoic in her grief. She gnawed her bottom lip bloody while accepting condolences, making arrangements, receiving a hot dish from a neighbor, and making an ever-growing list of things that needed to be done to prepare for Dougie's funeral.

Effham Falls was a small town, and news spread fast. The house was filled with people by the time the sun started to fall. Her father continued to sob. Her mother continued to chew her bottom lip until her mother's best friend, Betty, gently handed her a tissue and whispered, "Hon, you're bleeding."

And Addison during all this? She had become a silent shadow lurking in the corners, her breath coming in short gasps if she allowed herself moments of clarity. She had found one of his action figures lying on the living room floor and kept the little superhero clutched in her hands while a steady stream of words thundered on repeat between her ears: *Dougie is dead. And I killed him.*

Standing at Solveig's front door, she wished she had never met the witch. Wished she had been satisfied with her lot in life. But, no, she had to be greedy. She wanted more attention, wanted her parents to care about her as much as they cared about Dougie. Maybe, just maybe, there was a way to make things right.

Addison rang the witch's doorbell. A shadow passed the single lamp burning in the witch's bedroom. More lights flicked on, and Solveig was at her front door in a matter of minutes, wrapped in a long sweater, her long gray hair loose and wild.

The witch didn't appear surprised by her arrival. "Addison, shouldn't you be home with your—"

"Why didn't you say something?" The words burst from Addison's lips before she could think.

The witch's brows knit. "Say something?"

"You knew what might happen, didn't you?"

"Oh, dear child." The ancient woman brushed back her hair from her lined face. Behind her, the glowing eyes of several cats sitting on various perches in the foyer blinked through the dark. "Have you retained nothing I've taught you about the craft? You could have walked away. You felt the power of our spell. And you made your choice."

"I want to take it back." Addison wiped away the tears on her chafed cheeks. "Please. I didn't mean it."

Solveig clicked her tongue. "Oh, but you did. The heart always speaks true no matter the cruelty of a desire."

Fresh snot dribbled down Addison's face. "But my mom and ... dad, they're all ... I didn't mean for this to happen."

"You can say that as many times as you want, but it won't change what has come to pass."

Solveig's eyes narrowed as the warmth there blew away with the cold evening air. "You can't take it back. Accept the choice you made to me and to the moon last night."

"Choice? I didn't make a choice. I didn't know what I was saying—"

"Yes, you did." Solveig took the girl's hands into her gnarled grip. "Sometimes the spells reveal unexpected truths, and you must accept that truth." She turned Addison's shivering hands over, exposing the girl's left palm. The witch frowned, yanked on Addison's wrist, and bent to inspect the girl's hand. "You must not be weak in the face of death. You must accept the passing of your brother so his spirit can move on into the next world." She pressed her finger to a crease on Addison's palm. "There is a potential divergence here. Take care."

"I can't," Addison sobbed. "I did this. I'm a terrible person."

"So what if you are." The witch dropped Addison's hand, lips curled in disgust. "How many times have you complained about your parents leaving you at home alone while they are at the hospital? How many times did you tell me you wished your family paid more attention to you? You were jealous of your brother's hold on your parents. You have worked powerful magic. You should be proud of what we've accomplished."

"Proud? Only a monster would be proud."

The witch let out a crackling, hollow laugh. "My dear, if you do not accept what you have done, then I cannot help what happens next. Beware your sorrow. Your regret. A spell can change when the one who cast it doesn't accept the results."

"I don't accept. I want my brother back."

"Enough," Solveig spat. "A proper witch takes responsibility for their choices. A proper witch accepts what has come to pass."

"I'm not a witch." Addison rubbed her tears and mucus with the back of her sleeve.

"No," the witch said, backing from the open door, "clearly you are not. Go home, child. And accept the consequences of your actions." She shut the door in Addison's face.

Addison didn't have the strength to scream at the witch to come back and help her. She checked her phone—time to go home before her parents noticed her missing.

That night, Addison dreamt of her dead brother. He stood at the foot of her bed dressed in his favorite superhero-themed pajamas, the deep sucking sound of him gasping for each breath filling the room. She swore she could feel the weight of him as he sat down beside her, wheezing. His face remained in darkness, but he didn't need to say anything to accuse her of the horrible thing she had wished upon her poor sibling. Eventually, she fell asleep again, fitfully waking every hour or so to Dougie's rattling, cold breath streaming upon her face.

He visited her every night until his funeral. A small but unshakeable weight was at her side all night, his heavy wheezing pulling her from whatever other dreamland she had walked in moments before. His face and expression were hidden in the shadows while the faint streetlights from her window highlighted his downy blonde hair. His gasps stole the warmth from the room and by the time she woke fully, her own breath rose in a plume from her shivering lips.

Addison was barely present during the wake and the funeral at Hahn Funeral Home later that week. She wanted to apologize, but apologizing meant admitting her guilt. And if she acknowledged her guilt, would it change the spell? And in a good way or a bad way? She didn't want to find out.

People moved past her in a steady stream, muttering condolences, wrapping her in unwanted hugs, and promising that Dougie was in a better place. The whole town seemed to have come to say goodbye to the boy who spent more time in the hospital than in the community. Addison and her parents stood at the foot of his coffin as familiar faces such as Cindy Swanstrom, Sarah Moore, and even Jill Owens from the bookstore crept past. A handful of relatives from as close as Clover to as far as Florida stood over her brother's corpse, sadly shaking their heads.

Addison said nothing and did next to nothing. She stood there and let people's words and touches wash over her. She didn't even cry, for what would tears do at that point? Occasionally she grew brave enough to look at her little brother in his little suit in the child-sized coffin. She half expected him to sit up at any moment and raise a finger of accusation in her direction.

Time passed. Prayers were said. They moved from the funeral home to Dougie's burial plot to the gathering at her parent's place once her brother was put into the ground. Addison continued her silence, letting her parents prod her in the right direction, put her in the back of a car, and set a plate of food in her lap once they were home again. Her stomach curled at the sight. Eventually, the untouched plate was taken, and her mother suggested it was time for her to rest.

Addison didn't want to go back to sleep. What if Dougie showed up again? What if she couldn't keep her mouth shut and said something she might regret? Unfortunately, she couldn't find the words and ended up letting her father help her up the stairs to her room. He removed her shoes, kissed her forehead, and promised things would be better tomorrow though his words held little conviction.

Dougie returned as expected, settling upon the foot of her bed as he struggled even in death to breathe. His little body shook with the effort, and the wheezing seemed to come not just from him but from her bedroom walls too. She couldn't ignore him this time. The last week had taken too much out of her.

"I'm sorry, I didn't mean it," Addison whispered over the hem of her duvet.

Dougie sucked another ragged breath, his head bobbing with the effort to fill ghostly lungs. The room seemed colder than in the middle of Effham Fall's deep winters.

"Solveig tricked me. I didn't realize what we were doing."

Her brother didn't acknowledge her. Was the bed shivering with his effort?

"I didn't know. I'm sorry, Dougie."

The ghost's head snapped in her direction. The shadows covering his face shifted, revealing her brother's bone-pale face, mouth gaping open as he fought to draw another breath. Despite his sickness and his struggle, he once had soft, kind hazel eyes, often wet with the effort to stay alive. Now those eyes were round with abject fury.

He wheezed out, "Liar."

Slivers of cold poked through her blankets. "No, I mean it ... I mean, I didn't. I'm sorry."

Dougie's eyes widened farther. He leaned toward and hissed, "Liar."

"I'm-I'm not." Addison pulled her duvet over her chin as Dougie's icy breath needled her cheeks. "Please forgive me."

Dougie's small lungs heaved. "Never."

Unseen fingers wreathed around Addison's neck. "I didn't mean it, I swear."

Her brother's mouth twisted into an awful rictus. "Your turn."

The cold hands around Addison's neck clenched, cutting off her windpipe. She tried to cry out, but a coughing whistle came instead. The fingers clutched tighter. She thrashed, kicking away her blankets, clawing at invisible hands that gripped her throat tighter and tighter and tighter. The shadows on the edges of her vision grew darker and thicker. And through it all, Dougie silently watched her suffering, his breath coming easier than before.

She couldn't scream. She could only flail on her bed, seeking relief that refused to come. Her panic beat with the drum of her heart, the booms growing bigger and slower as each second ticked past. The dim world fuzzed. The haloed darkness tightened.

Her brother crept across the bed, sat on her chest, and gave a solemn nod. "Your turn."

Everything went black. Addison stopped fighting, dying to the sound of her brother's wheezing.

Until...

Addison's lungs opened, and she let out a scream. The night became morning. Sunlight flickered through her windows. The echo of her cry rang through her once-silent home.

"Addy?" Her father thundered down the hallway. He yanked open her bedroom door, his thin hair standing in several directions. He looked equally frightened and exhausted, eyes red from another poor night's sleep. "Addy, you okay?"

"I don't know." Addison continued to gulp down breath after satisfying breath. Nothing remained of her all-too-real dream. The bitter cold had left the room when her nightmare broke, and she was slick with sweat.

"Oh, sweetie." Her father rubbed his eyes and plopped in the same place on her bed Dougie sat every night. "Bad dream?"

"Yeah." Addison touched where the unseen fingers had crushed her windpipe. "Real bad."

"You've been so brave through all of this." He brushed a damp lock of hair from her forehead. "You don't have to be. Just let it out. Maybe it'll help with the bad dreams."

Addison let him gather her into one of his wonderful bear hugs. She melted into his warmth, feeling safer and more secure than she had in weeks.

She had to make this stop. Another visit from Dougie would finally tip her over the edge, and there was only one person who might be able to help her. Hopefully, Solveig would forgive her for their last visit.

"I had a feeling you would be back." Solveig opened her front door before Addison could second-guess her decision. The witch was garbed in her usual layers of black, and she had carefully wound her long, white hair into a simple bun.

"I just—I can't—I need," Addison stuttered.

"I know." The ancient woman raised a gnarled hand to quiet her. "Come, let me make you a cup of tea."

Solveig led Addison to her kitchen full of racks of spell ingredients, copper kitchenware, and a vast gas stove and range. An orange tabby and a black cat lazed on her enormous butcher block counter. The witch put the kettle on the stove and opened her tea cabinet. She studied the rows of small glass jars filled with everything from allspice to wintergreen, anise to wormwood.

Addison collapsed on the nearest stool. "My brother, he's—he's not really gone. I mean, yeah, he's dead. But—oh, God. And last night? I thought he was going to choke me to death. I have a feeling he might do it again."

"Of course he did." Solveig let out a soft sigh. "I told you to own what you have done. To accept the spell and let it run its course. But you acknowledged your brother's ghost. You've tethered his spirit to yours."

"What do I do? There must be something you can give me. Some amulet. Some prayer. Some mouse to kill or whatever."

"This town is the home of the lost souls, Addison. All it takes is one regret, one bit of unfinished business, and they stay forever. I told you to let it go, to accept what you have done. Now it's too late."

"Too late?" Addison sipped the hot, spicy tea.

"Until his spirit is satisfied, he will visit you every night. For the rest of your life."

"Every night? You mean, he's going to strangle me every time I go to sleep?"

"Yes."

"But there has to be something you can do?"

Solveig nodded solemnly. "There is, and that tea you're drinking is the first step. We need to try to untether his soul from yours. The moon isn't right, nor is the season, but we have no choice. Unless you want to wait until the spring equinox?"

"Spring? Seriously?"

"I figured not. Finish up that tea. I have to gather a few things first. Can you start a fire in my burn pit?"

"Of course."

"Good. Get a hot one blazing. Time to be brave, Addison. Time to be a witch."

The night was unnervingly still as Addison helped Solvieg place a steel grate over the fire pit and lift one of the witch's small copper cauldrons onto the grate. Solveig stirred the mixture she had prepared earlier until the potion began to simmer.

Solveig tossed a fist full of earth into the pot once it began to boil. "Luckily, I still had plenty of grave dirt in my sugar bowl."

Addison tucked her chin into her winter jacket. The temperature must have dropped ten or more degrees since they first stepped outside. The witch took a cheesecloth bundle out of her pocket, grabbed the sachet with steel salad tongs, and dipped it into the boiling brew three times.

Solveig waved Addison over. "Now come here. You need to toss this into the flames. And when you do, speak your brother's full birth name."

On the other side of the gently bubbling cauldron, Addison could see the faint shape of her brother. He wasn't as solid as when he sat at the base of her bed. She could make out the shapes of the trees behind him.

"He's here." Addison gulped, standing as close to the fire as she dared.

"Now, toss in the sachet."

Addison raised the soggy lump of cheesecloth. "Please leave me alone, Douglas James Andersen."

The fire flared when the cheesecloth bundle hit the edge of the fire. The cauldron momentarily boiled over before settling again. A sharp, bitter scent filled Addison's nose. Her brother grew more substantial. The rage on his face shone clearer than before. The witch uttered a series of phrases in Norwegian, tossing pinches of grave dirt between verses. The sound of Dougie's wheezing grew louder.

"Vaer borte!" Solvieg bellowed over the sound of Dougie's sucking breaths. "Ta sjelen din dit den hører hjemme!"

Dougie barreled around the fire faster than he had moved in life and flew at his sister. Addison shrieked and raced for Solvieg's back door.

"No, don't!" Solveig shouted.

Addison scrambled with freezing fingers to try to open the latch on the door, but she was so cold, even colder than the night before when Dougie strangled her. Small arms wrapped around her waist. Her brother's arms.

"Where I belong." Dougie gasped. His cold little body burned against Addison's.

The fire flickered and went out. The night collapsed around Addison. The last thing she heard before darkness fell was her brother's whispery giggle.

"Addison?" Solveig crept toward the girl collapsed against her backdoor. The fire had sputtered alive again after the boy's ghost disappeared into his sister. Had the spell worked? She was taking a chance by attempting something so powerful with a waning moon in the early winter months. But there was nothing else to be done. The boy's spirit would grow stronger with each night's visit.

The witch leaned over the girl so that the firelight spilled onto her face.

Addison shuddered and startled awake. She let out deep, heaving breaths. Her eyes went to Solveig's face, then to the sky, then to the fire, and back to Solveig. Addison tried to speak, but nothing came out.

Solveig pressed a hand to Addison's head. No temperature. But something was off, something her witch blood sensed.

"Addison, look at me."

The girl's gaze shifted to the witch. There he was. Addison's once dark brown eyes weren't quite the same. She now had one brown eye and one hazel one. Solveig had only seen Dougie from a distance a few times, but she knew.

"Shit." Solveig recognized a twinned soul when she saw one. "Well, let's get the two of you a cup of tea before I send you home. I should have waited for the solstice."

Theatre professor by day and writer by night, T.J. FIER's other works include many short stories in various anthologies. Her debut novel, *The Bright One*, is being re-released in September 2024.

THE STRANGER

Susette Quinn

JILL MADE ONE LAST round of the bookstore, checking that doors were locked, and things were tidy for the morning. The Tattered Cover had a friendly ghost in it for as long as Jill could remember, but since she and her friend Sarah Moore had solved his murder, Arvid had moved on. Jill missed the constant shuffling of footsteps and was surprised how comfortable she had become with them.

Giving a shout to Salem, her cat, and checking the cameras in the alley to make sure the coast was clear, she locked up and walked the five feet over to her apartment door.

Jill lived in a renovated apartment above the bookstore. With its large windows and natural light, it was the perfect space for her and Salem. She was extremely pleased with the view of Main Street and the square and with the updates she had made.

Grandma Evie had always wanted to own a bookstore. After Grandpa Hank retired, he made her dream come true. When he passed away, Evie threw herself into the store, using Jill for summer help when the city folks came to town. Jill inherited the building and the business in Evie's will and took it upon herself to make the upstairs her living space. New tiles and plumbing fixtures in the bathroom, appliances and backsplash in the kitchen, a facelift for the cupboards, a sanding of floors, and paint throughout made the space contemporary and livable.

The bookstore was thriving. Jill had been able to resurface the old check-out counter and get some comfy chairs to place around the store. Her bills were being paid and she had local customers who would place orders online during the winter months when they went south.

As she unlocked the door to her apartment, Jill had the uneasy sense of being watched. A quick glance up and down the alley provided nothing but a crow on a power line. She shrugged off the feeling and dead bolted the door behind her.

"There you go, Salem," Jill said as she gently deposited her friend on the stairs. Together they ascended into her kitchen.

Before she started supper, Jill knew she had better feed Salem. He had food and water in the store but would act as if he hadn't been fed all day. She opened the cupboard, and heard the angsty, feline 'meow' behind her, letting her know she wasn't moving fast enough.

"I'm coming, Your Highness" she said with a laugh.

Once Salem was taken care of, Jill was free to start her own supper. She had picked up a slew of fresh veggies at the local farmer's market and decided to sauté them with some lemon and olive oil, add some beans, and toss with some pasta.

Pasta boiling and veggies almost done, Jill poured herself a glass of Sauvignon Blanc to accompany her dinner. She plated her meal and carried it and her wine to her little dining room table. While she ate, she sifted through a stack of advanced reader copies that publishers had sent her and chose one to read after dinner.

After cleaning up her kitchen, she curled up in her favorite chair by the window to read. This particular book was written by an author new to the scene and Jill loved a good thriller. Salem perched himself on the back of her chair to look out the window at the goings on of Main Street.

A few chapters in, Jill felt uneasy; the hairs on her arms and the back of her neck stood on end. The feeling of being watched again was very strong. She tried to disregard it, but Salem's tail was doing a rapid twitch that only happens when he is talking to birds outside the window. The mighty hunter must be looking at something. Jill turned to see what Salem was watching, but with twilight shadows starting to grow, she didn't see anything other than Sheriff Sorenson's patrol car cruising by nice and slow.

"It's a little late for the sheriff but maybe he is covering for one of his deputies," Jill offered absentmindedly to her furry companion.

Out of the corner of her eye, Jill thought she saw something move in the shadows of the foliage in the square. She looked closer but didn't see anything. Maybe my eyes are tired, she thought, walking to the kitchen.

Jill washed her glass, checked her phone for any emails or messages from her family or friends, and decided to call it a night. The summer sun was fading fast.

The store wasn't due to open for a few hours, and Jill was busy placing orders for the next month when her phone binged. It was a text from her friend Sarah: Check the cameras and open the door. Jill smiled and glanced at the monitor. Sure enough, Sarah was standing in the alley with coffee. She unlocked the door, and her friend burst through it like a crisp breeze.

"I haven't seen you in like two weeks so I figured you wouldn't mind the intrusion. You work too much anyway. Here, Caramel Macchiato, just like you like it." Sarah pushed a coffee cup into Jill's hands.

"Thank you. Come in! Sit, sit! I am glad you dropped by, and I do love this coffee.," Jill said, still beaming at the prospect of spending a few minutes with her friend. "What have you been doing with yourself now that school is out?"

"Well," Sarah started, "you know how I have always wanted to replace my backdoor going into the yard? I am in the process of that, but then decided a new set of stairs with a small deck would be nice out there. Out of the grass and away from mosquitos, and all that. It's funny how one thing bleeds into another. My days are spent with power tools and trips to the hardware store."

"Wow!" Jill exclaimed. "That is quite the undertaking. I don't know if I'd be brave enough to attempt a deck and stairs, but I have the utmost confidence in your skills and I know it will look great. Do you need any help?"

"Only to christen it when I'm done," Sarah answered with a flourish. "And speaking of hardware stores, have you seen the new guy in town?"

"New guy?"

"I guess he bought the old Murphy place on the edge of town."

Jill was a bit confused. "Murphy place? It's derelict, unlivable. I don't think the roof is even intact anymore. How can he be staying there?"

"Hence the hardware store," Sarah replied. "From what I've been hearing, and I'm at the hardware store a lot these days, he's there just about daily. Comes in right before closing. The guys at the store were gossiping about him. I guess he knows what he wants and is doing everything himself. They also love his truck. Boys!"

"Well, this town could use some new blood. I wonder though, why here?" Jill mused. "What does he do for a living? And of all places to buy, the Murphy place? I have so many questions."

"Same! I should plan a trip to the hardware store just before closing one of these days," Sarah said slyly. Both girls laughed and the subject changed to their plans for the day and the upcoming Community Days celebration happening in a few weeks.

"I was given a large donation to buy kids' books and decided to give out books during the parade. Any child that swings by the store will be given a new book. I think I will set up a table out front on the sidewalk. That way I can chat with the kids and parents as well as watch the parade myself. It's a win-win," Jill explained.

"That sounds great," Sarah countered. "I'll be pouring beer for the Rusty Nail. They got a special permit to have a beer garden in the parking lot. Maybe the new guy likes beer and we can get a look at him."

"I'm sure he is far too busy for a small-town celebration, but we can hope." Jill winked. "Are you working during the day or in the evening?"

"I should be done about the same time that you lock up the store. I was hoping you might swing down for a beer and a brat. The firemen will be grilling again this year as part of their equipment fundraiser. It doesn't get any better than a ripped fireman cooking me dinner, even if most of them are married." Sarah giggled.

"That sounds perfect." Jill sighed. "I'll plan on that."

The next few weeks were business as usual for The Tattered Cover. Jill had the table set up with her display of books to give the kids. While putting the finishing touches on the window display to honor the event, she had that creepy feeling of being watched again. The store wouldn't open till 9 am and the sun was just starting to shoot its rays onto Main. She gazed around the square across the street, but other than shopkeepers prepping for festivities and a couple of birds, Jill didn't see anything peculiar.

The day went by in a whirlwind. Local author, Kathy Balsam, was on-site signing books and helping Jill out where she could. Jill felt like a thousand customers had come through the doors and during the parade, she and Kathy handed out books as fast as they could. When the melee settled, there were less than ten kids' books left over, Kathy had sold another forty-three books and both ladies were thoroughly exhausted. Jill flipped the Closed sign over and locked the front door. She heard a sigh behind her and smiled when Kathy dropped into an overstuffed chair with a bottle of water.

"I don't know how you do this," Kathy said. "My dogs are barking!"

Jill reiterated the sigh. "All days aren't like this. This day will make up for the less-than-stellar holiday season I had last year. I couldn't have done it without your help."

"It's all good. What is next for you? Cleaning up or heading over to get a beer and a brat?" Kathy asked.

Jill gave a cursory look around. The store was thoroughly decimated and the thought of staying and cleaning up was draining. "This mess will still be here in the morning. I think I'll buy you that beer for all your hard work."

Kathy laughed. "Well, I'll take it, but I'll have you know that I was just repaying you for selling more of my books than anyone else."

"You're a local celebrity. People beg for your books. Let's shut this place down and head out the back." Jill motioned for Kathy to follow her into the back room and went about shutting off lights. They checked the cameras to make sure all was well, locked up, and walked down the alley toward the beer garden.

About halfway there, Jill got that unsettling feeling of being watched again. She darted her eyes around but couldn't see anyone.

"What's going on?" Kathy asked, noticing the odd behavior.

"I think I'm losing my mind. For weeks now, I keep feeling like I'm being watched. It's probably in my head."

Kathy did a slow turn, checking all the windows and doorways. No one except a cat perched on a low roof. "Could it be that cat?" she asked, pointing.

Jill turned and looked directly at it. A shudder went down her back. It was as if the cat was looking into her soul. "That must be it. Let's keep going."

Arriving at the beer garden, Kathy and Jill immediately found Sarah at a table. Kathy joined her and Jill went to get them each a beverage. When she approached the table, she heard Kathy recanting the day's chaos.

"Right after the parade, we were swamped," Sarah countered. "It's been crazy over here too."

"Well," Jill said, raising her glass. "We don't have to think about work till tomorrow. To a job well done!" The girls clinked their plastic cups, and each took a sip.

They chatted and visited with people who wandered in and out of the beer garden. Occasionally, someone would join them at the table. They had brats and chips served by the Effham Falls Fire Department and were currently watching the band set up on a flatbed semi-trailer. Jill wasn't much of a dancer, so she planned to leave shortly after the music started.

As Jill scanned the crowd, she locked eyes with a man leaning up against the fence. He was maybe a little over six-foot-tall with dark hair swept back from his face in a way that looked just a little unkempt but intentional. There was nothing soft about him. Tall, chiseled features, broad shoulders and, from shoulder to thigh, his muscles bulged through his clothing. He had the most intense, hypnotic blue eyes. Realizing she was staring, Jill smiled and forced herself to look away.

Nudging Sarah, she mumbled, "Without being obvious, check out the guy along the fence."

After a beat, Sarah leaned in and commented, "He's gorgeous! I bet that's the new guy in town! He keeps looking over here, but he is definitely not looking at me. Oh God, he's headed this direction! Damn, he's sexy. He doesn't walk, he glides."

A few seconds later, a deep, smooth voice curled around Jill like a hug. "Excuse me, ladies. Is this seat taken?"

Jill seemed to have lost her voice. Sarah jumped in to reply, "No. Please join us. I'm Sarah. This is Jill. That's Kathy Balsam and Flynn Stewart. I don't believe we've met."

"The pleasure's mine. Beckam Porter," he offered. "My friends call me Beck. I've only been in town for a short time."

Beckam sat directly opposite Jill and her gaze was swallowed into the depths of those eyes. Thankfully, this was the moment Sarah had been waiting for and she continued the conversation. Jill's voice was in no hurry to return.

"Are you the one that bought the Murphy place?" Sarah asked.

"I am," Beckam answered. "I got it for a steal, but it needed a lot of work."

"It needed a roof, floors, walls and windows," added Kathy.

Beckam tore his gaze from Jill's and looked down the table. His chuckle seemed to vibrate in Jill's chest. "That it did. I should be able to sell it for a huge profit."

Jill felt like the warmth had been stripped from her when he looked away. What was it about him that had her so out of sorts? Those eyes? The velvety smooth voice? She needed to get it together.

Flynn was asking Beckam what brought him to Effham Falls when Jill's brain caught up to the conversation. Beckam mentioned he was looking to escape to somewhere quiet.

"I feel like we're interrogating you," Sarah added apologetically. "How are you getting along? Are you finding everything you need?"

"So far all I've needed are groceries, building supplies, and the occasional drink," Beckam answered, lifting his glass.

"Well, if you need any help, just ask. I'm pretty good with a drill and I have a few more weeks before school starts again," Sarah offered. "Flynn can be found at the fire station or the BarFly, Kathy runs the Nudi Retreat Center, and Jill owns the bookstore on Main."

"The nudey center?" Beckam asked, his eyebrow raised.

"I get that a lot. My artist retreat center is on Nudi Street. We wear clothes," Kathy stated.

"Sometimes," Flynn added under his breath. His comment received a gentle elbow poke from Kathy and laughs all around.

"A bookstore?" Beckam said, turning his gaze back to Jill.

And there went her composure again. "Um, yes. I inherited it from my grandma. It was her passion and now mine. I carry mostly new books but have a small historical section that is used and, of course, I carry Kathy's books." Jill stammered this out much too fast, trying to avoid Beckam's eyes.

"You're an author?" Beckam asked, turning his gaze back to Kathy.

Jill took a big breath and leaned into Sarah, "I'm going to grab one more drink. Do you need anything?"

"I'm good, thanks," Sarah answered.

Jill smiled at the group, shook her empty cup, and excused herself. She needed a minute away from Beckam to pull herself together. What was going on? Why was her breath stuck in her chest? Why could she feel him watching her?

She got to the makeshift bar and said, "Hey, Paul. I'll take another."

While she waited, she looked over the crowd, noting that some of the families with small children had left and groups of teenagers were hanging on the edges of the dance floor. There seemed to be far more security than she recalled seeing in past years. She found it curious that there were five officers covering the perimeter.

"Here you are, Jill," Paul said, setting her glass down. "Who's the guy at your table? I don't think I've seen him before."

"His name is Beckam Porter. Seems he's new in town. Bought the Murphy place," Jill answered.

"Really? That place is a dump."

"Supposedly he's renovating it—or rebuilding. Depends on how you look at it," Jill said with a laugh.

"Well, I wish him luck. Have a good night."

"You too," Jill said as she turned back towards the table.

The band was in full swing. The youngest were in the street, dancing along with a few older couples. The teenagers were debating whether to hang out at the street dance or run off to a field and have their own party. Conversation at the table had quieted due to the noise level and the difficulty shouting over the music. Sarah, Kathy and Jill were starting to feel the effects of the long day on their feet. Sarah stood and announced that she was going home.

"I'll walk out with you," Jill said, standing as well.

"I'm parked on the other side." Sarah frowned, pointing away from the bookstore.

"All good. I've walked alone before, and it isn't—"

"I'll make sure she gets home in one piece, Sarah," Beckam's smooth voice interjected.

Why did this comment fill Jill with both dread and excitement? She could barely talk to him, and he had to be the sexiest thing she had ever laid eyes on.

"Awesome. I'll call you in the morning. Store opening at nine?" Sarah asked.

"Better yet, bring me coffee," Jill added with a sly smile.

After saying goodnight to the others, Beckam followed Jill to the gate and past security.

"Goodnight, Sheriff. Hope your evening is uneventful," Jill remarked.

"Same, hon. Take care of yourself," Sheriff Sorenson quipped back.

Jill and Beckam strode away from the festivities in silence. Toward the center of the square, Beckam stopped and looked skyward. "The stars seem so much brighter here."

Jill slowed. "That's because we have very little ambient light to detract from them."

"Did you grow up here?" he asked.

"No. I grew up about an hour away but spent my summers here helping Grandma in the store. Even during college."

"Yes, the bookstore," Beckam added, tipping his head in the direction of the storefront. "Do you like it?"

"Running the store? I love it!" she exclaimed.

"That's good. It's nice to combine work with something we enjoy. Where are we going?" Beckam asked.

"Oh, I'm sorry. I'm so used to everyone knowing everything about me. I live above the store. My front door is really a back door from the alley behind the building."

"I suppose we had better get you home then."

They walked for a bit more in silence. Jill's head was spinning. Sex appeal oozed from every pore of him. Her pulse was racing, and her palms were sweaty like a school kid. But part of her was so uncomfortably nervous. She couldn't quite put her finger on why.

Maybe conversation would help. "What is it that you do for a living?"

"I'm a financial advisor. I have the good fortune of being able to work from anywhere that has Wi-Fi. I'm turning the old den into an office. As soon as the electrical was up to code, I had Wi-Fi installed and have been working a few hours each morning before starting the reno. It's not glamorous, but it pays the bills and allows me the freedom I want."

Between his voice and his eyes, Jill felt like she was caught in some kind of spell. Her brain was aware of the fact that the pause in conversation was hers to fill but her voice and body were struggling to stay present. "Where did you live prior to moving here?" she finally spit out.

"Chicago," Beckam announced. "I got tired of the noise and the busyness of the city. I wanted wildlife and evening walks on a country road."

"You're going to want to watch for mosquitoes. A swarm of them will suck the life right out of you."

Beckam's eyes had a humorous twinkle. "Thanks for the warning."

"This is it up here," Jill said, pointing toward her door. "Thanks so much for walking me home, Beckam. It wasn't necessary but was very kind of you."

"Beck. Please."

"Beck."

"I should confess. Kindness wasn't my intent. I really just wanted to spend more time with you and the opportunity presented itself, so I grabbed it."

His voice draped over and around her, and Jill felt almost off balance listening to him. As she took out her keys, he continued.

"I'd like to see you again. Call on you, take you to dinner, a movie, anything you would like. Would that be okay with you?"

"Um, uh," Jill stammered, her voice caught in her throat. Why was she so dumb struck by this man? He wanted to see her. She should be gushing but she was struggling to form words. "That would be nice. I'm at the bookstore every day except Monday. You can reach me there. Thanks again."

As she turned to put the key in the lock, she caught sight of a patrol car slowly passing the end of the alley. With Beck right behind her, Jill couldn't put more thought into it. She unlocked the door and turned to say good night, but she was alone. Beck was gone. Stunned, she looked up and down the alley. She hadn't imagined being walked home, had she? Where could he have gone? Was she losing her mind?

She went inside, reset the alarm, and checked the cameras in the alley, as if he would materialize again. The only thing moving was a raccoon walking across the top of a nearby dumpster. Dropping onto a dining chair, Jill shook her head. What had just happened? He was there on second and gone the next.

"Salem, I might be losing my mind," Jill sputtered. Then she realized that her cat was behaving oddly. Salem was lying on his side, purring and reaching out to something. Or someone!

"Who is in here with me?" Jill asked the empty room.

The faint reply came out of thin air. "It's Arvid."

"Arvid?" Jill sighed warmly. "What are you doing here? Is everything alright?"

"Need to warn you. Danger is near," Arvid continued.

"You stayed with me last time I was in danger too and I appreciate that, but I have security and cameras now. I'll be fine. You don't have to worry."

"I'm staying," Arvid protested. "Need to conserve energy. Go to bed. Tomorrow will be here soon."

"It's not like I can make you leave. See you in the morning. Or hear you," Jill said, turning toward her room.

The next morning, Jill got ready for work early. The store was still a mess from the previous day and would take some work to tidy. She said 'Hi' to Arvid but got no answer, made a quick breakfast, then she and Salem were on their way down the stairs as the sun made its debut. Upon entering the store, she discovered much of the mess had been tidied up. All the doors were locked, and she knew of only one person who would have done this.

"Arvid, you didn't have to. If you have to conserve energy, this is definitely not the way to do that. It's appreciated, thank you." Jill spoke to the air around her.

A very faint "You're welcome" came the reply.

Jill smiled and finished the little Arvid had been unable to accomplish. Just as she was headed into the back to do the office work for the morning, a book tumbled off a shelf and hit the floor with a thud. A book on supernatural creatures lay on the floor.

"Arvid, I am guessing this is some kind of clue to why you are here. You rest and I'll try to take a look at this today," she said to the seemingly empty room.

A few minutes later, Sarah arrived with coffee. She buzzed through the door when Jill opened it. "He walked you home! Tell me everything."

"There isn't much to tell," Jill explained. "We had some conversation, he's a financial advisor from Chicago and he likes stars. Then he just disappeared on me."

"Wait. What? What does that mean?"

"I wish I knew. I'm as confused as you are. One minute he's asking if he can see me again, and the next he's nowhere to be found. Gone. Poof."

"He wants to see you again! Wait. I don't think I follow," Sarah added. "Explain, please?"

Jill described the walk home, the idle conversation, Beck asking to see her, turning to unlock her door and turning back to an empty alley.

"People just don't disappear," Sarah said. "Did you roll the camera back?"

"No, I looked at the alley after coming in but didn't rewind," Jill admitted. "I got sidetracked by Arvid."

"Arvid? Arvid's back?" Sarah asked. "There's a lot to unpack here."

Jill nodded. "There really is. Arvid was in my apartment when I got home. I can faintly hear him talk to me. He says there is danger, and he is staying. Then he spent the night putting the store back together after yesterday." While she spoke, she was busy pulling the footage from the camera feed. "OK, here we are." She motioned for Sarah to come around the desk.

They watched as Jill and Beckam rounded the corner into the alley and walked toward the building. Jill put her key in the door, a car went past the end of the alley and, 'poof', Beckam was gone. Jill was alone in the alley.

"What the hell just happened?" Sarah wondered aloud. "Can we do that frame by frame?"

"I'd like to know as well," Jill exclaimed, rewinding the feed.

Sarah and Jill watched it numerous times, frame by frame and on a loop. One second he is there and the next, nothing. Finally, they had to admit they had no answers. It was time to unlock the store and get the day started.

Jill pointed to the book Arvid had given her. "Arvid knocked that off a shelf this morning. There must be a clue in it, but I don't have time to look right now."

"Well, I do. Mind if I hang out back here for a bit?" Sarah made herself comfortable at the desk. "Of course you don't. Shoo!" she said, waving Jill toward the front of the store.

Community Days events were happening all week. There had been a pancake feed that morning, which would be followed by events for children and family. Jill unlocked the door and got the coffee brewing. A steady stream of people needing help finding things ensued. Around noon, Sarah announced she had to leave and was taking the book with her but would call later that night.

By the time Jill locked the door, she was wiped out and seriously contemplating temporary help for the next year. The last family hadn't been very good about watching their three kids so, with a sigh, Jill went about righting things. She tidied up, put away stacks of books, and wiped down the coffee station. Giving the store a once over, she was startled by Beckam- Beck- standing outside the door and waving.

Before she could reach for the door handle, something grabbed her arm. Arvid very forcefully said, "Do NOT open the door."

Conscious of Beck watching, but wanting to address Arvid, Jill smiled. "I would love to open the door but the minute I do, someone will find their way in and I am done for today. In more ways than one," she said, stepping near the glass to be heard better.

"That's alright," he seemed to purr, his voice floating through the glass to envelope her. "I was passing by and saw you still here. Have you thought any more about a date? You mentioned having Mondays off. We could go to dinner. Or you could come out to the house, see the changes I've made."

Arvid shouted, "NO! Stay in public. Do not go to his house!"

Jill could have sworn Beckam's gaze swung to Arvid at the right of her. Could he see him or hear him? "Dinner would be nice. La Piazza has great pizza, or The Rusty Nail has a decent menu."

Beckam's gaze returned to Jill, and with a smile he said, "Lovely. Can I text you?"

"Of course," Jill replied, rattling off her number so he could type it into his phone.

"Till then." Offering her an endearing smile, he gently touched the glass with one finger. If the window hadn't been there, he would have booped her nose. He offered one more hypnotic grin and disappeared out of view.

Jill walked to the back room, turning off lights as she went. Once out of view of the windows, she said, "Arvid, do you want to explain yourself? Not only did you grab my arm but you yelled at me. And I think he can see you! How is that possible?"

"He isn't what he seems. He's dangerous. You cannot invite him in or be alone with him. Do you understand?"

"No, I don't," Jill barked back. "Can he see you? Or hear you?"

"Probably both. He isn't sure that you can though. I won't be able to protect you as well as I can here, so you must be surrounded by people at all times."

"This is ridiculous. Finally, someone is interested in me. Plus, he's drop dead gorgeous!"

"Was that a jab at me?"

"No. Yes. Maybe." Jill laughed. "I just don't understand what's happening."

She collected Salem and went upstairs to start dinner. Arvid was quiet the rest of the night.

Jill talked to Sarah that evening. The book Arvid had left them was on mythical monsters like Bigfoot, Chupacabra, Elementals, Shapeshifters, even Vampires and Werewolves. Sarah wasn't sure what to focus on. Jill recanted the visit from Beckam-including the adorable, virtual nose boop, Arvid's reaction, and how she was sure Beckam could see Arvid.

"So," Sarah wondered. "Arvid thinks Beckam is dangerous but what is the connection to the book?"

"Is he saying Beckam is a monster?"

"Well, he did disappear off your video. We still can't explain that. I'll take another look at the book."

The girls hung up and Jill tidied up before bed. When she turned off the lights in the main room, her cell phone pinged with a text from Beckam: *Good night, Jill.* Did he know she was going to bed or was this a coincidence?

Jill went back into the darkened room and directly to the windows to look up and down Main. There was nothing there, no one standing or walking about.

Turning away from the windows, Jill gasped when she caught sight of a shadow figure a few feet behind her.

"You're not crazy. He's out there," Arvid informed her.

"I can't see him," Jill said.

"You can't see him in this form. You're protected. Sleep."

There would be no further answers to Jill's many questions. Arvid had gone silent.

Jill continued to get texts from Beckam over the next few days, but it was the goodnight texts when she turned off her lights that frazzled her nerves. They had agreed on La Piazza for dinner that night and Jill was both excited and on edge. She told herself she was just nervous. Beck was going to pick her up at seven and Arvid had been trying all week to get her to cancel.

Shortly after six o'clock, Jill saw movement in her periphery.

"Tell him you are running late and you will meet him there. Don't ride with him," Arvid said.

"Aren't you being a little over the top?" Jill asked.

"In that truck, you are as good as alone with him. Drive yourself."

"You can't be serious?" Jill protested

"I'm very serious. I can't protect you in his truck. You need to listen if you are going to go on this date."

"Fine," Jill conceded, then pulled out her phone to message Beck. *Ran some errands and am running late. I'll go straight to La Piazza and meet you there,* she texted.

After a beat, the reply came: *If you're sure. I am happy to wait.*

I'll be on time if I go straight there, Jill typed.

See you soon.

"Happy?" Jill shot a dirty look toward Arvid's voice.

"Not unless you cancel," Arvid answered.

Jill checked the mirror one last time. She had opted for a sundress, noting that she could use a little sun. She spent far too much time inside the store. Slipping on sandals, grabbing her bag, and telling Salem she would be back soon, Jill armed the alarm and left for her date.

Moments before seven, she stepped out of her car and caught Beck sliding out of a huge Dodge Ram with windows so dark they couldn't possibly be legal. Her stomach did a little butterfly kick at the sight of him walking toward her. Jill thought, "Sarah was right. He glides."

"Hi," Jill said "Thanks for understanding the change in plans."

"It's no problem," Beck said, his voice like silk as he leaned in to give her the slightest of hugs.

Jill's tummy did a somersault. His scent, woodsy and spicy, seemed to wrap around her. As he pulled back, he lifted her chin to look right into her eyes. Jill felt like she was on a cloud. Those blue eyes were mesmerizing. Beck led her to the door and, before she knew it, they were seated.

The server, a frequent visitor to the bookstore, fell all over herself in Beck's presence but managed to get wine to the table without spilling. After having a conversation about favorite pizza toppings, Jill and Beck decided they were quite compatible, and Beck ordered a pizza to share.

"How is the house coming along?" Jill asked.

"When I can get the supplies I need, it goes very well," he answered, rolling his eyes in exasperation. "I hadn't factored in how frequently, or rather how infrequently, a small-town hardware store gets shipments when I decided on this project. It feels like I wait forever to get what I need. I've been ordering directly from the manufacturers to speed things up. I have most of the kitchen, a bedroom, and one bathroom done. In between, I work on the landscaping."

Jill shook her head. "It seems like a huge undertaking. It's been years since I have seen the house, but it was barely a frame. To have a roof, water, and electricity plus two and a half rooms done seems like a lot."

"I suppose it is. I'd like it to go faster. It would be nice to have you over," Beckam replied, playing with her fingers on the table.

Jill noticed Beck's gaze shift to a spot behind her a second before she heard Kathy say, "Look who's here!"

Kathy and Flynn, out with another firefighter, a deputy, and their respective wives, were being ushered to the table next to Jill and Beckam. As the group took their seats, Kathy introduced them all to the 'new guy in town'. Beckam was bewitching them all and when the server returned, he instructed her to put their drinks on his tab.

"That was kind of you," Jill mentioned.

"It's a small thing," he said. "Tell me about yourself. Did you always want to take on the bookstore?"

They filled dinner with getting to know each other, regardless of how Jill struggled to form words. Why did Beck's eyes have such magnetism? The butterflies made it hard to eat and she felt like time was standing still. The air felt heavy, but that didn't make sense. Each time Beck reached across the table to run a finger down her forearm or over the back of her hand the heat at Jill's core would flare.

As Kathy and Flynn's table was leaving, pausing to say their goodbyes, Beck paid the check, and walked Jill to her car. Outside the restaurant, he took her hand.

Jill was weak in the knees. At her car, she leaned against it for some stability. Beck took her face in his free hand and leaned in to kiss her. Jill's entire insides did a flip. He paused, waiting for a sign of consent. Jill, sucked into the depths of his eyes, nodded and he closed the minute distance between them.

Tender at first, Beck teased and caressed her lips with his own, slowly building until he was toying with her tongue. Jill pulled him closer. His entire body was pressing against her and still it wasn't enough.

He broke the kiss and whispered, "We could take this to your place."

Without thinking, Jill nodded and pulled him back in for another kiss.

With a glint in his eye, Beck asked if she wanted to leave her car and ride with him. A small warning sounded in Jill's head "No. I'll drive. You can follow me."

He gave her one more kiss, leaving her breathless, and walked to his truck. Jill climbed into her car and tried to pull herself together. What was happening to her? She never behaved this way. Or maybe she had just never had the opportunity. Her thoughts were swirling. She would get this out of her system and deal with tomorrow when it came.

Jill pulled into her spot behind the building. Beck put his truck directly behind her. She got out of the car and almost pounced on him when he shut his door. She couldn't get enough of him.

He pulled away with a sexy smile. "I'd rather not do this in the alley."

Jill nodded, reaching into her bag for her keys. As she staggered the few feet to the door like a drunk person, Beck supporting her, two cars came screaming into the alley from both ends. Startled, Jill dropped her keys. Before she could recover, Sheriff Sorenson was out of his car and ordering Beck to step away from her. Instead, he stepped closer.

"I'm warning you. Step away from her!" Sorenson shouted.

"Sheriff, I'm sure this is a misunderstanding," Beck replied, reaching for her hand.

But Arvid already had Jill's hand and was moving it away from Beck's. "Stay with me," he whispered.

There were four officers pinning them up against the wall of the store.

"There's no misunderstanding. I know what you are and this ends here. Step away from Jill or I will shoot!" the Sheriff ordered.

Beck laughed. "Boys, you can't hurt me. This is a waste of your time. Get back in your cars and I'll let you live."

Jill was so confused. Arvid was steadily pulling her farther from Beck's reach.

He would let the officers live? There were weapons pointed at him and that was his reply?

"Last chance," Sorensen offered.

Suddenly, Beck was gone and a large wolf stood in his place. The wolf growled, hair bristling, and sprang at the sheriff. Arvid tugged Jill hard and sent her sprawling. Gunfire erupted all around her, prompting her to instinctively cover her head.

"Jill, stay where you're at," ordered the nearest deputy who Jill recognized from the table next to them during dinner.

She felt Arvid help her sit up and she could see what was left of Beckam. The wolf was gone but so was the gorgeous man she had come to know. What lay in the alley was unrecognizable. A skeleton on its stomach with its head turned to the side, and the skin seemed to be shriveling up before her eyes.

"Looks like one of us got him in the heart, Sheriff," exclaimed one officer.

"Sure does. I need to call in the experts. Stay here, and keep your body cameras on him," Sorenson commanded before stepping away to make a call.

The body, if one could call it that, continued to degrade. Gaping holes in the skin were appearing and it was flattening, as if the bones were disintegrating to dust.

Jill started to cry but couldn't pull her gaze away. The Sheriff ended his call and came around what was now almost completely ash to help Jill to her feet.

"Are you hurt, hon?" he asked.

Jill shook her head.

Sheriff Sorenson wrapped his arms around her in a hug. "It will be ok. I'll explain as soon as I can. Can I call someone for you?"

"Sarah Moore," Jill choked out.

The sheriff motioned to a deputy and walked Jill to his car. He sat her on the edge of the seat. "She'll be here soon. Try to relax for a minute"

Out of view of whatever that was, Jill sat with her head between her knees, trying to get her breathing regulated. She heard Arvid shuffle close to her.

"He's dead," Arvid explained. "You're safe now. You don't need me anymore. I have to go; my time is up. Goodbye, Jill"

"Arvid, don't leave me," Jill whispered, but he was already gone.

It seemed like hours had passed but was mere minutes by the time Sarah arrived. The alley was filled with a smattering of people Jill had never seen before, some in plain clothes and others in biohazard suits taking pictures and samples. Sheriff Sorenson gave Sarah permission to take Jill inside and said he would check on them before he left.

Sarah took Jill upstairs and started tea. "Do you want to talk about it?"

Jill recanted the date and how she brought Beck back home, the sudden appearance of police cars, shouting, Arvid pushing her down, and the gunshots. "He disintegrated. Before my eyes, he turned old, then he shriveled up and turned to dust"

"That doesn't make sense," Sarah said, trying to wrap her head around it. "Hopefully, the sheriff will have some answers."

It was hours before the sheriff rapped on the door. Sarah let him in and he dropped his large frame into a dining room chair. He rubbed his face and apologized for taking so long.

"Jill, Beckam Porter wasn't who you thought he was. He was a vampire who could shapeshift. He could be a shadow, bird, or the wolf that you saw. I had heard through the pipeline that there was one of them headed this direction but when we got an anonymous tip letting us know it was here, I called in the experts. They blended in with the tourists and helped us keep watch. That thing had it's sights set on you for a while. They've been watching him since he bought that house and they had seen him in the square after dark," he said, pointing toward the front windows.

"So all the times I thought I was being watched, I really was?"

"Seems so. I panicked a bit when I heard he was following you home from dinner. He would have either turned you or killed you if he got you alone. We loaded up with silver bullets and came as fast as we could. You're a smart girl though. You knew to stay out of his reach and dropped to the ground at just the right moment."

Jill sent Sarah a knowing look and said, "I had a guardian angel's help, Sheriff."

Born and raised in Wisconsin, SUE QUINN transplanted to North Dakota in the late 80's. She raised her two girls in Fargo and is proud to see them take wing on their own. She is a full-time bookkeeper and part-time bookseller. When not busy with her friends or traveling, she can be found writing or editing. She has published short stories in *Tales From The Frozen North, Welcome To Effham Falls*, and *Tales From The Water's Edge*.

THE NECROMANCER OF EFFHAM FALLS

Michael Pickell

A CAWING CROW FLEW past me. I had been digging for some time, as evidenced by the waxing moon. Saint Barbara's cemetery was far enough from Effham Falls that no one would see what I was doing. Stealing bodies, no matter the reason, was always frowned upon. I wiped the sweat and dirt off my face and decided I needed a breather.

They say you shouldn't walk towards the edge of holes. At some point, the part you are standing on could cave in, and you'd be swept in. But it was I who had dug this in the first place, and it made a good spot to just sit and look up at the stars. What do people do outside in the middle of the night? Probably not steal bodies, or more specifically, bones.

Earlier that day, I scouted the cemetery for the older dates so that I would most likely get bones. Also, the newer graves are filled with concrete to prevent this sort of thing from happening.

A breeze picked up and brushed my cheek. Off in the distance, the crow still cawed. Maybe to warn the others of my presence. For a moment, I collected my breath to focus on the task and why I was doing this in the first place. The spell I needed called for bones, and Effham Falls was so small that people would notice when others had disappeared. They would talk and soon there would be a friendly cop coming to have a chat with me.

After catching my breath, I hopped back into the grave and resumed my work. Maybe a half hour later, my shovel hit a wooden casket with a deep thud. I removed the dirt off the lid and opened the treasure box. I smiled and whistled, happy to give my sore arms a chance to rest. And just as I predicted, there were a bunch of bones with clothes on. I then collected my loot. It was the last set of bones needed to complete the number called for in the spell.

I had everything I needed. After years of studying the craft of necromancy, I was so close to completing it. Then I could raise my lovely Anabelle from the dead.

Sitting at the edge of the bar were two guys arguing about the stock market. Who fights about how well the financial sector does? Seriously, I was bored.

I sipped my ale and let my mind wander for a bit. I had taken a few days off from all of my research. Called in sick at my temporary job at the hotel. Yes, I had to get a temporary job because I was paying for my apartment on the West Coast and for a place to stay here. I had a large savings account, but I wanted to make sure it wasn't all spent by the time I got back.

"And I'm telling you, I've had bad luck in the stock market ever since that witch Aggie Baggie messed with those dolls."

"That's super superstition, my friend. Pure superstition. Whatever that old bat does, it doesn't affect stuff like the stock market."

"She put a hex on me that day. I can still see her evil eye staring me down." The guy made the sign of the cross, then took a swig from his beer.

"Wait, did you guys say witch?" I tried to keep the excitement out of my voice.

A real witch. Someone who could help me raise the dead. Someone I could talk with about necromancy.

"Yeah, Aggie Baggie. The town's witch. Don't you know who she is?"

"I just moved here."

"Figures."

I finished up my ale and set the glass down roughly. This conversation had given me an idea, and the direction I needed to go if I wanted the spell to work. With a mock salute, I left the bar.

It didn't take long before I found her house. Just a little search of the public archives at the library. But when I knocked on her door, she greeted me with a raised shotgun. And her appearance was exactly the way the drunk stock brokers described her: long frizzled salt n'pepper hair, an ancient dress, and thick spectacles.

"I'd leave Effham Falls if I were you, Norman Porter." Agnes shifted the gun as if indicating which direction I needed to go.

"How do you know my name?" A shiver ran down my spine.

She must have been a real witch. I heard she didn't leave the house much. At any rate, she had a gun pointed at me.

"I know all sorts of things about you. You think you're this 'rad' magician, a necromancer. But you're nothing, and you should leave town before you get yourself hurt."

"I'll do no such thing, you old bat. They all said you're crazy."

"Then get off my property."

Agnes fired her gun past my shoulder. My heart fluttered. For a second, I thought I was going to die. The smell of gun fire invaded my nose. My ears rung, especially my right. She was batshit crazy. She smiled a toothy grin towards me. I stepped back. She didn't lower her gun. I kept my eyes on her the whole time I backed out of her yard.

Truthfully, I didn't think she would help me. Talk around the town, along with the archives, told me she was older than dirt.

The gate squeaked as I opened it and shut it again. I gave her the bird as I walked along the sidewalk towards the bar. This spell would need some serious planning.

Light shined through a crack in the window. Was it already morning? I studied all the copies of maps I made of Effham Falls. If my suspicions and the archives were correct, the biggest concentration of magical power lay in the middle of town above the old mine. And as far as I could tell, the old bat's house was at the center of all that power. But how was I going to harness it? She wouldn't let me near her house. And if she was the witch everyone said she was, she'd have a charm to prevent me from entering her lawn.

I made myself some extra strong coffee and looked over all the papers I had spread over the table and walls. Summer solstice was the next day, and I needed to figure out how I would carry out this spell. I put the cup before me, sat in the chair, and chanted off the spell of refreshment. Instantly, all the bad energy and the remaining alcohol oozed out of me like a golden fume. I watched as it floated up above and the air absorbed it. Moments later, my body was as refreshed as if I had slept a full night's sleep. It wasn't a spell I could do every day because eventually the lack of sleep would catch up to me, but every now and then it helped.

The brightness of the morning sun didn't bother me as I strolled across the town. It was time to test out my theory, to see if Agnes had actually put up the charms that would block me from entering her yard. When I got to the gate, I tried to put my hand through it but couldn't. I pounded on it and my hand wouldn't budge the gate. She had done it.

For the next twenty minutes, I scouted the area to see if there were any other places that would work for the spell. The neighbor's backyard would do. I had a rough idea of where the mine was, and I put stones in the lawn marking one of the tunnels. A man briefly looked out a window, which was my cue to leave the backyard.

Back on Main Street, I made mental notes about all of the houses, trying to guess which ones had prying neighbors. Every now and then, Aggie showed up in one of her windows, watching me case the area. After I collected the lay of the land, I scurried back home so I could get some real sleep.

I donned the black robes. They weren't so much for effect, but so I wouldn't be seen in the night. The bones and other items for the spell were in a black bag. As the sun dipped lower in the sky, kids were still playing outside, but after nightfall, the town was quiet. I slipped out of my rental home to Agnes' neighbor's house. It was too dark for me to see if she was peering out the window, but it didn't matter. She could watch me all night for all I cared.

At the far corner of the guy's yard, I plopped down the bag of bones and stuff. Using the spade I brought, I dug a small hole for the candle. I set up the ritual space, with a small altar and candle in the middle. All the bones were laid out in a circle.

I spotted a flash of white pass in one of Agnes' windows. Soon, though, I would have my power as a necromancer, and there would be nothing she could do to stop me.

When the moon waxed to its peak, I lit the candle and put it on my altar. Sparks of red, yellow, and orange danced before me. Sitting in front of it in a meditative pose, I chanted. Talking about the laying of the bones in the circle, I described to the spirits my process of contacting them. The spell was about enticing the spirits of the dead to aid me in this endeavor, to have them be a part of me, to join me so that I could use this power.

The wind picked up, tossed my hair. My chanting grew fervent. I called on the spirits that inhabited the dolls. Still, the flame of the candle held, and no strong wind would ever put it out. It was my energy, my time as a necromancer came, and I seized the night.

Spirits like white flames rose from the lawn. Some of them had faces and evil grins, others were only blurs. My voice grew louder. I didn't care if all the people in the neighborhood woke up. I was a necromancer at last!

Then, the ground shook like a mini earthquake. The balance seemed to shift, and I didn't know what it was. The ground below me fell away, sending me through a hole.

A sinkhole.

Nothing in my books on magic mentioned this. I fell for what seemed like forever, but it must have just taken a minute or so. I stopped midair but rubble kept on going until it crashed on the floor. I was in a cave with tunnels leading in different directions.

Wafts of decay assaulted my nostrils, a coppery tinge in the air that smelled like I was in the pit of an outhouse. The thud of dirt landing sounded like a thunderstorm, and I couldn't figure out why I hadn't hit the ground too. Dirt hitting the back of my head, and my back stung like getting hit by hail. I tried to squirm out of the way but couldn't move. I was suspended in mid-air as if caught in a spider's web. My breaths were shallow. Anxiety ran down my spine like an electrical current.

I could hear noises, though where they came from I couldn't be sure. There was a crunch of dirt and bones here and there and the slithering of what I thought was a tail. It was out of my sight, but each step terrified me. The hair on my forearms stood. Goose pimples covered my arms. My pulse quickened.

"Ho, ho, ho. Well, look at this lost soul," said a disembodied voice.

"Who are you?"

Two burning red balls of light floated before me. "You should have listened to the old hag."

"What do you want from me?"

"What do I want? I want for nothing, and if you hadn't stumbled into this place, I wouldn't be talking with you. Stupid fool."

Before the sinkhole, I felt the power of the spirits enter me. So maybe I had enough to do something. I focused on raising spirits and found that I had enough magic to summon more ghosts. Spirits rose from the ground below. But the thing before me only laughed.

"Do you think what little spirits you were able to conjure could help you now?" The red eyes tilted for a moment.

My body sank into an imaginary web, but not my entire body. My arms and legs stayed put. My joints snapped like a chicken wishbone, and pain seared through me. The pain felt like someone was drilling holes in all my sockets. Like the worst root canals I had ever experienced, but in my joints. I let out a scream.

"I'm going to enjoy consuming you."

I whispered a small prayer to whichever deity or spirit might be listening for all this pain to end soon.

MICHAEL PICKELL currently resides in Seattle, WA. He has been published in the Nebraska Writers Guild Anthologies *Voices from the Plains* Volumes 1 and 2. He has written articles for Food & Spirits Issues 21, 27 & 28. His self-published collection of Haiku poems can be found on Amazon: *Across*

Distant Galaxies. He also has a short story in the Moorhead Friends Writing Group Anthology: *Tales from the Water's Edge*. When he isn't writing horror stories, he enjoys hiking and photography.

LIGHTS OUT

Suzi Wieland

"YOU'RE FAMOUS. YOUR PICTURE and everything in the Effham Falls Gazette." Ruby whacks me with a rolled newspaper and tosses it onto the bed. She picked it up after breakfast from the front desk of the hotel.

"I am not." I sigh and heave my suitcase onto the stand.

I don't want to be famous. Don't want anybody to know my name. And I definitely don't want to be called a ghost detective extraordinaire. I just want my life back. I want to walk by a cemetery without being grunted at.

My damn back aches so bad. Three floors and no elevator in the hotel is hard on a flabby fifty-year-old body. But eating healthy is so difficult on the road. Ruby is forty-seven, though, and doesn't have my problems.

I lean down, pick up the newspaper, and spread it on the top of my suitcase.

Ghost Detective Extraordinaire to Visit Effham
Falls
By Renata Avila

Famed ghost detective Krista Mellon will be visiting our very own Effham Falls. Mellon was invited by twelve-year-old Taylor Whittle to try to solve the disappearance and murder of her great-grandfather, Marvin Whittle, who went missing from his hardware store in May of 1964. "My grandma has told me so many stories, and I feel bad that nobody knows what happened,"

Whittle wrote in her letter to Krista Mellon. "She deserves to have peace."

Marvin Whittle's body was found behind the First United Methodist Church, but the case remains unsolved to this day.

Young Taylor wrote a beautiful letter about her great-grandpa and what it would mean to her and her grandmother," Mellon said in reference to the case, "and I just knew I had to come try."

Mellon's new calling as a ghost detective started after her fiftieth birthday. "I don't know why it happened, and I don't know how, but on the night of my birthday, there was a blue moon, and suddenly, the next day, ghosts started seeking me out."

The ghosts don't actually speak to her, Mellon said, but she feels their emotions, and they lead her back to their graves. There, she does her detective work, and she's able to glean enough clues about their murders to give to the authorities. So far, her information has led to the closing of ninety-two previously unsolved crimes and thirty-two arrests. "I'm just happy to be giving closure to the families of these victims."

In Part 2 of my article on Krista Mellon, we will reveal exactly how she gets her information from the ghosts. Stay tuned. And please join us for a reception welcoming her to Effham Falls on Thursday at eleven a.m. at the Rusty Nail Bar and Grill.

"Pretty typical of a small-town newspaper, isn't it?" Ruby chuckles.

We both grew up in dying rural towns. Effham Falls doesn't seem so bad, though, with its thriving downtown and lovely parks. And that waterfall, its namesake—we drove by it, and it's so beautiful. We'll have to check it out when we have more time.

"At least it wasn't like the newspapers when I was a kid. Our weekly paper was still sharing how Mrs. Busybody went to visit Mrs. Snootyville for tea." The newspapers were half gossip rags back then. "But yeah, Renata was good to talk to. She's only like twenty-seven. Hasn't become cynical or jaded yet."

Unlike me. But I have a great reason. When you're constantly surrounded by poor lost souls who were violently murdered and just want to move on, it's hard to stay bright and cheery. Their gruesome bodies are sometimes hard to look at.

Renata is a little pushy, but not so bad—she's a journalist after all. I had to tell her three times that she couldn't come with us to the reveal, which is what I call it when I find the story the ghost wants to share. Ruby is the only one I allow with me since she knows how to behave and won't scare the ghosts away.

"You showering before the party?" Ruby asks. "Don't use up all the hot water."

I snort. She won't let me forget the time we visited a small town in northern California, and my twenty-minute shower emptied the water heaters, according to the desk clerk at least. This hotel is older but is still in decent shape.

"I think we'll be good."

Ruby's been my best friend for over thirty years now. Been there for the divorce of my awful first husband and the death of my beloved second. And now she travels the country with me, making me laugh and keeping me organized. And sane.

I wish she could go in my place to this welcoming reception, but it's me they want there, not her. Even though she's the fun one. I'd much rather be in my hotel room enjoying the silence. Because it never lasts long enough.

I rub my eyes and scowl. "A full moon. How fitting."

It shines bright in the sky tonight. I don't know if the full moon kickstarted my supernatural abilities, but it was there the first time I ran into a ghost.

"The moon will help us see, at least," Ruby chirps from the passenger seat.

The Effham Falls Cemetery lies just a mile outside of town, bordered on one side by the Niijii River. And thank goodness we have that full moon tonight because the only other light is from poorly spaced streetlights along the paved road. And several of them are out. We ditch my car and step onto the grass, the dark headstones spreading before me. The hot, acerbic air sits heavy in my chest. It's wrong. All wrong. Graveyards usually fill me with peace, but this one is off. Maybe that's why I'm in such a foul mood.

"Do you smell that?" It almost smells like there's a pile of rotting eggs hidden somewhere, but I doubt that's the case. Maybe there's a landfill close by.

Ruby sniffs the air, her hands on her hips. "Smells like fresh-cut grass."

Not to me.

The hairs on the back of my neck prickle. Stone after stone stands at attention like wary soldiers, and I can't help but feel that someone is watching us. It's not a feeling that ghosts usually give me.

"Yeah." I shake off the uneasiness. No reason to get her riled up, but that sour stank isn't sitting well in my stomach. And now I know what else is wrong.

The noise. Or lack of it, rather.

It's silent.

No buzzing cicadas like outside of the hotel.

No grasshoppers or crickets.

Nothing. Absolutely nothing.

"Lead on, fearless leader." Ruby claps me on the back, and I about jump.

Nothing is wrong here. I'm just on edge because... well, because... I don't know.

We pass grand headstones and simpler ones, and some graves only have flat markers. They don't have a columbarium here, the newest trend I've been seeing, but I'm sure it'll pop up soon.

"There it is." I point to the gray granite headstone.

Marvin A. Whittle
Born February 14th, 1932
Died October 25th, 1964

"Only thirty-two years old. And the murder left his poor widow to raise those three young children all by herself." Ruby lets out a sigh. "At least she had a good support system."

A man in coveralls suddenly appears behind the grave.

I stumble backwards and put my hand over my racing heart. I should be prepared for the ghosts' appearances, but I never am.

"Boo," Ruby says softly and grins. We've done this enough times, and she knows what happened.

The man's body fades in and out for a few seconds until it finally solidifies into a black-and-white form. The one thing I can't figure out is why the ghosts don't appear in color. Well, that's not the only thing, but it's the one that bothers me the most.

"Hello, I'm Krista." I give him a warm smile to reassure him I'm safe, but there's no animosity rolling off him like some others have. He's way over six feet tall with broad shoulders, and he's good-looking with his thick dark hair and big eyes. He's missing a tooth, which sort of makes him look even more adorable. "I'm here to help you."

He grunts, a grin spreading as he raises his hand to me over the headstone. It's too bad that the ghosts can't actually talk to me—or that someone hasn't invented a grunt translator. It'd make my job a lot easier.

I offer him my hand, but it passes right through his, and he gives me a surprised look.

"That's how it usually goes." I laugh, dropping my now-damp, heated hand to my side. I've never felt anything solid, but their touch always leaves my skin moist and warm.

Ruby kneels on the grass with my bag, pulling out everything I need.

"Your family invited me here," I continue. "Your great-granddaughter actually. Taylor is a little spitfire. She—"

He throws his head back and laughs. Then starts grunting, like he's rambling off a story about her. His face is bright and cheery, the opposite of so many ghosts I run into. No doubt he's had visitors to his grave quite often. There's no speck of loneliness in him, which is so common among the ghosts I free.

Because that's essentially what I'm doing. Solving their crimes—even if it doesn't end up with a conviction—gives the ghosts permission to move on. They just need someone to see their story, to acknowledge and share it.

Marvin's hands wave animatedly as he grunts at me, and I can't help but smile.

"He's telling me about his family, I'm guessing," I tell Ruby, and Marvin stops. I point to her as she stands and dusts off her knees. "This is my friend Ruby."

He waves to her, and I chuckle. "She can't see you. Or hear you." I turn to her. "He's saying hello."

"Hey, Marvin. It's great to meet you. I heard so much from your great-granddaughter and daughter today. Taylor is such a sweetheart." Ruby is facing him, her eyes flitting around.

"We're here so you can tell your story," I add. "And I hope that will allow you to move on."

His head turns to another grave beside us, and his shoulders droop. All the joy has left his face, and he trudges to the matching headstone next to his.

Josephine L. Whittle
Born September 26th, 1934
Died October 25th, 2015

She never remarried, according to Taylor's mom. Never even tried to look for love again.

"I heard she was a remarkable woman. And I'm sure you've missed her a lot." I step closer to Josephine's grave. One time in this strange journey I've been on, I ran into the dead spouse of a murder victim. She died of natural causes years after her husband.

As far as I could tell, the two ghosts lived side-by-side in a graveyard for forty years, never knowing that the other was beside them. Never able to escape the pain of their losses. Until I was able to reveal their story. I'll never forget when their eyes opened to one another, the joy and happiness on their faces, and the sense of peace as they moved on together. Stories like that are what keeps me going.

Marvin runs his hand back and forth over the top of the gray stone, his pain filling me, and I pray that he's able to see her again.

I can't say for certain that 100% of the ghosts I run into have moved on, but I've seen it happen enough. And I don't want to think about the ones who still refuse to leave—the ones whose suffering is too great to allow them peace.

"How about I start so you can see your beloved Josephine again?" I smile at him, and the gratitude in his eyes almost makes me tear up. I quickly explain how I'm unable to understand him talking to me but that he'll be able to share his story another way.

I kneel in the grass before his headstone, all my tools ready. First, I spray the stone with my water bottle, then wipe the towel over it a few times to remove all the dust and moisture.

I unroll a large piece of paper and hang it over the grave. Marvin just watches us as Ruby steps behind and tapes the paper down while I kneel in the front. I pick up my black crayon that looks like a charcoal briquette. It's about two inches thick, and I made it myself from melting others down. It's much easier to grasp than the thin crayons that little kids use. When I was in the midst of my Crayola years, I never imagined how I'd be using these crayons one day.

I run the crayon back and forth over Marvin's name and dates of birth and death. As they show up on the paper, Marvin creeps closer, but Ruby just sits back and watches.

Once his name and the dates are completed, I slide my crayon off to the side of his name, over the flat, smooth stone. There are no grooves underneath, but a picture begins to emerge as if there were. A rectangle. I keep rubbing, back—forth—back—forth—and the shapes fill in. Windows on the front of a building. No, two buildings right next to each other.

I keep going, revealing maybe a sun above the buildings—but not a sun. A face. And then a second face. I slide my hand back and forth across all the blank space on the paper, the black crayon coloring it all in.

A sense of urgency fills me. I'm close. So close. I just know that I'm going to find my answers. The family will find *their* answers. But they'll have more questions too. Marvin was murdered in 1964, and the killer is most likely dead. They might not get justice, but it's a start to the end of the story.

My wrist throbs, and I want to switch hands, but using my left hand doesn't work. I wiggle my back because it's starting to ache. Sometimes my rubbings take twenty minutes, and sometimes they take hours.

The crayon continues to create images that shouldn't be. Not only because there is nothing behind the paper but due to the accuracy—it looks more like a sharpened pencil did the drawing and not a blunt crayon. Also, I am no artist. I'm unable to replicate anything that shows up on my graveyard papers, though I've tried many times.

Finally, no more images appear when I rub. Just lines that go back and forth.

I sit back and take in the whole picture.

I was wrong. It's four buildings next to each other, that I recognize from downtown. The outside two have no details, but the inside two show me exactly what they were. The Neon Rose Lounge and Fluff'n'Fold Laundromat. Above them are the faces of two men. One with a bushy beard and the second with a mustache. The latter, with the dark glint in his eyes and his smarmy grin, makes my skin crawl.

"Is this who killed you?" I point to the mustached face, and Marvin grunts. "And you were murdered at the laundromat?"

He shakes his head.

"At the bar?" I glance back at Ruby, who's quiet.

Marvin nods.

"And this guy"—I point to Bushy Beard—"He... did he help?" Marvin gives a no. "Was he there?"

Yes.

"And this is where they found your body." I had drawn a picture of First United Methodist Church, which is still in town too. I knew he'd been discovered at a church and had checked out all three before coming here, but I didn't know which one it was. The picture shows a row of bushes outside and a dark shape, his body, stuffed underneath the distinct window.

Yes.

The only other pictures are of a twenty-dollar bill and a woman's face. It's not much to go off of, and I usually have more. Time for rapid fire. My very own game of Twenty Questions. Although sometimes it's fifty or more.

"Is that Josephine?" I ask.

Yes.

"Does this have something to do with her?"

Yes.

"Mustache Man. Did he hurt Josephine?"

Marvin's face wrinkles up, and his brows raise, though he doesn't respond otherwise.

"Was he going to hurt her?"

He nods vigorously and points to Bushy Beard.

"Him too."

Yes.

"And you tried to stop them. And Mustache Man killed you. At the bar."

Yes.

He grabs his neck with his hand and squeezes.

"You were strangled by Mustache Man."

The relief flows off Marvin, his face glowing. I need to ask more questions. The more information, the better. And I don't know what the money means.

"Did you owe—"

Martin's head whips around, and he stares at Josephine's grave. Then his head tilts up. An intoxicating scent hits me, like I've stepped into a field of hyacinths.

No, no, no.

I want to yell at him to stop, but I have no control over the situation. And even if I could stop him, I wouldn't deny him this next step.

His smile broadens, and his body starts to fade. The air is fresh and light, like a spring day, and I can't help but feel happy for him.

"He's gone." My body even feels lighter right now.

"Already? That's quick." Ruby comes over to me, and we look down at the paper taped to the headstone. "Did you get enough information?"

"I don't know. It'll depend on if anyone can identify the two men. The murderer is connected to the laundromat somehow. Maybe he worked there. Or owned it. We'll see."

I sniff at the air. That sour smell is back, filling my nose and turning my stomach. Perhaps the wind changed.

A cloud passes over the moon, and the cemetery darkens like someone switched the lights off.

"God, that smell. It's awful." I rub my nose. "You still can't smell it?" I bend down and remove the paper from the headstone while Ruby gathers the other tools.

"Nope, luckily not, I guess."

"It's making me queasy. Is there some kind of factory somewhere close? Maybe a sugar beet plant? Uff." That doesn't explain why I didn't notice it when Marvin was here though.

I straighten up and look around.

Oh shit. I suck in a hard breath.

There are bodies everywhere. Ghosts. Mostly men but some women. Grunting at me. Standing behind other gravestones. Between them. Walking toward me. Toward us.

One has a big gash in his neck. Another has a hole in his bare chest. A third—he's holding up his hand, and it's missing all its fingers. So many injuries. So much death.

I back up, my hands clammy. There's too many of them. This cemetery has maybe five hundred graves. All from the past hundred-plus years.

"There's... there's..."

It's not possible. There can't be this many murder victims in a small-town cemetery. Over fifty. Or maybe a hundred. Wave after wave of gory ghosts are coming closer. They're almost here.

"What's wrong?"

They grunt at me from the left. From the right. From all over. The sounds vibrate in my chest, getting louder and harder. My body is so hot, and my feet feel like they're glued to the ground.

Krista, Krista, Krista...

They have no voices, but they're calling my name. They want me. They're coming after me.

They're grunting at us. A swarm of the dead. An army.

The paper falls from my hands and curls up on the grass.

"They're... they're all over. They're coming..."

"What?" Ruby squeals, her head whipping around.

"Hundreds of ghosts." I grab her arm and jerk her to my side. "We need to get out of here. Now!"

"Let me get this straight." Sheriff Craig Sorenson looks up at me from his desk, a pile of rolled-up grave rubbings in front of him. Rubbings that explain exactly what has been happening at the cemetery. "You want me to dig up some graves because you think there's more than one body in them?" He gives Deputy Frantzen an incredulous look.

"Yes. I don't know how many yet. I couldn't get them all last night, but I'll keep going until I document each person's story."

Ruby and I fled the scene two nights ago, but the guilt sat heavy in my stomach. Those ghosts didn't want to hurt me. They just wanted someone to listen. Just like Marvin. And so I gathered my courage and dragged her back the next night. They returned, and although I couldn't count them all because they kept moving around, I'd guess between seventy and ninety.

"The evidence is all right here." Ruby grabs the nearest roll and unfurls it. "This one. See. It shows a picture, the same picture as all the others do. And they also have other information."

She unfurls a second paper and holds them both open. The first paper shows a casket with two bodies in it. Additional drawings on that paper show a house and a knife dripping with blood. The second paper shows the same two-bodied casket, but its other pictures include something I swear is the St. Louis Arch with the city skyline, along with two buildings that look like they belong downtown. It also shows two men, one pointing a gun at the other.

I didn't interview the ghosts like I had Marvin. I should have done that with at least a few—it was stupid not to. But the ghosts kept calling me from one grave to another to do their rubbings.

Deputy Frantzen runs a hand through his hair and stares at Ruby. "This is a bit preposterous."

"But you saw how her rubbing led to them solving Marvin Whittle's crime. You know this is real." Ruby, my biggest supporter, is always there to stand up for me. "We have thirty of these."

Sheriff Sorenson shakes his head. "I wouldn't say that is solved yet. Just because she remembers the two Graff brothers doesn't mean they did it."

Marvin's daughter identified the two men pictured in my rubbing. Brothers who died before the year 2000—one owned the laundromat, and the other owned the bar next door back in the 60s. We don't know the full story, but they're on their way to unraveling the mystery—I know it in my heart.

"But it will be solved. And so can this other mystery. And if you can just dig up one of these graves to prove there's a second body there, you'll—"

"You didn't say who these other bodies belong to. We haven't exactly had a surge of missing people here. Or any missing people, really. Not only in our town but in the county." Sheriff

Sorenson folds his arms and leans back in his seat. "And you want me to go ask a grieving family to let us dig up their loved one's grave."

My whole body deflates. This is the problem. The grave rubbings show the name of the local person buried—the one we know about—but the rubbings also show that there are second bodies in those caskets. I believe all the additional pictures belong to the second person, yet I don't know who they are.

Deputy Frantzen folds his arms, the smirk still on his face. "Randy would get a big kick out of this story if he heard what you two girls are suggesting. Hahn Funeral Home has been passed down from generation to generation. It's a respectable business."

Girls. The word grates on me like nails on a chalkboard.

I clench my jaw, and my head is throbbing.

Sheriff Sorensen laughs. "Yes, I don't imagine Randy Hahn is out there murdering people and stuffing them into his coffins."

Antagonizing them will do no good here. They'll never believe us, and I don't know what we can do. More rubbings. That's a start. Interview some ghosts to try to get some details. I have to do everything I can to solve this mystery. There are so many lost souls who deserve peace.

But we're set to leave after my interview with the reporter, and we have to be in Eau Claire by tomorrow night. Then Ruby and I are driving to Davenport and Springfield. I also have that stupid mammogram appointment I'd scheduled months ago, so I have to get home to Louisville.

I scan my mental calendar. Three weeks from now, we have a break.

"I'm not giving up on this. At the end of the month, we're returning." Or I'll return if Ruby doesn't want to, but I know she will.

"You do that." Sheriff Sorenson gives me a patronizing grin that I want to smack off his face.

Ruby and I take our leave, and I fume all the way to the car.

"So what's your plan?" she asks as she tugs on her seatbelt.

"After we finish this tour, I'm coming back on our break. But I don't think I'll mention this to the reporter yet. She's sure to put it in her story, and people will probably be less open to the idea. Especially if she interviews the sheriff, and he calls us dumb or something." I rub my temples, trying to get rid of my headache.

"Once I do more rubbings, I'll talk to the townsfolk. If I can convince one person to let us look and we find that second body, then the sheriff will listen."

"Maybe we should fly in for this one. We can rent a car and drive from Minneapolis."

"Good idea." I picture all the sad faces I saw in that graveyard, each and every one with a story to tell of their own.

I can't let those ghosts down. The ghosts deserve justice, and there's got to be someone—just one person in town—who'll believe us.

The door slams, and I jolt up, wavering on my feet. Little pins prickle across my skin like my feet have fallen asleep. All the blood rushes to my head, and I feel woozy for a second. But then it goes away, replaced by an ache in my back. Again. Being fifty sucks.

"What the hell was that?" a gruff voice says, and I blink my unfocused eyes. Deputy Frantzen is standing in front of a door, his face twisted into a snarl.

The room. It's cold, like the air conditioning is on high.

"Relax," another man says. I don't recognize him, but his smarmy grin sets me on edge. He leans against the counter of the room we're in. The space has gray cupboards, sterile countertops, a small sink, and a bland tiled floor, but it doesn't feel like a hospital room. And the second man isn't in scrubs.

"You almost fucked it all up, Boone," Deputy Frantzen spits. "I knew we shouldn't have trusted you."

"Hey, bruh, you didn't want to go down to Louisville. I did you a favor."

"Gentlemen, settle. We're all good here." A third man waves his hands, standing behind a raised metal table. Randy Hahn. I remember him from the welcoming reception. We only spoke briefly before the mayor interrupted us. It was too bad because Randy is nice to look at—a man who's aging gracefully.

"What's all good?" I close my eyes for a second, willing away the throbbing in my head.

"You almost got the wrong one." Frantzen stalks toward Boone. "You almost—"

"I got the job done." Boone pushes off the counter and rounds the metal table, heading for me. He's looking me straight in the eye, and a memory flashes in my head. Him in my kitchen late at night. The stink of a sweaty body, his foul breath. His ugly, dark eyes.

I jump out of his way, but he passes through me like I'm air, and stops.

My mouth drops. My stomach heaves. My body feels so hot.

He stands in front of an empty wood casket lined with silky pink bedding, a strange look on his face. Then he wipes his forehead and rubs his hands on his pants.

"Where is she? How does this work?" Boone stuffs his hands down the side of the casket.

"Let me do it." Randy pushes him away. He sets aside the pink pillow and folds the shiny pink lining back to reveal the bottom. "There's a false floor in here. You can't just pull it up." He grabs a tool with a beveled edge and sticks it down the side near the corner. There's a small pop, and the corner rises. He nudges Boone again and repeats the move on the other corner. Then uses his fingers to raise the thin piece of wood.

I gasp.

It's me. Or what used to be me.

"God, she's ugly." Boone snorts. "What'd you do to her?"

I am. My face is pale and stiff. My eyes closed. My nose flattened. And I'm wearing a t-shirt and shorts. My pajamas.

But I'm standing right here. I'm alive.

Or at least I feel alive.

I touch my heart to see if it's beating, but I can't feel anything. I search for my pulse on my wrist.

Nothing.

"The noses and bodies get smushed sometimes. I can only add four inches to the casket height, or else people will notice. I'd rather not cut up the bodies if I don't have to. She just barely fit." Randy Hahn speaks like he's talking about stuffing a suitcase into a trunk, not a dead body.

My dead body.

"I'm not really dead, am I?" I ask.

"How did she know what was going on?" Boone asks.

"I dunno." Deputy Frantzen runs his hand through his hair as he sighs. "I'm pretty sure she didn't talk to Renata Avila yet, so only the sheriff knows, and he thinks she's a kook.

And the friend you knocked out..." He scowls at Boone again. "Hopefully, she'll be too distraught over her missing friend to even imagine this is connected to Effham Falls."

The memories hit my mind in flash after flash. Ruby and I watching a movie. A knock at the door; Ruby answering it while I refilled our wine glasses. Her squeals of terror and the thump on the floor. Boone rushing for me with a shocked look on his face.

Then nothing.

Oh no, Ruby.

"Did you hurt her?" I try tugging his arm, but my hand passes right through him. He better not have killed her. But no, that's not what Frantzen implied. She must be alive.

The weight on my heart lifts. I'd feel so guilty if I'm the reason she's dead.

Randy Hahn replaces the board in the casket. "I'll just glue this shut, and it'll be all ready for Phyllis Smith. Poor woman. The cancer just spread too fast." Randy tucks the bedding into the side tenderly.

"What number is this?" Deputy Frantzen knocks on the side of the casket.

"Seventy-eight."

Boone lets out a long whistle. "You've been busy."

Randy grins wickedly. "That's over the last ten years. Word's been getting out lately across the country, and I've had more people interested in sending me their worm food."

I gasp as Boone snickers.

"I'm in the wrong business." Deputy Frantzen huffs.

"That you are, my friend." Randy pats Frantzen on the shoulder as he passes by. "Good thing I need a dependable man helping me out from time to time. Especially when some crazy lady shows up claiming there's ghosts in the graveyard." He holds the door open for the two men, and Boone and Frantzen shuffle out.

Randy stares at the casket holding my dead body, then flips the switch by the door.

And the lights go out.

SUZI WIELAND writes in a variety of genres and has self-published horror and suspense stories and some fairytale retellings. She has also published contemporary young adult novels under the name Suzi Drew. When she's not writing, she spends time with her family and friends and her sweet and fluffy dog. She also works as a freelance editor and gets to edit fantastic stories for her job.

FAMILY SECRETS

Robert D. Moore, Jr.

TORIE OPENED THE BACK door of Wallflower and leaned out to look around. The parking lot behind the string of businesses was cracked concrete faced with crumbling brick walls. Pretty facades were something for the front of the businesses and street traffic, not the back. Deep shadows stretched out toward the few cars left in the lot.

Finally, she stepped out, closed the door, and locked it. Now it was time to walk to her car. She tried to follow her mother's advice to look confident and walk normally, but the more she thought about the dark, the more nervous she became, and the faster her steps.

"Hey there, baby!"

Torie almost broke and ran when she heard the cheerful male voice. A tall, muscular man stepped out of the shadows to her right. He was wearing a light jacket, black in color, even though the summer night didn't warrant it. With a rolling swagger, he moved in front of her.

"I thought you'd never close up tonight."

"Listen, Mark, I've already told you three times that I'm not interested," she said as she backed away from him. She stopped for a second then moved suddenly to get around him. Mark shuffle-stepped to stay in her way, making it clear that such a ploy would not work.

Smiling, he shook his head. "And I've told you you're not thinking this through." He moved toward her confidently.

That did it. A panicked Torie darted to the side, but Mark laughed and lunged to grab her arm. He swung her around at the wall of the diner, and she hit it with a grunt as the air was knocked from her lungs. Mark followed, grabbing her again, and bringing her arm up against her back painfully. Pressed between the hard brick and his bulk, she couldn't catch her breath.

"Tonight, I'm going to show you what you're going to be getting with me." Growling like an animal, he flicked his tongue along the edge of her ear. Torie tried to sob but there was nothing in her lungs.

She gulped before managing to gasp, "Please don't do this, Mark. Please. I won't tell anyone." Mark just laughed at her.

"Do that some more. I like it when a woman begs."

He pulled her back from the wall but hitched her arm higher behind her, and reached around to fumble at her belt and the fastening of her jeans. Torie tried to twist and turn to make things more difficult for him, but the pressure on her pinned arm limited how much she could move before searing pain made her stop. Instead, she took a deep breath, ready to let it out in a scream.

"I'll pull it out of socket if I have to, and if you scream, I'll hurt you even worse."

Deft fingers got her belt unfastened and the snap undone. Torie's free hand beat feebly at Mark's as he unfastened her pants, but he hitched her bound arm higher, sending searing pain through her shoulder, and she stopped. His lips brushed her ear, and he purred as he inched the zipper down. Torie shook with an unvoiced sob and wished something, anything, would happen to stop him.

Mark started pushing her pants down but had barely begun when a sharp sound echoed from up the alleyway toward Orange Avenue. The sound came again and became identifiable as the sharp clack of boot heels striking concrete.

Frustrated, Mark growled. "Everything's fine, do you hear? I have a gun. I'll shoot you and whoever's interrupting our fun." He turned to Torie and said, "Get your pants up."

He let her go. She straightened up and did her best to fix her appearance in the few seconds they had.

The steps came closer, and there was the distinct, acrid smell of cigarette smoke in the air. A dark form approached them, slipping between the shadows, much as Mark had done. Tall and slender, the figure walked toward them with an unhurried, rolling gate. Orange light flared from the coal of a cigarette as the figure took a drag. When the light lit up the face of the newcomer, Torie's heart raced with hope and dread.

"Mom?"

"Hello, dear," the figure said in a silky, smooth voice. "Is everything alright?" She took another drag from her cigarette.

Torie gave Mark a nervous glance, then looked back at her mother. "E-everything's fine, Mom. What brings you out tonight?"

"Oh, I just had a feeling there might be trouble tonight, what with that guy stalking you and all."

The entire time, her mother's eyes never left Mark's. His hands went into his jacket pockets. She took a final drag from the cigarette, dropped it, and crushed it out with a ruthless twist of her boot, then stepped closer.

Torie shook her head rapidly, hoping her mother would take the hint and just leave. She feared what Mark might do to her, but she was more afraid of what he might do to both of them if her mother didn't leave.

"Everything's fine, really. M-Mark just came...to walk me to my car."

Torie's mother lit another cigarette. She exhaled a cloud of smoke as she put the lighter away.

"Hello, Mark, I'm Selene. It's a pleasure to meet you." For the first time, Selene's eyes flicked to her daughter. "And you're a terrible liar. We'll have to work on that." Her eyes shifted back to Mark's. His expression tightened, and his smile became forced.

"It's a pleasure to meet you too, Selene." He sounded pleasant despite seething inside. "I was thinking of taking Torie out for a drink or two if that's alright."

Selene took another long drag on the cigarette and exhaled a plume of thick smoke. "No, it most certainly is not alright. In fact, I think Torie's going to go home right now, and you and I are going to have a nice...chat."

"Mother—"

Selene cut her off with a shake of her head and a cutting gesture of her hand. "Leave. Now."

Mark looked Selene up and down, taking in her slender, lithe shape. Her golden blonde hair framed her face and draped down onto her shoulders like a mane. She wasn't as nicely curved as Torie, but she was pretty. She was certainly too pretty to be someone's mother, especially someone Torie's age.

"Yeah, Torie. You go on home. I'll catch up with you later since your mom wants to have a talk with me." He was through with pretenses, so he grabbed Torie's arm and shoved her off toward the parking lot, keeping his other hand in his pocket.

Torie hesitated, but Selene gave her a slow nod as she watched Mark. Not understanding why her mother would stay, Torie hurried to her car.

Once Torie's taillights disappeared, Selene drew a final drag and flicked the cigarette away carelessly.

"You should make this interesting and run," she said in a low hiss.

Mark laughed a cold and condescending sound. He drew a gun from his pocket. "No, you should make this interesting and just strip."

"Strip, hmmm?" Selene murmured. "Yes, that might be best." She started unbuttoning her shirt and continued to talk. "You know, I'm not Torie's real mother." She finished unbuttoning her shirt and flipped it open revealing herself to be naked beneath.

A distracted Mark said, "Is that so?"

"Yes. You see, I found her abandoned in the woods. Such a pale, puny, pink, and mewling thing." Selene heeled off her boots, still moving slowly and methodically.

"I had no children of my own, so I decided, 'What the hell?' and I have raised her as my own ever since. I've even pretended to be human and got a job of all things." Her eyes glittered in the low light as she shrugged out of her shirt and worked on her pants. "It's going to be nice to drop the charade even if it is just for a brief time."

Somewhere along the line, she must have lit another cigarette, because smoke puffed from her nostrils. Mark didn't notice, or care, that her hands were empty. He was licking his lips as he watched her undress.

"You're a crazy bitch," he said with a laugh. He stopped laughing and brandished the pistol. "But you talk too much. Finish stripping and get over there against the wall."

Selene stepped out of her pants. "No, you get against the wall, or maybe start running like I suggested." Her voice was still a silky caress, at odds with her chain-smoking habit.

Mark opened his mouth to say something, but his intended words turned into a scream. She struck fast like a snake, grabbed his wrist, and twisted. Bones snapped like dry twigs and ivory spikes tore through the jacket. The gun dropped to the broken concrete. She grabbed him by the front of his jacket, lifted him completely off the ground, and threw him against the wall. He hit with enough force to lose his breath and gray out.

"I told you to make this at least somewhat interesting and run." Her voice was no longer a silky tone, but a low, guttural growl. Her eyes weren't just glittering. They glowed with a menacing red light, the pupils now vertical slits.

Mark regained his breath and couldn't believe what he was seeing. The shape of the woman stretched out and thickened. Even in the low light, he could see the sheen of scales covering her skin. He didn't need another warning. With a cry, he turned and ran. He'd made it twenty yards up the alley when he heard an animalistic growl behind him. Somehow, he ran faster.

He'd almost made it to Orange Avenue when he heard the clacking on the roof above him. He didn't slow down but glanced up and cried out at what he saw. "Oh god!"

A long, gleaming, serpentine form with scales of gold and green flowed along the edge of the roof. Talons that flickered in the low light like silver spikes gripped the edge of the building and dug into the brick. A great golden mane surrounded its head, and fleshy whiskers drooped from the end of its long snout. Glowing red eyes stared into his.

The monster opened its mouth and a gout of flame billowed forth. Mark leaped to the side, avoiding the fire, but still feeling its blistering heat. Another cry, this one more of a sob, and he ran across the avenue and cut north toward Main St. Selene watched him go and chuckled.

Effham Falls isn't a big town, so Mark's flight soon took him beyond the streetlights and sidewalks. He barreled into the trees and undergrowth at the edge of town with his lungs burning. Selene stayed on top of the building, watching. She waited — long enough that Mark slowed to catch his breath. He thought he might get away among the trees, or maybe she would let him go.

Selene sprang from the top of the building and slithered through the air until she was above the streetlights and nothing more than a passing shadow below. She followed Mark's path and wound her way silently through the trees. When Mark stopped, she dropped on him, pinning him to the ground with a great clawed foot.

Mark screamed. "Please! Let me go. I'll leave Torie alone. I'll disappear, leave Effham Falls forever. Just let me go."

The claw lifted from him. Reptilian lips peeled back from ivory fangs in a vicious imitation of a smile. Selene's voice vibrated with a purr as she said, "Do that some more. I like it when a man begs." A forked tongue flicked out to lick the side of his face.

Mark's eyes widened and he scurried backward but was hindered by the useless arm cradled against his chest. Smoke billowed from Selene's mouth, and she flicked him with a silvery talon. Mark cried out in pain as he rolled over his disabled arm.

"Run, little morsel. You haven't made this very interesting."

Scrambling to his feet, Mark ran. Fire sizzled behind him, but he didn't turn to look. He wound and twisted his way through the trees and crashed through brush. The sounds of pursuit followed at a slower pace, but he couldn't keep going. His breath came in ragged gasps and his legs burned from exertion.

As he slowed, there came a rushing sound behind him. He dodged blindly but the razor point of a talon still scored down his back. Mark stumbled forward and fell. Jagged spikes of bone from his arm stabbed into his chest. He tried to scream but only managed a gurgling groan. With a delicate touch, a claw rolled him over to look up into those gleaming red eyes.

"I can't just let you go, you know. Later, you'd just start thinking it was some hallucinogen in the smoke. Then you'd bother Torie again." She brought her snout down to his face. Smoke rose in wisps from her nostrils. "And I would do anything for my daughter." The snout drew back, and Mark gave one last scream that cut off sharply.

ROBERT MOORE is originally from the Mississippi/Louisiana Gulf Coast but has managed to find himself in North Dakota now. He's an astronomer and geologist who likes to poke at the question of why planets and stars exist in the first place, and he likes to write stories that he hopes are at least somewhat entertaining.

LET ME DREAM IN A QUIET ROOM

Alexander Vayle

ANDREW PUT HIS LAST thousand bucks on black and watched the marble drop.

Roulette was a dumb game. A beginner's game. A game for people who wanted to look like gamblers but didn't know what the hell they were doing. That being said, roulette still had its place, and that place was firmly at the end of the line. After a little fun on the video slots, after chewing out idiots for splitting tens against a face card on the blackjack tables, and after a few gorgeous—but still second place—poker hands, then and only then came roulette. Because roulette was a game fueled by desperation, and that night Andrew's tank was full.

One hundred forty thousand dollars had come and gone over the last year. The money arrived in a lump sum with a little help from a nine-millimeter, which now lay in the bottom of a river outside Shitsplat, Minnesota. It went a chunk at a time. Some on a sixty-five Mustang that he'd recently crashed and abandoned, some on top-shelf booze and lavish dinners, and a whole lot at the casino, where the rooms were three hundred bucks a night and the gambling was more. He could have (and probably should have) rented a dumpy apartment to save some dough. However, dumpy apartments don't come with cable and room service. What's the point of risking a robbery if you don't treat yourself to the good life?

However, the good life don't last. No sir. For guys like him, the good life comes in hard-earned bursts and spurts, and this round had all but sputtered out.

The marble skipped and jumped over the wheel. In a few seconds, he'd either have two grand or zero. He'd pocket the two for seed money on the next job. Or he'd walk out with empty pockets to face an unforgiving night. A night whose wind would blow a little message into his ear, saying, "Tough shit, pal. Take it like a man. Oh, and here's a little rain for good measure."

The wheel spun. The marble clicked a few more times, then settled in.

Andrew cruised down Highway 37 in his new-to-him car, an '88 Chevy Celebrity. She wasn't a beaut. Rust from those darn Minnesota winters. Whopper of a dent in a rear quarter panel, probably from sliding into an intersection (again, courtesy of those darn Minnesota winters). The years hadn't been kind, but her previous owner did a fair job where it counted. The motor purred. The oil sticker had two thousand miles to go. Nice set of radials. All in all, a satisfactory machine for the price he paid—that being zilch. Which was exactly what he had left after the marble had hopped out of black and nestled into red.

In the backpack next to him were the items that had helped him acquire his new ride—duct tape, heavy gauge wire, gorilla glue, and a screwdriver. In Andrew's opinion, any criminal without said items wasn't really a criminal. He'd swapped plates with another vehicle, even replaced the trunk's Celebrity logo with a Century logo he popped off a junky Buick. A bit of glue, a minute's work, and voila! At a glance, he was driving a Century with cold plates. A classic car guy might note the distinction between the two old vehicles, but the average young, dumb cop wouldn't have a clue.

The gas might get him two hundred miles. If not, he'd end up with his thumb out before sunrise. It'd be close. But one way or another, he'd be in The Falls by breakfast.

Effham Falls. Andrew never thought he'd go back. Not after a score from such a prominent family. He'd never followed up on the aftermath of that encounter. It was bad juju to look back. Even worse to return to the scene of a crime; any idiot who ever robbed a man knew that. Then again...

The Falls had treated him better than any other town he'd lived in. Real work and honest pay during the week, rounded out with some midnight jobs on the weekend for a little tax-free fun money. He'd made good connections on both sides of the law. There'd even been one guy, Bill, who he was close to calling a friend. Never mind that he'd left Bill behind, unconscious and bleeding from his guts. Hadn't been his doing. Though he did wonder, from time to time, whether Bill was still alive. Who knew? Not Andrew. Or was he Greg the last time he'd been in the Falls? Or Jacob? Andrew had used so many names he couldn't keep them straight.

Whoever he had been didn't matter. That man had left town with a sack full of cash—a rare beast in a world of digital transactions. The man heading to The Falls wasn't just different in name. No, the time away had changed him. An extra thirty pounds. Thank you, gluttony. A heavy beard and a cleanly shaved dome. Now in his forties, nature was making fast work of his hairline anyway.

For the final touch, he added glasses, a la Clark Kent, picked up at a gas stop months ago and intended as a disguise, but maintained when he realized he actually needed them.

Yes, Andrew was as close to unrecognizable as a man could get. At least on the outside. His core, on the other hand, was in question.

At 4:17 a.m., Andrew rolled into town with the needle riding on E. No matter, the car had served its purpose. Time to ditch it. West of a dumpy little street named Harm's Way was a trailer park. Within that park, an empty lot had been turned into a junkyard by the locals, much to the ire of the city. Busted cars, old washers, all matter of items in the take-it-to-the-dump-later category. Andrew pulled into the trailer court in the lingering dark and parked next to the shell of a white van. He popped the hood, pulled the positive cable to kill the engine, then walked away.

The benefit of such a dismal neighborhood was that people minded their own business. He could have pissed around with the car for an hour, and not a soul would have bothered him. Also, crime was a matter of daily routine. The Celebrity/Century would be gone in a day, in pieces if not as a whole.

The eastern horizon was glowing. Birds tweeted the daybreak. Andrew needed a place to bunk down after the long drive. He strolled over to Harm's Way. His old partner-in-crime,

Bill, lived there (if he still lived), but that wasn't a stop he'd make. In fact, he avoided Bill's side of the road altogether and found an abandoned house at the north end that looked ripe for squatting.

Andrew rattled the front knob. Locked. He moseyed to the back. Locked. He put a hip into the door and heard a crack—louder than he liked, but quieter than needed to raise a fuss in such a neighborhood—then struck once more and the ancient door gave in.

The main floor held nothing but dust and a few black trash bags. The upper cabinets had toppled from the kitchen walls and lay broken on the floor. The sink was gone, leaving a hole with a few copper pipes that made Andrew think of snakes peering out of a pit.

He ignored the basement. Creepy damned places, especially in old homes. The feeble light of his phone would only make the setting worse.

Upstairs, he found a bathroom that smelled like something had died there. At least he hoped it died, because he wouldn't want to meet something that leaked such a rotten stench and still moved. The first bedroom had a stained mattress on the floor and a dismantled frame next to it. He checked the second bedroom and—as the door creaked and his light shined in—Andrew gave an eyebrow-raising expression one might when they opened a long-lost tomb.

Inside sat a chest of drawers, a writing desk with a gooseneck lamp, an oval rug with three rings of color—gold, red, and green—and the bed, believe it or not, was still made.

Score, Andrew thought. Then, the moment of victory faded. There were nicknacks in the room. A cup of pens and pencils. A faded wall calendar with once-bright lettering over a photo of a waterfall, asking the reader to "Visit Friendly Effham Falls!" Beneath that sat a handful of paperbacks sandwiched between hand-shaped bookends. Andrew didn't look, but he was certain the closet would be full of clothes, as would the chest of drawers. The find was too good.

Not another squatter. Everything's covered in dust. Why empty the house and leave this? There was a story to the room that Andrew wasn't sure he wanted to know. What he was sure of was that he no longer felt like this was a score. He'd stayed in abandoned houses plenty of times. They were eerie. A guy didn't always sleep well, but this was different. His neck prickled as if being watched.

Andrew shut the door, went back to the other bedroom, and flipped the mattress over. The other side was stained too, but not as bad— and it was dry.

He pulled a brush and toothpaste from his pack, spat the foam on the floor, then lay down and imagined he was back in the hotel—king-sized bed, fresh sheets, buzz of the air conditioner—so maybe when he fell asleep, he'd return there. But he couldn't. He thought of the little room, and sunk into dreams of laying down in the bed that had been awaiting a guest for so many quiet years.

A scratching inside the wall woke Andrew up. He tried to ignore the sound, but it persisted. Then he was annoyed. And then, of course, he was awake.

His watch read 3:09 p.m. His stomach felt tight, and a vice clamped down on his eyes—the sign of an encroaching migraine. He hadn't eaten since his last extravagant meal at the hotel, just before check-out the day before. A pile of waffles, half a hog's worth of bacon, yolky eggs, OJ and fruit, and...now there was nothing.

What a difference twenty-four hours made. But that was the rollercoaster of Andrew's life, ever since the days of his youth when he realized he could take his brother's toys on a whim. The act was never thought of as stealing. The concept of ownership simply didn't make sense. Andrew wanted the toy. He took the toy. If his brother wanted it back, he could take it. Or at least he could try.

That mentality hadn't served Andrew well, but he'd stuck to it all the same, catching little rewards here and there, strung along by the hope of a bigger payoff. When you boil it down, thieving was simply gambling. A bit riskier. A lot less governed. But the stakes were only limited by one's imagination. Though maybe he'd gone high enough.

Andrew got off his stained mattress and stood in the middle of the room. The place stank. A waft of the decaying thing in the bathroom. A mildew smell from the mattress and, now too, from his hoodie. Dry shit from the little fella *skritching* away inside the wall. A prevailing oldness to everything that mimicked how Andrew felt about his life.

Crime was rapidly becoming a younger man's game. Andrew's hot-wiring skills—taught to him by his father—were fast becoming irrelevant as newer vehicles dominated the road. Kids had access to more money than he could dream of by sitting at a computer and hitting the right keys. He couldn't even type. Cameras in every business, on car dashes, on phones. It was sickening. The end of an era. The problem was, he'd known this time would come. The only thieves his age were one of two persuasions: rich or broke.

Andrew grabbed his backpack. The headache wouldn't be dismissed until he ate. Then he could think. But not now. Not with a vice threatening to pop his eyeballs like fleshy water balloons.

As Andrew exited Harm's Way—taking a wooded path that ran from an unkempt park out to Fisher Avenue—he peeked at Bill's house. If he could catch Bill mowing, the little part of him that still wondered about his buddy's fate would be set to ease. Except he couldn't see his buddy. Or the house. Because that house didn't exist anymore.

Andrew stood amidst the scraggly trees like a gaping Peeping Tom. Where Bill's house once stood, now lay a plot of flat earth and weeds.

Dead. The first word that popped into his head. Again, with a slight expansion. *Bill is dead.* Then the final thought in his trilogy, *I killed him.*

He hadn't. Not directly. He'd only persuaded Bill to partner with him on a robbery, which had gone both good and bad. Andrew had walked away with over one hundred forty thousand dollars of now-pissed-away cash. Bill hadn't walked away at all.

Andrew stood for a moment of reverie. Or respect. Or dumbfoundedness. Eventually, he told himself he wasn't at fault for the demise of his almost-friend. After all, Bill had agreed to the crime—his first, and unfortunately, last. Andrew shook his head and whispered, "See ya on the flip side, Bill," then continued on.

The food was easy. The ploy, well-used among the poor and hungry. Walk into a grocery store, grab a cart, toss in random shit. Somewhere during the course of shopping, you tuck a summer sausage and a block of cheese into your pants. Then ditch the cart—perhaps with a patting of pockets and a disappointed shucks-I-forgot-my-wallet headshake for a little flare.

Andrew ate in Ackley's Park, a busy middle-class spot where his good-but-dirty clothes wouldn't stand out. He sat against a tree, slicing hunks of sausage and cheddar with a pocketknife while watching families come and go.

He'd never understood the attraction of family life. Kids seemed like a great deal of work with questionable payoff. He knew guys who'd fallen into the trap. All they did was bitch. The wife was on their ass. The kids were expensive and annoying. More than once he had heard an exasperated dad say, "School can't start soon enough."

Yeah, it was all bullshit. At least that was the story Andrew had told himself the last couple of decades. But lately, the telling required greater frequency, and each pass needed more convincing to choke down.

To validate the path he'd set—not that he needed validation, mind you—Andrew eyed a couple of young brats engaged in a tug-of-war over a baseball mitt. Another mitt, identical to the naked eye, but inferior in some way known only to squabbling kids, lay at their feet. A mother strode over and wedged herself between the two. Andrew expected harsh words, maybe a good swat on the ass for the both of them. Instead, the woman knelt and spoke what might have been a magic spell for how quickly attitudes changed. The boys giggled. One conceded the favored mitt, grabbed the one at his feet, then the pair sprinted off. The mother sat in the grass and watched. A droop to her eyelids said she'd known little sleep lately; a hint of a smile on her lips said she didn't mind. Andrew looked away.

The thought occurred to him—not for the first time, but perhaps more consciously—that all his buddies' bitching was superficial. Those complaints rode the cognitive surface. Appreciation, on the other hand, ran a little deeper. It was the soil to the complaint's weed.

If that theory was true, every complaint about marital head-butting might have masked a period of bliss or at least contentment. After all, no one goes out with the boys and talks about the great day they had with their wives. They vent about the ugly stuff, and that's what gets all the attention.

The afternoon and evening went by in a wandering daze. Andrew passed the headquarters of a construction company he once worked for. He thought about the checks he'd earned. What felt like a pittance at the time suddenly seemed like a mountain of gold.

The library was a good sanctuary for a few hours. The coffee was weak but free. A sign read "Donations accepted, thank you!" He tested the lock on the wooden money box to make sure someone hadn't left it open. He tried to pick up the box and found it nailed to the table.

At 9 p.m. a pleasant voice announced the library was closing. They'd be open again at 9 a.m. the next day. Please come again.

When Andrew stepped out, the sun had been reduced to a burnt-orange line, pressed low on the horizon. Still, he wasn't ready to retire to his abandoned abode, so he walked. No real direction or destination. Just movement.

A drink sounded good. Something to dull the sharp points in his thoughts. Hustling pool at the Rusty Nail might get him one. Though if he'd be recognized anywhere, that would likely be the place. The Barfly was the next option. He'd never spent time there, didn't even know if they had a pool table, but he could do a walk-through and lift untended glasses. Andrew aimed for downtown.

On an otherwise quiet block, a man stood talking to someone through the glass door of a bookstore. A tall, dark, and handsome fellow. Irritatingly so. Exuding a mystery and charm Andrew had never—and would never—possess. As the conversation came to an end, the man touched a finger to the glass, a delicate, but somehow powerful gesture, as if he brazenly marked something or someone he craved.

Andrew planned to give him a wide berth, but the stranger turned and their eyes met. Street fights were nothing new to Andrew. He was accustomed to challenging stares and bravado. This wasn't that. If anything, the stranger was concealing his strength. The man smiled a too-perfect smile, and Andrew's stomach turned. He didn't want a drink anymore. Under his breath, he muttered, "Screw downtown." Then turned back and walked around the corner.

Soon, the sounds of the city quieted. Lights grew more sparse. The business district gave ground to residential, then residential segued into a forested park that ended at the shore of the Niijii river. To the south stood the Atlas Bridge, alive with headlights running east and west. To the north were the mighty Effham Falls, from which the city took its name. Andrew thought of the old calendar in the quiet room, the beautiful picture of the falls. It was as good a place as any to whittle away time. He turned left and headed to the sound of water.

The east side of the falls was meant for observation. There was a groomed picnic area, a landing marked "Scenic Viewpoint", and a railing supporting plexiglass panels the little ones could press their faces against. The west side, where Andrew was, had a more challenging approach. A hill rose steeply to meet the crest of the fifty-foot falls. Where a cement stairway had been years ago was a tract of dirt—the decrepit stairs having been removed to discourage exploration.

Andrew took his time, weaving back and forth to the top, uncertain of why he accepted the challenge instead of going through the park where the earth rose in a longer, more gradual approach. However, once he began, the heat in his lungs and the tight muscles of his legs felt good. Foreign—he couldn't remember when he'd exercised last—but good.

At the summit, Andrew was met with a chain suspended by a dozen steel posts, cordoning off the area. Worn placards hung between each post which read, "Unstable Terrain. Do not approach."

Andrew had heard the story. Before his time in the Falls, the city attempted to build an observation area. An over-confident engineer wanted a concrete slab instead of simply leveling the land. He got his way. Within a week, the ground crumbled and the whole thing slid into the drink. The written story claimed there were no souls aboard. The whispered version disagreed.

That was a long time ago, with no excitement since. Andrew lifted the chain and walked in.

A patch of crabgrass swayed in the breeze, ten feet from the edge of the falls. A yard light from the east side put a twinkle on scattered bottles and broken glass, but the grass seemed free of debris. He settled in and closed his eyes.

The unending rush came to his ears. Infinite variations of splish and splash and hush. Like the smell—earthy at first, then a shift in the air turned it fresh and flowered, then cool and damp. If God had made one place on Earth solely for soothing the nerves, that place was a waterfall.

And if anything could break such peace, it was the rattle of a chain.

Andrew snapped a look over his shoulder. A man had a hand on the chain, lifting it as if he were about to crouch under. The man froze when he noticed Andrew. A moment passed as the two stared at one another.

Even in the dim light, Andrew could see the man was older than him by a good fifteen or twenty years. Slender to skinny. Sparse gray hair. He wore a windbreaker, stretched down due to the weight of something in the front pocket. Cylinder-shaped. Maybe a can of pop.

The old man took his hand off the chain and straightened. "I, ah, guess I'm not supposed to go on that side of the fence."

Andrew scanned the vicinity and shrugged. "Don't see any cops."

The man looked around as if to confirm. "Well, I won't tell if you don't. Mind if I join you?"

Andrew turned back to the falls. Peace would have been nice. A moment to think. On the other hand, he couldn't recall his last real conversation. He raised a hand and waved the man forward.

The chain rattled. Footsteps fell over soft ground. Andrew eyed his approach. The old man, perhaps sensing Andrew's caution, eased himself to the ground a good half dozen paces away.

"I'll be honest." The stranger leaned a bit and put a hand to his mouth. "This ain't the first time I've cheated." He smiled a wrinkle-laden smile.

Andrew raised an eyebrow. "Cheated?"

"Crossing the fence. I come up here from time to time. I even snuck a couple of these." He slid a can of Miller High Life out of his right pocket, then a second from the left, which Andrew hadn't noticed. "I could share, if you're a drinkin' man, that is."

"I am." He always had been. Heavy in youth. Moderated as the hangovers began to outweigh the fun.

"Here ya go." The old man tossed a can into the grass. "They're warm. The cold gets to my teeth."

Andrew didn't mind. He picked the can out of the grass and drummed his fingernails over the top.

The old man cracked his beer and sipped loudly at the foam. "This is a good place for thinking, isn't it? Is for me at least."

Andrew popped the top and gave a hard blow at the foam, spraying it into the grass. "Sure."

"Not being nosey or anything. Just that I've never had company up here before." He faced the falls and appeared to address the water as he muttered, "Apologies, Justin. Real company is what I meant." He shook his head. "Boy, that don't sound right either."

"Who the hell's Justin?" Andrew asked. The idea there might be a third, unseen person atop the hill stirred an unease in his gut.

"Oh, he-he-he's not here. Not in-in the sense ah' you and me, that is. Justin is my...was my nephew. My sister's kid." His eyes drifted over to the falls. "He..."

Drown. Jumped. Died. Fell. Any number of words might have filled the blank. But the old man's sad eyes, the fact he took his recess atop a litter-strewn hill, said plenty. This meaningless patch of earth was likely the last place his nephew ever stood.

"They said—they being the authorities, that is—they said Justin...did it himself. Gloria, that's his mom, her and I knew better. He was a quiet kid, but he talked to me. Maybe because I was a little shy as a youth too. Kindred spirits, you know? He was quiet, but he wasn't sad. He wouldn't have done such a thing. They didn't believe us, so they put it in the papers. Right in the damn paper for everyone to see. Local teen commits..." The old man tossed a hand in the air, as if shooing away the word he didn't want to say.

The confession caught Andrew off guard. The openness. He was no bleeding heart. For the most part, Andrew believed if bad shit happened to other people, it was because they probably earned it. But now and then...

He took a drink, cleared his throat. "Sorry about your nephew. Must'a been some kid."

"You bet he was. Good mom too. She passed a few years back. Tumor." He tapped a crooked finger to the top of his head. "She wasn't upset to go. She knew he was waiting. But sometimes..." He glanced at Andrew, then turned back to the falls. "I don't know."

"Sometimes what?"

The man wiped his mouth with the sleeve of his windbreaker. "Sometimes Justin talks to me. But that type of thing doesn't happen, does it? So I guess that means I'm falling off my rocker."

A memory surfaced in Andrew's mind—the funeral for his stout German grandmother, decades ago. As he'd passed the open casket, hardly tall enough to see in, she'd said, "Brush your teeth, mein gutes Kind." Her voice had come to his ears as clearly as the hymn being sung in the background. He'd answered, "Okay, Oma."

The memory had never wavered. Never faded. And he'd dutifully brushed his teeth twice a day ever since.

"Weird shit happens. Unexplainable shit. Anyone who tells ya different doesn't know as much as they think. Or maybe you are falling off your rocker. Screw the rocker. It ain't all it's cracked up to be."

The old man smiled and nodded. "You've an unorthodox approach to diagnosing sanity. I think I like it. I also think I need to water a shrub, if you'll excuse me." He set down his beer and grunted to his feet, then padded away. A zipper unzipped, and the sound of pissing over dirt offered a diminutive mimic of the waterfall.

Andrew wondered how much beer the old man had at home, if, perhaps, he lived nearby and whether he had a warm couch a guy might crash on. And did he keep much cash on hand?

The piss trickled to a stop. One last squirt. Stopped again. A zipper re-zipped.

In a tone a bit lighter and more congenial, Andrew called over his shoulder, "So, when your nephew talks to you, what does he say?"

No immediate answer. The old man walked back to his spot. His eyes glistened in the lamplight as he stared into the falls. "Justin always tells me the same thing; he says he's lonely down there. And on that note, I'm afraid I'm going to have to bring this friendly conversation to an end." He reached to the small of his back and produced a handgun.

Andrew didn't move. He should have gotten up to piss at the same time, even if he didn't need to. Equal footing and so forth. But the man's kindly demeanor had made him lower his guard. The gun, however, wasn't aimed at him. Not yet. It simply hung from the end of a thin arm.

"My nephew's not down there anymore. I know that. They never fished out a body, but the years take care of things. There might be some bones left, buried in the mud. Maybe spinning around in the currents. The part that counts is up there with his mom. Least it's supposed to be. But when he talks, boy, he talks. Clear as a bell. And it about scares me to death thinkin' he's been pulled back here somehow. It scares me to think his mom is worried about him again." The old man turned to Andrew. The gun remained low.

"I got my head scanned. More than once. Plus a whole slew of other tests. I wanted to make sure there wasn't a tumor rooted in there, like my poor sister. Had to make sure I wasn't talking to a glob of cancer cells." He shook his head. "Leads me to believe what I'm hearing is real. Even if it's not, I can't risk it. And for that, I'm awful sorry." He reached into a hip pocket, pulled out a long, thin cylinder, and screwed it to the end of his pistol.

"I used to be a cop. Dreamed of becoming a detective. That never happened. I worked the beat, mostly. Spent the last few years shuffling papers. It paid the bills. Funny thing is, I never shot at someone 'til after I retired. 'Til after Justin started talking to me." The old man racked the slide. "Now I've given my nephew more company than I care to say. It keeps him quiet. For a little while." He raised the gun and motioned for Andrew to stand.

Andrew stared into the small, deadly void at the cylinder's end. He turned right and saw the park. Left, across the falls to the empty landing. Last, he peered over his shoulder along the river's bank. The cloud cover allowed enough moonlight to see the muddy slope of the shore, but there wasn't another person in sight.

"Just us, partner. This isn't a very popular stop." The old man motioned again. "I'd prefer you do it yourself, but either way, you're bound for the water."

With a racing mind and no plan but delay, Andrew got to his feet. Slowly. "Mind if I finish this?" He shook his can. "Only take a min—"

"Walk." The old man lowered the barrel to Andrew's feet and fired in a single motion, either supremely confident in his abilities or not caring where the bullet flew.

A hot pain lit the side of Andrew's left foot. He cussed and lifted his leg, holding the wound while dancing a hopping dance until he tipped forward. As he fell, he saw the man reach out—not to attack, but to steady him. The old guy's instinct had taken over, and that instinct said to help. He had a good heart. Too bad for him.

Andrew's injured foot touched down and seething pain raced up his leg, insisting he couldn't stand. Self-preservation slammed onto the other side of the scale, bringing along a flood of adrenaline. He dug in, turned his stumble into a bull rush, and smashed his shoulder into the old man's chest.

Ribs cracked. The man's breath shot out in a foul-smelling gust. The gun went off—no pain this time. However, where Andrew had hoped for a nice clean tackle, he'd only managed to put them into a spin. His momentum brought them around once before they toppled. When they did, Andrew tried to position himself on top, so that the impact might knock the gun free. But there was no impact. Because there was no longer ground beneath them.

The wind rushed by, accompanied by a fine spray of water. The old man's scream was lost in the waterfall's intensifying crash. Andrew kept his eyes shut as they plummeted toward the river. The water, nestled between two sharp rises, would be black. The old man's face would be the picture of helplessness and horror. There was nothing to see he couldn't already imagine. So, he held tight and hoped—perhaps prayed—they'd miss the rocks. The wind shrieked through the curves of his ears. Then the men struck the water like a meteor of flesh and bone.

The Niijii River widened out just south of the falls. The water slowed as the surface area increased, giving the floating body a lazy, almost relaxed appearance of a man who might be snorkeling and simply riding the current.

Years ago, the city had partially dammed the river with a load of rip rap to form a fishing pond. As the body bumped head-first into a broken slab of concrete, it began to rack and spasm. Flailing arms slapped at the wet blocks, gained purchase, and pulled with what little strength they retained until the man was lying across the slab.

He tried to breathe, but only uttered a series of short, thick sounds—not unlike plunging a toilet—as his stomach pumped in and out. Then a stream of vomit and river water gushed from his mouth. He drew breath, and the process repeated.

Eventually, the man finished and flopped onto his back. The dull moonlight lit his shaved head and set shimmering highlights in his wet beard. However, the glasses (a 'la Clark Kent) had been lost.

After a rest, Andrew sat up and gave himself a once-over. His body felt pummeled, but unbroken. He looked at the falls, the height he'd dropped, and checked his body again. Fingers, toes, everything in working order. Sore and burning—like a machine that'd been running with no oil—but alive. He shook his head in disbelief and uttered a short, dry laugh.

Andrew landed near the west side—the park side—of the river, less than fifteen feet from shore. The old man was nowhere in sight. Nor was anyone else. No sirens, no shouts. Just another quiet night in Effham Falls. And that didn't sit right.

How could such an event go unnoticed? Less than an hour earlier, an old man had struggled up a hill to visit a long-lost nephew. Then he was gone. Perhaps rolling in the same ceaseless eddy as poor Justin's bones.

However, it easily could have been Andrew, gone to join the dead. He'd have slipped from the world to the woe of none. What a diminishing thought, that something so precious as life could end unnoticed.

And there bloomed the most demonstrable, yet frightful, revelation Andrew ever had: Death was easy.

The old man had been deleted in a matter of minutes. Would the connection between them ever be made? Doubtful. No witnesses. No history. The gun was gone. The man was gone. Andrew's wound—painful, but not terribly deep—would never be reported. Besides, this wasn't murder. The death was one part accident and one part self-defense. He'd only wanted to bat away the gun. Right?

Andrew slid into the water. The cold water felt good on his wound. On his whole body. Refreshing. Renewing.

He swam to land, then pondered where to go next. But not only where. There was something bigger coming to mind. Not a place, but a path. Lately, he'd doubted the road he was on and struggled with the question of whether he should redirect to a straight and narrow life. Steady paycheck. Food on the table. A warm bed. It could be done. Perhaps not well, and he wouldn't be happy, but it could be done. However, that was not the answer.

The real answer had been there all along: Go harder. If you're going to be a criminal, be a goddamn criminal. He'd often been hesitant to pull the trigger, in the most literal sense. If the event with the old man taught him anything, it was that life comes and goes. Natural as the setting sun. So, speeding up the inevitable might not be as taboo a crime as he'd always thought.

Andrew needed to rest and consider these ideas. He took off his shoe and tore his sock into a binding. The abandoned house was too far of a walk. Tomorrow, perhaps, he'd return to the quiet room. His fear of that place had been irrational. Ridiculous even. There was comfort to be had, and he would have it.

As he cinched the bandage, a connection sparked, like a mental welding of thoughts. He wondered if the quiet room had once belonged to Justin. The tragic ending, the undisturbed items. Yes, Justin slept there. He dreamed in that room.

And not coincidence, that Andrew crossed paths with the boy's uncle. No, the meeting was set up by Justin when he tacked up the waterfall calendar, thus tipping the first domino that would end with his dear uncle joining him in the afterlife. Divine intervention was too heavy a term, but fate had a nice ring to it.

Andrew could only put weight on his heel and, even then, his limp was pronounced. However, the bridge wasn't far. From experience, he knew there were "accommodations" on both east and west sides where the land rose to meet the structure.

After a painful ascent, he found himself by the sheltered area beneath the bridge's footing—little more than a three-foot crawl space where the homeless tended to gather. Andrew crouched and started in. Before he vanished, he turned and looked over the city one last time. She was peaceful, like a defenseless child, lying asleep. He smiled at what tomorrow might bring. For an instant, the moonlight caught on two rows of strong white teeth. Then he slunk into the shadows and was gone.

ALEXANDER VAYLE is a longtime member of the Moorhead Friends Writing Group and author of supernatural thrillers, crime, and suspense stories. His collection "Among the Stray" was published by All Things That Matter Press in 2021 and more of his unique, character-driven stories can be found in each of the MFWG anthologies. When not writing, he works as an RN and enjoys the outdoors with his wife and four children.

THE DIRGE

Daniel R. Haynes

THE NIGHT FOREST IS silent as the wayward traveler, a bearded lumberjack, somehow senses that the hour is approaching midnight. So quiet are his surroundings that he can almost hear the progression of the heavy fog filling the woods with its ghostly dense mists.

He realizes that he has been here before and yet he remains lost.

His anxiety builds as he readies his ax like a Viking warrior of old, although he is unable to identify the bane of his dread. It is as if he is expecting a known threat that had somehow been pushed so far back into his memory that he could no longer recall its origins or in what form it might manifest.

He can only speculate that it must be some suppressed horror of such magnitude as to threaten his sanity should he dare to acknowledge its existence.

The fog begins to envelope him in its ever-thickening embrace. Like a cold damp blanket suffocating his soul, it holds him in place in its paralyzing grip. He can scarcely breathe and releases his grip on his ax which disappears into the hazy abyss.

Trembling violently and sweating profusely, he suddenly realizes that he is completely naked in this nightmarish wilderness. His perspiration compounding the intense chill that had already enveloped him.

Then the atmosphere abruptly falls deathly still. As if time had suddenly frozen.

In the distance, a horrifying howl cuts through the foggy night forest and the traveler's blood runs cold, knowing it is not the howl of a natural wolf but something far worse.

It is the relentless mournful dirge of some condemned lost soul that has been consigned to the body of some unholy beast, cloaked within the shadows of the wilderness. An unnatural creature that has targeted him as prey.

He can feel its unseen demonic eyes locked upon his helpless form. He can feel its malice and its hunger.

The howl does not waver but is continuous and growing closer to the petrified traveler, whose eyes bulge wide as he begins to hyperventilate with its approach. Still, he can do nothing but brace for his inevitable fate.

Overhead, he hears the upper branches of the tall trees give way in a cacophony of thunderous cracks and snapping. As if the howl was now crashing through the treetop canopy and descending upon him from the night sky in some phantom physical form.

The demonic wail then contorts into an earsplitting shrilling whistle, before striking the forest floor amongst the close-knit trees, beyond the traveler's view. Still, the force of the impact is such that the sonic concussion propels the traveler from the forest and back into his conscious host, who tumbles off his couch and onto the floor with a violent thud.

Doug Jansen came to with an abrupt start on his living room floor and looked about his darkened furnished apartment with a sense of dazed confusion. His naked body drenched in cold sweat, although his in-floor furnace projected enough heat to keep his modest abode toasty warm.

His mini apartment complex sat isolated on a rural two-lane interstate outside of town. His full-sized unit sat in the middle of the structure and was flanked on either side by smaller efficiency-styled units whose residents pounded loudly in unison on the adjoining walls to protest the disturbance.

Panting heavily, his breathing eventually began to slow along with his rapid heartbeat as his senses slowly came back to him. His surroundings once again familiar, he realized that he was back home in Effham Falls, Minnesota, and not back in northern Iraq. That an incoming mortar round had not, in fact, struck outside his apartment door and that he was in no immediate danger.

"Damned dream," he cursed under his breath, as tiny rivulets of sweat trickled down his face to slide beneath the concealment of his dark beard.

He huffed an irritable sigh as he braced against the couch and pushed himself up to one knee, pausing to decide whether he wanted to stand or just hoist himself back onto the cushions and return to his slumber. Yet, while the latter option sounded more enticing, he instead rose unsteadily to his feet.

"This is getting ridiculous," he grumbled.

It had been two full years since his return from the Middle East and subsequent separation from the Army and yet the disturbing dream persisted. Always manifesting in the same manner with little or no alteration in the details.

Still, as torturous as the recurring nightmare was, he considered himself fortunate that it, alone, was the extent of his PTSD. He knew that there were thousands of others who suffered far worse and he remained grateful that he did not have to count himself among their numbers.

That did not, however, prevent the memory of incoming mortar rounds that would strike on a regular basis. The impacts of which had rattled his bones and had on several occasions knocked him from his bunk and onto the floor of the prefabricated sleeping quarters. Two-man rooms that had been erected for the soldiers so that they would no longer have to bed down in the moldy abandoned buildings of their surroundings.

Even so, he had never bothered to seek out the professional counseling services provided by the VA, choosing to face his demons, alone. Knowing they were the byproduct of the combined manifestations of both his military and civilian lives, he felt as if he could deal with the disturbing images on his own. He would just have to find a way to reconcile the two and exert his mental control over them.

Since his release from the Army, Doug Jansen had established himself as an up-and-coming lower-tiered author of horror fiction with werewolves being a favorite subject of his. An aspect of his life that surely must account for the horrifying howl he would repeatedly hear in his recurring nightmare.

He had also been a star middle linebacker for the *Effham Falls Lumberjacks* high school football team when he was younger. Reasoning that was why he would always appear as a lumberjack in his nightmare. Also as a player, there had always been thousands of eyes upon him in the various stadiums, accompanied by persistent howling and chanting.

As for his being nude in his dreams, he could only attribute that to the fact that he had always slept nude since his return from Iraq. A practice that he, himself, was hard-pressed to account for other than he found the routine more comfortable than donning sleepwear.

Due to both his fascination for and belief in cryptids, he would also often write fictional tales of Dogmen and Sasquatch, two species of cryptid as having been reported by hundreds of self-proclaimed eyewitnesses throughout the decades. Which might also account for the forest surroundings in his nightmare.

Yet it had also been a contentious topic that his on-again-off-again girlfriend, Tammy Ravenwood, had often discouraged him from writing, adding additional emotional stress into the psychological equation of his troubled sleep.

Being Native American, she had tried in vain to caution him of such forbidden lore of her people. Tales of demonic entities and spirits that took the physical form of cryptids and were never to be mentioned or even brought to mind.

Eight years his senior, Tammy, a divorcee, had also been his former coworker when both were employed as municipal utility meter readers for Effham Falls. She had also given him one hell of a memorable intimate send-off when he prepared to ship out for military service.

While deployed, she would write to him religiously while expressing her desire to cultivate their relationship upon his return to the States. A proposal that Doug had been more than willing to endorse.

Unfortunately, that was when the damned nightmares first began and eventually doomed their relationship. When Doug would spring up in bed drenched in sweat, alarming Tammy in the process as she lay next to him, often taking her several minutes to calm and reassure him that he was home and safe with her.

"Douglas, would you please stop writing about the woodland spirits?" Tammy would often plead. "Can't you see that they're the ones plaguing your dreams?"

Doug would only smile warmly and reply, "Honey, you know I can't now. The series is taking off and I've just signed an additional three-book contract with the publisher."

It was to be a repeated argument between the two, without resolution.

Needless to say, regardless her love and affection for him, she could no longer bring herself to remain with him.

Although they had made several attempts at reconciliation, each effort had proven futile because the nightmares that plagued Doug's subconscious would serve to drive a deeper wedge between the two.

After the inevitable separation, Doug had found it difficult to sleep alone in the same bed that they had shared and could not bring himself to invite another woman into that bed, let alone, his life. He then found himself spending most of his sleeping hours on the couch, although it had posed its own hazards.

Oftentimes, his nightmares would cause him to flail about in his sleep, resulting in him smacking the back of his hand atop the coffee table that was positioned in front of the couch.

He soon after repositioned the table in front of the loveseat that sat perpendicular to the couch and before the front window. A fortuitous decision in light of his just hitting the floor instead of the thick wooden furniture during his most recent night terror experience.

Standing shakily, Doug glanced over to the darkened doorway of his bedroom with a sense of melancholy. Phantom memories of Tammy standing there in her see-through lingerie as she seductively grinned and crooked her finger in a beckoning motion for him to join her in a night of passion, filling his mind.

It was a somewhat cruel vision, yet one which he had conjured on numerous occasions, as if attempting to rub the emotional wound so raw that the nerve endings would cease to register the pain. Sadly, to no avail.

"Damn it, Doug," he chastised himself. "What are you doing? It's over between you two. Let go and turn it the hell loose, already!"

As if on cue, Doug was startled by the abrupt and unexpected factory-set ringtone of his cell phone, no doubt designed to bore into the very core of the owner's soul and cause heart palpitations.

"Shit!" Doug cursed. "I've gotta remember to change that thing."

He then restlessly ran his fingers through his hair to vent his frustration.

Swinging about, he directed his gaze down to the brightly illuminated phone screen that sat on the coffee table. He then redirected his gaze up to the digital readout of his clock radio, positioned on the top shelf of his television stand. The luminous digits displayed 4:34 AM in the darkness.

He scratched his head and grumbled, "What the hell?"

Who would be calling him at this hour, he wondered, before irritably reaching down for the phone? But his heart caught in his throat when he saw the caller ID display.

Another dream?

He sat down heavily on the loveseat, before taking a deep breath and pushing the answer button.

"He-hello," his raspy voice stammered.

"Well, it's about time. What took you so long?" the tinny, electronically altered voice of Tammy inquired.

"Tammy?" the stunned voice of Doug challenged.

"Who else would it be, doofus?" she playfully chastised.

Feeling slightly overwhelmed, Doug chose his next words carefully.

"Well, no one, really. It's just that you're one of the last people I'd expect to hear from," he awkwardly replied.

There was a brief silence on the other end before Tammy sighed and submitted, "You just had another one of your nightmares, didn't you?"

Stunned, Doug challenged, "Yeah. How did you know?"

"I-I'm not sure, exactly," she stammered. "I just woke and felt the sudden need to check on you. Are you alright?"

Doug hesitated, before replying, "Yeah, sweetheart. I'm good. Just the same old, same old. Nothing to worry about, but it's good to hear your voice."

"It's good to hear yours, too," Tammy confessed.

There was then an awkward silence between the two before Tammy offered, "Well, I guess I'll let you get back to sleep. I'm sorry if I woke you."

Doug quickly offered, "Oh, no. I was already up, hon."

Please don't go, he silently pleaded.

"Okay. If you're sure. I guess I'll let yo-"

"Say, Tam, since we're both already up, how about I take us out for breakfast?"

There was a brief pause, before he heard, "Sure. That sounds good."

"Great. Just let me shower and throw on some clothes, then I'll swing by and pick you up."

"How 'bout I just meet you at The Wallflower in, say, an hour?" Tammy countered.

"Well, I was thinking more along the lines of forty minutes, but I know how long it takes you to get ready, so okay," he playfully goaded.

"That's enough out of you, mister," Tammy giggled.

"One hour, then," Doug declared.

"Date," she confirmed.

They both ended the call with Doug repeatedly reminding himself that it was just breakfast and that he should not get his hopes up.

An hour and a half later, Doug and Tammy were sitting in a cozy little booth in *The Wallflower Diner*, making small talk and basically just catching up. Doug had already downed his second cup of black coffee, while Tammy absent-mindedly stirred the cream and sugar into her second cup, as well.

Likewise, Doug had already devoured his sausage and eggs while Tammy recalled how he had once informed her that his feeding abandon had been a byproduct of Army discipline. Eat fast and whenever you can, then move on with your mission.

Tammy, meanwhile, daintily ate her breakfast at a more leisurely pace.

"So, how goes your latest book?" she inquired, prior to taking a small mouthful of egg.

Doug shrugged and replied, "Slower than I'd like, but it's getting there."

Tammy glanced down at her plate momentarily before lifting her gaze and locking eyes with Doug. All pretense of casual conversation erased, her beautiful hazel eyes now conveyed a serious intensity.

"Douglas, there's something I've been meaning to tell you," she began.

Aside from his late mother, only Tammy addressed him by his full first name and Doug braced for the worst.

Tammy pensively began with a weak smile, "Damn, this is harder than I thought."

Doug sighed deeply, before encouraging, "That's okay, hon. I'm ready when you are."

His false bravado touched her and a tear began to roll down from the corner of her eye as she sighed, smiled, and with a quivering voice quipped, "Why do you have to be so damned nice and understanding all the time?"

Doug shrugged and flashed a quick wink as he replied, "It's my curse."

Inside, however, he could feel his heart begin to freeze up and break apart in anticipation of whatever portent of gloom his former girlfriend was about to impart on him.

Tammy chuffed a weak chuckle and dabbed at her tears with a napkin between sniffles. But she quickly collected herself and again locked eyes with the man for whom she held so much affection.

Shaking her head with sincere remorse, she steeled herself and announced, "Nathan and I are getting back together. We're going to move to Seattle to get away from our past, here, and try to make our marriage work."

Doug was stunned.

He had been expecting a punch to the heart, but he had not been expecting the woman he loved to announce that she was reconciling with her abusive ex-husband. It was almost as devastating as the mortar rounds that used to knock him from his bunk in Iraq.

"Please, say something," Tammy softly pled.

Doug eventually cleared his throat and focused. He wanted his response to be in a tone of mature civility, in sharp contrast to the emotional maelstrom he was now experiencing.

With downcast eyes and in a low and barely audible voice, he managed, "We-well, I suppose four years of marriage would be too deep of an investment to just let fall by the wayside."

When he lifted his gaze to meet hers, Tammy saw in his eyes something disturbing that she could not identify, although it did fill her with dread.

"Good luck with that," he coldly intoned, before breaking eye contact.

He then rose and pulled out his wallet.

"Douglas, please?" Tammy attempted, in effort to dissuade him from leaving before they could talk it through.

Her pleas, however, were in vain. He dropped a wad of bills on the table and turned to leave without speaking another word. As far as he was concerned, there was nothing left to be said that would not either end in a heated argument or compound the pain he already felt.

Tammy thought to call out, to go after him, but this was a small town and she did not wish to make a scene. Instead, she merely stared down at her unfinished breakfast, wondering why her life had to be so emotionally complicated.

There could be no avoiding the path they both must take now. A revelation that deeply saddened her.

Doug was feeling a powder keg of complex emotions well up inside him. Aside from the obvious heartache, there was also the overwhelming sensation of betrayal, justified or not. The heart rarely made distinctions in such matters.

He consoled himself with the logic that his abrupt tantrum-like exit should make it easier for Tammy to move on without her attempting further contact. Although he now cared little for her emotional well-being.

He first thought to shut his phone off but, instead, simply blocked her number since he knew that she would only leave voicemail messages that he would be too weak to ignore.

Entering his car, Doug knew that he had to get away. At least for a little while.

But where would he go?

There was a national forest nearby. He would shoot for there.

The morning sky was overcast, matching his mood perfectly as when he calmly pulled from his parking slot and headed out of town, the late September breeze added just the right bit of chill for this area of northern Minnesota.

This had begun as one of Doug's most promising Autumns.

Book sales were good. The previous Sunday, the Vikings had won their third game in a row with the promise of a powerhouse team for the remainder of the NFL season. Next month was the annual Anoka Halloween Festival, which Doug had planned to drive down for to make the most of his favorite holiday season with Tammy by his side, until she dropped that emotional bombshell on him back at the diner.

Fortunately, there were few tourists visiting the forest during this time of the year, and fewer still this early on a Tuesday morning. A revelation that gave Doug some small measure of relief as he would not be exposed to happy couples and families celebrating their love while enjoying the beauty of the wilderness.

Doug pulled into a parking slot near the mouth of a well-marked hiking trail and sat in silence as he replayed the events of the morning. Cringing with the memory of Tammy's announcement, while trying to convince himself that she might have a change of heart if he would just phone and apologize for his behavior.

"Never apologize, soldier. It's a sign of weakness," he remembered was often repeated by superior ranks in the Army during the course of his enlistment.

With that in mind, he checked the charge on his cell phone, and finding it satisfactory, he exited his car and made for the woods.

Wearing only an insulated flannel shirt, jeans, and hiking boots, he entered the trail and was quickly swallowed up by the forest. His boots made a soft rhythmic thumping percussion on the semi-hard packed earth as he route-stepped down the path without care to a destination and unconcerned as to what adventures might lay ahead.

Thirty minutes into his hike, he was just beginning his ascent of a steep hill when he was struck by a wind gust carrying a horrendous odor. A stench so foul as to cause Doug to bury his face within the top of his flannel shirt in a vain attempt to shield his olfactory from the oppressive assault.

"Holy shit!" he swore. "What the hell? Must be a dead animal around here somewhere."

Judging by the intense odor, however, it would have had to have been an animal of immense size. The reek was overwhelming and smelled as if the corpse was at least a week old.

It was a speculation that gave Doug to pause and ponder what type of dead animal it could possibly be and how had it died.

Natural illness? An accidental fall? A predator?

The latter supposition sent a chill down his spine when he felt a set of cold eyes lock onto him from within the woods.

Hungry eyes. The eyes of a predator.

Doug slowly turned in a three-hundred-sixty-degree full circle, while attempting to maintain his stance on the incline of the hill. Calmly surveying his surroundings without making any sudden movements that might trigger an attack from his unseen stalker.

He had almost completed a full circle when he froze in place. His eyes locked onto a massive dark object that was partially concealed by a stand of trees, further up the hill and slightly to his right, no more than fifty yards from him.

The creature stood upright, although it slightly swayed and had to use one of its hands to steady itself by gripping a tree next to it.

Even at that distance, Doug could make out the massive appendage as having elongated jointed digits that were not so dissimilar to those of a raccoon. Each finger tipped with a thick black claw that dug effortlessly into the trunk of the tree.

Doug thought he might pass out from shock when he also recognized two pointed canine-like ears atop the creature's massive head. Giving the beast the all-too-frightening semblance of a Hollywood werewolf.

As if to confirm his speculation, the creature slightly turned its head so that its elongated muzzle could be defined in silhouette by the fading light of the forest. Its demonic eyes never shifting from its human audience.

There could be no doubt as to its identity now. This creature was a Dogman. A cryptid canine-like monster so large it was reported as having battled the mighty Sasquatch on numerous occasions.

Doug felt his pulse and heartbeat increase at a dangerously rapid rate when he realized that he was now actually confronted with one of the more terrifying cryptids that, until now, he had only written about in the fictional context of his novels.

But this was not merely the image described by hundreds of eyewitnesses in various cryptid audio podcasts. This creature was standing before him as an apex-dominant living monument of flesh and fur and it was what was exuding the horrible stench that tainted the air.

As if having sensed Doug's recognition of its identity, the creature resumed its pose so that it was staring straight down its snout at the human intruder. Its eyes a luminous amber color that resembled two lighted windows in a distant dwelling atop a hill in the darkness.

Then, as if having sensed the terror in its human prey, the creature added to the horror of its appearance by baring its gleaming white fangs in what could only be described as a sadistic contorted grin.

The monster was actually *smiling* at him.

Doug could feel his knees begin to buckle as if they could no longer support his weight, but he willed himself to stand firm as he prayed to God for divine protection. A prayer that was swiftly answered as he felt the strength suddenly return to his legs.

Interpreting this as a sign to stand his ground, Doug defiantly locked eyes with the beast. He then slowly raised his phone in an attempt to video the nightmarish cryptid.

In response, the Dogman narrowed its eyes and glared down into those of Doug's, while issuing a one-word telepathic warning: Don't.

The creature then emitted a deep rumbling growl that penetrated Doug's bones and affected his nervous system to the point of near paralysis. It was the infrasound tactic often used by large predators and had been reported as having been employed by various cryptids, as well.

A common report that Doug could now verify.

Doug now realized that the strength was returned to his legs in order to flee, not stand his ground.

It was a revelation that he was quick to act upon as he turned and weakly began to stumble back down the path. His strength and balance gradually returning as he put more distance between himself and the real-life werewolf as quickly as he could.

To his horror, however, he could hear the demonic beast match his stride as the gigantic monstrosity tore through the woods paralleling the hikers' trail. Effortlessly plowing through the dense undergrowth, while almost joyfully panting and snarling as if it were a family dog running through a field of weeds in a game of tag with its master.

But when the creature abruptly exploded from the woods and onto the trail in front of him—a snarling, salivating monster that was at least eight feet in height with the girth of a gigantic grizzly bear—there was no illusion of it being a family pet.

Doug released a terrified scream as the last thing he saw were the flashing fangs and slashing claws of the Dogman as they descended upon him. Then the darkness of the creature's fur enveloped him completely in the crushing embrace of its powerful arms.

The last thing he heard was the monster's thunderous howl which nearly ruptured his eardrums. He knew that it was his own death dirge and had one last prophetic thought, befitting an author. The title for his final book.

Doug's Death Dirge.

He had to admit it did have a nice ring to it.

The howl then crashed down upon him as he screamed and flailed about wildly, flinging himself off the couch and onto his living room floor with a resounding thud. And once again his neighbors expressed their displeasure of the commotion by banging on the adjoining walls.

Doug, however, seemed not to notice.

He looked wildly about the darkened room as his chest heaved from his frantic panting and his naked body glistened in the cold sweat that matted his chest hair. His senses were taking longer than usual to fully return and he briefly felt as if he was losing his sanity, before falling back onto the floor with relief as he realized he was home.

Just then his cell phone rang and from the floor, he reached up to grab it off the coffee table. Regarding the caller ID with a mild sense of confusion, he answered.

"He-hello?"

"Hey, sleepyhead. We still on for breakfast?" the tinny, electronically altered voice of Tammy cheerfully inquired.

"Ye-yeah, babe. Sure," Doug breathlessly assured her. "Meet you at The Wallflower in about an hour."

"Good, 'cause I got some great news for you. For us," she excitedly declared. "I'm about to make you a very happy man!"

Doug then perked up and sat up.

"Really?" he tested in disbelief.

"Yep. I can't wait to see the expression on your face when I tell you! See you soon," she chimed. "Oh, by the way, I love you."

Stunned, Doug could only reply, "I-I love you, too, beautiful."

They both then ended the call without another word, but the smile on Doug's face could not be contained. Still, he pondered what this great news could be because it certainly did not sound as if she was about to break it off with him and return to her ex.

He quickly rose to his feet and was about to head to the bathroom for a badly needed shower when he heard a faint scratching at his front door.

Turning, he slowly approached the door and listened as the scratching sound appeared to proceed along the outer wall toward the window, no more than five feet from the door to his right.

Curious, he braced himself upon the cushions of the loveseat and carefully parted the curtains. As he peered out into the early morning darkness, the lone streetlight in the front parking lot revealed only a dense layer of ground fog that rolled lazily over the modest lawn and hedges.

Puzzled, he momentarily turned from the window in an attempt to rationalize what he had heard. But when the light streaming through the window was suddenly blotted out by an enormous shadow, he turned back to find the entire frame filled with the dark-furred silhouette of the Dogman.

The monster glared down on him with its salivating grinning jaws dripping thick drool on the windowpane. Its demonic burning amber-colored eyes, narrowed with murderous intent, conveyed a message into Doug's mind.

I need no longer hunt you through your nightmares. I've found you now. You should have heeded your woman's warning. She sends her love and apologies.

"Tammy?" Doug exclaimed in disbelief. "Noooooo...!"

Sitting in *The Wallflower Diner* Tammy casts her gaze downward as the imagery of the attack played out in the reflection of her cup of black coffee. She prayed that the evil shape-shifting spirit of her ex-husband, Nathan, would make it as quick and painless as possible.

Lightly shaking her head, she softly lamented, "Oh, Douglas. Why wouldn't you listen to me?"

DANIEL HAYNES is an Army vet who served as both a Helicopter (Huey) Mechanic/Crew Chief and then as a Civil Affairs Specialist. Daniel's passion for classic horror films/monsters began when his father would buy, build, and paint monster models for him. *The Wolf Man* was his favorite and continues to serve as inspiration for the unique and frightening characters he creates today.

THE SHOE

Chris Stenson

THE SINGLE HIGH-TOP CANVAS sneaker rested partially hidden in the tall grass along the Old Mining Road #2 that headed north out of Effham Falls. Peter would have never noticed it if he hadn't pulled off to check his messages. *No texting while driving*—that was his safety mantra. It was white – just out of the box bright white – which made the irregular red spots on its surface stand out vividly. Was it paint? Food coloring?

Peter always wondered about lost shoes. He pondered their origins, who owned them, and why they'd been lost or left behind. Whenever he came across a lost shoe, he collected it. Multiple boxes of mismatched singles were stacked in his garage. Peter was a shepherd collecting lost souls. They gave him feelings – intuitions and insights into their owners – and he only had to hold them long enough to allow the visions to wash over him.

A speeding logging truck passed close to the car, forcing Peter back into his vehicle. A cloud of dust obscured his view of the prize. When the air cleared, the shoe had disappeared. Peter rushed out of the car and knelt on the hard-packed gravel road. Large black flies swarmed around a pool of blood. Their incessant buzzing drove a nail of pain into his temple. He inhaled the lingering rich coppery scent of fresh blood. Filled with dread, he sighed, closed his eyes, and mumbled a prayer he thought he'd forgotten. "Mary, Mother of God, pray for us sinners."

Peter placed his hand upon the pooled blood, then jumped to his feet to survey the area. The chest-high grass in the ditch had been trampled, revealing an obvious trail leading to the edge of a forest. He took one step and stopped. *Why am I doing this?* A few years ago, his world had been torn apart and God had abandoned him. He was broken, but not destroyed, so what more did he have to lose?

Droplets of blood and drag marks made following easy. He slowed when he approached the edge of the trees. Twigs snapped somewhere in front of him, and leaves crunched. Swallowing the lump in his throat, Peter needed to find courage. He followed the path to a clearing. A dilapidated house obscured by overgrown bushes and a small tree sat deep in the shadows. The tar paper siding lay in tatters, and vines grew out of the holes in the moss-covered roof. Peter expected the trail to lead to the fallen porch and black maw of where the front door should have been, but the tracks led to a different door, one propped up against an ancient stump. A coat of tacky blood covered the enameled knob, and an odd-shaped red handprint embossed the peeling paint of the door.

Peter considered calling the police. He assumed the blood belonged to the person who lost the shoe—at least that had been his experience. He possessed a gift. Or maybe it's a curse. Whenever he held one of these lost shoes, a picture formed in his mind. He would know what had happened, he could see and follow the owner's invisible footprints, but he never experienced this without actually holding the shoe. Over the years, a handful of the shoes' owners had been killed by drunk drivers, a dozen or so of the shoes had fallen off handlebars and been forgotten, and one parental kidnapping resulted in the child losing the shoe he'd found. He never found the owners of some.

But this was different.

The weathered door leaned against the stump at an angle, the rusted hinges flat against the pine needles, leaves, and debris on the forest floor. Peter first walked around, then he bent to inspect the underside of the door. He reached into the shadow the door cast and immediately ripped his hand back. The cold and vileness were too much for his soul. He leapt to his feet and sprinted out of the forest, instinctively heading to a spot where the sun shone the brightest. A sadness he had never experienced suddenly engulfed him as he dropped to his knees, thanking God for each breath he took. The evil hiding behind the door needed to be exterminated.

He sat on the ground until his shivering abated and the unpleasant sensations passed. Peter didn't understand how or why, but in his gut, he knew that the owner of this shoe was a kidnapped girl, that she was special, and that he needed to do everything in his power to rescue her. He climbed to his feet and headed back to the clearing.

Movement in an upstairs window of the abandoned house caught his attention. He pushed aside a few branches and willed himself forward. With each step, his confidence grew, and he made it to the front of the porch.

A green-eyed teenage girl stood in front of the missing window. She was holding a shoe that matched the one he had seen beside the road. "He likes beautiful and special children. The girl is now ours," she said in a commanding voice.

"Who are you?" Peter asked, as he tried to make sense of her words.

"I'm a collector. Someone you don't want to mess with. Forget about the child. She won't be missed."

"Hey... I care."

The girl shrugged, ducked back into the shadows, and disappeared.

On every side of Peter, high-pitched giggles filled the air. Yellow eyes glowed deep among the trees and in the dark recesses under the house. The atmosphere now cold and uninviting, he took a step back. *Am I being warned?*

Peter steeled his nerves and stepped toward the house, gingerly ascending the stairs to the porch. Wet decayed boards covered the surface, and when he inched forward the wood sagged but held. He took another step, then another. The house groaned, as if protesting his presence.

In front of the doorway, a large gap appeared in the floorboards. Peter pulled out his phone, turned on the flashlight, and pointed the light into the black fissure. He thought his long legs might be able to reach the other side, but if he slipped, who knew what monstrosities lived in the darkness? He didn't want to find out but decided to try anyway.

He jumped, but his foot punched through the dry rot, plunging his leg into the large void under the porch.

"Damn it anyway." He pivoted and plopped down on the threshold.

Two red pinpricks of light rose from the inky blackness. He braced himself and pulled. His leg wouldn't budge. The pinpricks of light narrowed and transformed into multiple pairs of eyes. He yanked again, and something yanked back. Several hands held his ankle in a vice-like grip. His foot lost all feeling. A sliver of wood poked his calf like a sharp needle. Something slimy crawled up his leg. His sock became soaked with blood. Venomous, hostile thoughts pulsed through his mind. He knew that the creatures below, if he left them to their own devices, would devour his flesh.

He threw his weight backwards. The rotted wood splintered, allowing him to break free, and he scrambled into the entryway. Two filthy clawed hands reached through the opening, trying to grab him. He pulled himself to his feet and, against his better judgment, limped into the kitchen.

In the center of the room, most of the floor had given way, exposing the fetid water of a large cistern. A decomposing body floated facedown.

"What the hell?" Peter squeezed his eyes shut to quell his racing heart.

A teenager dressed entirely in black, her many metallic piercings glinting off the foul waters of the reservoir, sniggered and pointed at the floating body. "Do you want to be dead like her?"

"N-No..." Peter stuck his quivering hands in his pants pockets. "Who are you?"

"A gatekeeper." The girl smiled, small fangs pushing past her lips. "This isn't a nice place after dark."

"What is this place?"

"A doorway."

"A doorway to where?

She shrugged.

"I'm going up. Are you going to stop me?"

"I don't need to."

Peter followed the trail of small wet footprints and droplets of blood up the deteriorating staircase. Red eyes glowed between the cracks in the wood, daring him to take a misstep. The girl with the green eyes waited at the top. A door just past the landing stood ajar.

"I want the child," Peter said to the creature with the poison-colored eyes.

"She's in there."

Malicious voices from Peter's past filled his mind.

Implore the evil inside you and give into your lusts.

Sink deeper into your own despair.

A sense of evil, along with a corrosive burning and itching, settled upon Peter's skin. Invisible hands clutched at his clothing. He stumbled to a broken window and contemplated grabbing a large piece of broken glass. A way to end this nightmare forever.

God has demanded a sacrifice. Yours. It only hurts for a second.

Son, join me. You left me alone to die.

Peter's fingers twitched. "No."

Do it. Do it now.

Peter ignored the temptation and pushed aside the cobwebs covering the opening.

The house now stood on top of a crag, no longer residing in a small grove of trees on the outskirts of Effham Falls. Vertigo struck Peter at the sight. He wavered on the edge of collapse and vomited.

"What...is...this...place?" Peter asked for a second time once he got his bearings.

"Your nightmare." The green-eyed girl opened the door wide. "She's yours. Go to her."

Peter shook his head, and the voices began again.

Chickenshit.

Death waited for Peter on the other side of the open door, but he staggered forward anyway. A sound, a whisper, something just at the edge of his hearing, prickled his skin. Gloom settled on him like a heavyweight. No doubt in his mind that the green-eyed girl was death.

Peter did his best to push the malicious voices from his mind, but his uneasy malaise persisted. This house defied understanding and logic. He didn't know why, but he knew he needed to save the kidnapped girl at all costs. He also somehow knew that going through the door on the second floor meant death. As crazy as it sounded, Peter knew he needed to find the key to the abandoned door outside. It might be the safest way of reaching the girl.

The feral children with the red eyes who hid in the shadows of the house petrified Peter. Their aggressive postures and lips curled in vicious smirks made him cringe every time they glanced his way. He made sure of his steps as he hurried down the stairs.

"Are you staying longer?" the girl dressed in black asked him.

"This place needs to be condemned." With added bravado, he added, "Tell your boss that I don't scare easily."

"You should be terrified."

"Are you a vampire?"

She shrugged. "I'm not sure. Maybe a hybrid."

"You are a godless creature, are you not?" Peter pulled his mother's crucifix from underneath his shirt. He wore it as a reminder of his failures.

The girl flashed her small fangs. "That only works in the movies. But I'd love a taste of your pretty boy blood."

Peter recoiled.

"Just a little taste, pretty please."

Laughter chased Peter outside and into the sunlight. With each breath, he expelled the vileness from the house. He didn't think he had the discipline or the courage to enter the house again. Confession and Mass might be the only things that would cleanse his soul. A deep corruption blossomed within him. The temptations that the house whispered were almost too much for him to bear, but he needed to inspect the door one more time before he left.

The abandoned door appeared even more weathered than it had earlier, its corners now swallowed by time and the forest floor. Peter brushed off the amassed debris and found that the enameled handle gleamed like polished bone. When he grasped the knob, a cold vile hatred surged through him.

Innocent souls would die if he didn't act soon, but did he have the moral strength to combat evil? He didn't have a choice. Saving lost souls and preventing the spilling of innocent blood was his calling, his redemption for past sins.

He willed his legs forward. The world around him slowed. His limbs grew heavy, and a dark fog clouded his mind. The tree line was within reach. A short sprint, but he stumbled and fell to his knees. He tried to pull himself up by grabbing a branch but didn't have the strength. He let go, fell forward, and was asleep before he hit the ground.

Peter's eyes snapped open. Shadows slid along the ground, weaving between tree trunks. The songs of the night creatures filtered through the branches as dusk settled over the stand of trees like a thick blanket.

The children had gathered, and they were watching him. Judging him.

He sat up and gasped for air. Time had vanished. Several hours of Peter's life had simply disappeared.

Eyes the color of rotted leaves glared at him through the fading light. He crawled to a tree and pulled himself to his feet. When the dizziness stopped, he took a step toward the road.

The circle of eyes tightened.

"What do you want?" Peter asked.

The feral children, now sporting fangs of their own, all chanted, "You fall dead." Their otherwise angelic faces gleamed with hatred and leaked venomous intentions.

Peter considered himself a brave man, but one wrong move and he feared that they'd rip him apart.

The circle opened and the green-eyed girl stepped in. "Be gone." She dismissed Peter with a wave of her arm.

He stumbled out of the grove of trees. The children followed behind, making sure that he left, that he could not return. The outlook for saving the kidnapped girl's life appeared bleak. *How does one find a key for an abandoned door?* Peter peered into the shadows. Someone had used the door at least once, so a key existed. He just needed to find the right one.

He stood in the gently swaying grass as the sun dipped lower in the sky. A symphony of night sounds drifted from the trees. The house had simply vanished, but he knew he would search the heavens to save this girl.

All week long, nightmares haunted Peter's sleep. His soul had been damaged so long ago and had never healed. On Saturday afternoon, he stepped into Saint Barabara's Catholic Church for the first time since his mother had died years prior. He opened the door to the confessional and knelt when he heard the familiar sound of the divider sliding open.

"Bless me, Father, for I have sinned. It has been ten years since my last confession. I have lost my faith and my way. I walk in darkness, for God has abandoned me."

"How can I help you find your way back to God's flock?" asked the priest on the other side of the screen.

"May I ask you some questions that have been nagging me for years?"

"Yes, my son."

"Father, do you believe in evil, that people and places can be inherently wicked?"

"Men can do evil, but they aren't born that way," the priest answered.

"Why does God let evil exist?"

"Man has free will."

"How does evil corrupt?"

"In a moment of anger or weakness, evil quietly slips into a man's soul, waiting for an opportunity to infect."

Peter spent the rest of the day contemplating the priest's words, walking the street, searching for old keys. He found some but didn't think any would fit. Before bed, Peter knelt in front of his bed and prayed. In the morning, he took his mother's rosary and crucifix and returned to Saint Barbara's.

A beautiful young woman sat in the pew in front of him. Her dress hugged her in all the right places. Sunlight streamed through the stained-glass windows and lit her blond hair on fire. Her perfume, warm and intoxicating, circled Peter's head and filled his mind with troubling thoughts of lust and inappropriate sexual acts. Her handshake and smile went straight to his groin. Though he did his best to control his lustful thoughts, they steamrolled through his mind. All through the Homily, his mind kept undressing her. She starred in his own personal adult movie.

After mass, the young woman waited until Peter left his pew then stepped beside him. "I can help you with all your problems," she whispered, glancing at this crotch before sliding a piece of paper with her number into his hand.

The elderly lady handing out the weekly bulletin glared at her and said, "He doesn't need your type of help."

The young woman said something under her breath and headed straight for the front doors. Before exiting, she glanced over her shoulder and gave Peter an inviting smile. He needed a cup of coffee, a donut, and a quiet place to regroup.

In the friendship hall, after he collected his cup of coffee and donut, Peter found a table where he could sit. An old woman pushing a walker, the same one who had handed out the bulletins, sat next to him.

"Good morning," Peter said.

"Good morning, Peter."

"How—"

"May I be blunt?"

Peter nodded.

"She's a vicious killer."

Peter knew who she was referring to, but he asked anyway. "Who are you talking about?"

"That young woman you drooled over during mass."

"A killer?"

"Was your mind full of sexual thoughts all through mass?"

Peter blushed and nodded.

"Did she invite you somewhere?"

"How did you know?"

"We've dealt with her kind for centuries. She's the Blood Countess."

"I don't understand."

"Evil walks unfettered between realities, no longer content with hiding in the shadows. They feed on the blood and souls of the innocent. They want our children—our hopes, our dreams, our salvation. We need to stop the Dark Ones and time is running out. You can help. Trish, the reason you went to that house, is special. She is the Guardian's future."

"The rundown house in the woods?" Peter asked.

"Yes, the house is a way station for transporting innocent children to their deaths, the place where they harvest their souls.

"Who are you?"

"We are the keepers of the keys of knowledge, the guardians of the doors between worlds and the ancient librarians of Alexandria."

"I'm only one person. What can I do?"

"Help us find Trish. Bring her back alive. But remember, if you fail, fear and despair will give birth to a new dark age."

"How can I do this? I lost my faith years ago."

"Having faith didn't mean you believed in only one God. It meant you believed in something, a higher power or even one's self."

"I'll try."

The old woman cupped Peter's hands in her own, her skin warm and soft like ancient vellum. The wrinkles and age spots told a story of knowledge, caring, and longevity. She placed a key on his palm. "This is what you seek. It is a special key. This instrument will open abandoned doors and let you travel where you need to go. Abandoned doors are wild and have gone feral. They used to have a specific destination, but now where they lead may change. Don't let your mind wander. Concentrate on your destination and always lock the doors behind you. Find the girl."

The house glowed wherever the moonlight hit. Peter found the abandoned door after several minutes of digging through leaves and deadfall. He took a deep breath and reached into his pocket for the key the old woman had given him. A small hand clutched his jeans.

"Holy shit, you scared me," Peter said to the child holding onto him. "Why are you here by yourself?"

"Sir, my mommy says there are no such things as monsters, not real ones anyway." The young boy smiled. "But she lied," he said before lunging at Peter's neck.

The boy's small, pointed teeth ripped the collar of Peter's shirt, nipping his flesh, and drawing blood. A small rivulet ran down his neck. The boy stepped back, licked his lips in anticipation of more. He flexed his body, ready to spring again. Peter held his crucifix in front of him, hoping to hold the boy off long enough to try the key and escape.

"Your God doesn't scare us."

"Us?"

"We are but a few, but we will become many."

Peter pulled the key from his pocket. The boy snarled and stepped back.

"A Guardian."

Peter ignored the boy and inserted the key. The mechanism clicked and the door opened to a dark void. He knew if he stepped through, his faith would be tested, but he believed in this cause. He closed his eyes, said a silent prayer, and entered.

Traveling somewhere else reminded Peter of falling. Not the cartoon type—flashing before your eyes, things rushing by—but more like falling down a pitch-black elevator shaft without the splat at the bottom. He now stood in a dimly lit corridor lined with doors. A single torch flickered. Shadows danced, the light undulating and twisting into shapes. He gazed at all the different entrances. Where did all these doors lead? Different worlds? Different periods of time? How many would he have to try before he found the right one?

The feeling of not being alone prickled his skin, and a strange sensation gnawed at the back of his mind. He glanced at the darkness over his shoulder. A cold draft slid along the floor, shifting, moving, and changing.

"Weren't you supposed to lock the door behind you?"

Peter spun around. A different boy stood in the wavering light of the entrance. A drop of sweat slid down Peter's back. He ignored the ache building in his throat. "What's your name?"

"Bobby." A sly smirk parted the boy's lips, exposing razor-sharp fangs. "One of the two Bobbies. I'm the bad one."

"I'm Peter."

"You know she doesn't want you to find the girl, don't you?"

"Yeah, I know. Do you know why?"

"Trish has special blood and an unnatural soul. The Dark One has special plans for her."

"Are you here to warn me? Threaten me?"

Bobby laughed. "No, just to slow you down."

"What is this place?"

"Corridor of lost souls."

The boy slammed the door shut and before Peter could lock it, it faded away. "Shit." Until he found the girl, he would have to watch his back. He hoped this would be his last mistake. He grabbed the torch off the wall and stepped into the eerie, yawning darkness.

"He's waiting here for you," a voice whispered.

After Peter took two steps, the pressure in the corridor shifted. Malice and an unknown tension hung thickly in the air, constricting his chest and turning each of Peter's breaths into a laborious effort. A chill clung to his spine and took root. Something truly evil was down here with him. Up ahead, a figure swirled in the flickering light of the torch. Laughter came from the darkness. Ancient sins, an ancient hunger, a demon from Peter's history waited. His mind slipped into the past. His nightmares still refused to let him go.

A keen wail of despair filled the tunnel. Grief clutched Peter's heart when he recognized the voice – a mother who never forgot what she had lost emerged from the darkness. Her eyes told the story while Peter kept his downcast.

"You bastard. You killed my son."

He had. The court had ruled it a tragic accident, but Peter knew the truth. He had been distracted, fiddling with the radio when the three-year-old dashed across the icy street. The snowbanks were high and Peter hadn't seen the young boy until he was in the middle of the road. He slammed on his brakes and swerved, but he didn't miss. The boy thumped under the right front tire and his lifeless body lay under the truck.

Peter had jumped out and hurried around to the front of the car. One of the boy's boots lay several yards away. Peter kneeled and took the boy's cold hand. Blood oozed from his mouth.

"Momma," the boy wheezed, "Momma, I hurt."

The mother pounded her fists on Peter's back as the boy took his last breath. "No, no, no. Please, God, not my Scotty."

"I tried to stop..." The rest of Peter's words failed.

That same mother now wailed and shrieked like a banshee. She brandished a curved blade and waved it in the air. Peter jumped backwards. He had made another costly mistake by not bringing a weapon. He thrust the torch at her, but she knocked it aside. She swung at Peter's face, grazing his cheek. In the near darkness, he threw himself against the wall. A sharp pain pierced his chest. He reached into his shirt but found no blood. The crucifix his mother had given him on her death bed lay mangled and melted against his chest, but the Guardian's key still dangled from his neck, unharmed. He ripped the key from the chain and held it between his fingers.

The woman snarled and flung herself at Peter again. He struck first, pressing the key into her forehead. The skin in contact with the key sizzled and turned black. The stench of sulfur filled the small space. The gash festered, green puss dripping down her face, dissolving into wisps of smoke that curled around her head. The demon burst from the woman's body and howled in agony before vanishing.

Peter crept forward in silence, scrutinizing each door as he passed. *How will I know which one was the right one?* The ghosts of his past clung to the walls, hiding in the shadows, whispering, taunting him, and softly chanting, "Child killer. Child killer." Their words gnawed at his conscience until he began to doubt himself. He closed his eyes and took a deep breath. He took another breath and exhaled slowly. He believed in himself and his ability to find lost souls.

A phosphorescent handprint, like the bloody one he'd found on the door in the clearing, marked one of the doors. His pulse quickened. He inserted the key, but the door wouldn't open. If he wasn't successful in finding an exit, would he wander this corridor forever? *Am I a lost soul?* By saving Trish and the other innocent children, he hoped to redeem his life and save his own soul. He squeezed his eyes shut and said another silent prayer.

When he opened his eyes, he saw footprints glowing faintly on the hard-packed dirt floor for a split second. He gripped the key tighter and prepared to defend himself.

After Peter passed several doors, a young boy resembling Scotty stepped into the light of his torch.

"You're a bad man," the boy said. "You're a very bad man."

Peter told himself this creature wasn't really Scotty, just a manifestation of the evil that wandered these halls.

The boy rushed him. As Peter fended off the attack, someone or something jumped on his back and wrapped its arms around his neck. Pinpricks of sharp pain seared his neck. Images of the potential life of a young Scotty flickered through his mind as the venom of the malevolent Scotty's bite spread faster than poison. Peter flung the second Scotty over his shoulder and used the key to stab the boy who now hung on his legs. A dark line raced through his veins, dropping him to his knees. He was suffocated by the reality of what would happen if he failed in his quest. The key vibrated and began to glow.

On all fours, the two boys snarled and approached, this time staying out of reach of the key. Peter crawled toward the door, terror inched up his arms and legs. His chest constricted again, and he struggled with his next breath. Some form of pestilence still coursed through his veins, blackening his skin as it traveled through his body. Between bouts of lunacy and unconsciousness, he followed the glowing footprints until he reached the next door. His hand shook as he inserted the key, then he fell through the doorway as it opened abruptly. Making sure to lock the door behind him this time, he collapsed into a pile and slipped into a fitful sleep.

Peter woke, rolled over, and vomited mouthfuls of black bile all over the blood-red floor. Bone-white worms wriggled in his puke. His head pounded and his soul, just like his stomach, was void of substance. Where had he ended up?

He pushed himself to his knees and stood on wobbly legs surveying the room. Gauzy figures shaped like children hung by their hands from the balcony of a church. Splashed with what appeared to be copious amounts of blood, a stripped-down altar filled the front of the room. The place reeked of despair. Every board, every nail, had been inundated with evil.

Why had the door led him to an abandoned church?

Behind the altar, a man dressed in black, a white collar clipped to his shirt, stepped into view. Overhead, the child-shaped figures floated, their eyes wild with fright, their mouths locked in a never-ending scream.

"Behold," the priest said, raising his hands, "the harvested souls of our children."

"Those are children's souls?" Peter balled his fists and strode forward. "Who in the hell do you think you are?"

"Father Abrams."

Peter was tired of asking the same question, but the events, the people, and the places he experienced were surreal. "What is this place?"

"A collection center for the innocent souls and blood."

"Take off that collar. You're not a man of God."

The priest laughed. "They're using you. Do you want to die for them? In the end, darkness will prevail."

"Give me Trish."

"She's ours."

"Your kind has corrupted the innocent and the pure. You have used our children in dark rites for too long. Father, I beg you. You must resist being exploited by evil." Peter shook his head in disbelief. Where had that come from? Was the Guardian's key something more than just a key?

Just before the sun dipped below the tree line, light streamed like a river of blood through the only stained-glass window that remained. The beam, dark, viscous, and intense, bathed the priest in ghastly shades of red. His eyes glowed demonically.

In the hole-riddled roof, Peter caught glimpses of the sky. Thunder, like the pounding of horse hooves, rumbled. Jagged bolts of lightning ripped the sky apart. Four dark riders appeared on the horizon. Peter knew that death approached.

Father Abrams chanted an invocation. Peter picked out a few words of Latin, but the rest made no sense. The priest reached into his pocket, pulled out black sand, and tossed it into the air. Powdery smoke swirled above his head, invoking some type of dark spirit. A phantasm. The mist settled and congealed into a familiar figure. The creature elongated, its protrusions mimicking arms and legs while muscles bulged, and fingers stretched into dangerous weapons. The disfigured and hideous face of the child he'd killed appeared; its lips curled into a snarl.

"Hello, Peter. Are you ready to die?"

Why did evil come in familiar forms? Peter's worst nightmares always involved that tragic day.

Lightning cracked and thunder boomed. The flashes were so bright that Peter had to look away. The weathered steeple burst into flames.

"My God says no!" Peter yelled.

"Your god is not here," it said.

The fire spread and the smoke grew thicker, the heat more intense. The larger-than-life Scotty backed Peter into a corner. The fire popped nearby, and boards groaned under their combined weight. The imp grinned and stepped closer. Peter was hemmed in. With a shudder, the floor gave way.

The pair fell into the catacombs beneath the church. Peter hit hard. The creature lifted his head and in the flames' dancing shadows, its eyes were more animal than human. With teeth bared, he sprang at Peter.

Seized by terror, Peter didn't move. The creature crashed into him, pinning him to the ground. Jagged, broken teeth gnawed at Peter's throat. As the intensity of the pain soared, Peter's hands frantically searched the ground for a weapon.

Father Abrams' silhouette, framed by the growing flames, peeked over the edge of the hole. "The Dark Riders are here. Give up and give us the key. You're fighting a losing battle."

"No." Peter writhed, throwing his battered body against the unmovable weight. Blood and saliva dripped down his chest. His strength waned. His vision narrowed. He touched the key and was struck by strong images of what was to come. The Dark Ones had ambitious goals. The end of hope, the extinguishing of light and innocence. He started to shake with fright. He fumbled the key while switching hands and watched as it slipped from his hand.

All around him, frantic shadows rose from the depths of the catacombs. He lunged one last time and pushed through the pile of bones until he found something cold, thin, and sharp. The energy from the key filled his every pore. He drove the key like a blade into the back of the creature's skull. A scream rattled the church, sending embers raining down upon them. The brief bursts of light exposed a tunnel leading into the depths of the catacombs.

A normal-sized Scotty, not the mangled child from his nightmares but an intact boy with a youthful glow coloring his cheeks, stood in front of him. "Peter, I forgive you."

Peter bowed his head and wept.

Loud voices and the sound of horses neighing pulled Peter from his reverie. He wiped his eyes and groaned when he stood. He pushed his battered body forward and limped in the direction of the tunnel. Blood still dribbled from the superficial neck wounds. The creature had infected him with some type of corrosive venom, and it still coursed through his veins, devouring his hope. With each step, a different part of his body complained. Mounds of bones, small children's bones, were scattered everywhere. He realized he needed to hurry, but he feared he might be too late.

A thin layer of condensation covered all the surfaces of the tunnel. Tiny rivulets streamed down the walls and pooled on the floor. As the passageway descended, the temperature decreased. Peter shivered, but a feverish sweat beaded on his forehead and wetted his shirt. The darkness pressed in all around him. The deeper he traversed, the blacker and narrower the tunnel became. The constant drip, drip, drip of water toyed with his mind.

"Child Killer. Child Killer," his conscience whispered.

The poison gnawed at his self-confidence. He didn't think he would find the next door. The ghosts that walked by his side agreed and kept telling him he was a failure. Maybe he was.

He stopped and blinked twice, not sure if what he saw was real or just part of the delirium he was experiencing. Trish's luminous footprints appeared on the stone floor in front of him. As he followed them, the sweet cloying scent of rotted flesh permeated his senses. Time passed slowly as he limped along. With each of his steps, good and evil played a tug-of-war with his soul. Several times he leaned against the wet walls to rest. Each time, the voices told him to lay down and his worries would be over. Nobody would find his body in this labyrinth, and nobody would miss him. Despondency had taken hold when Trish's glowing footsteps ended at a blood-splattered door.

Peter didn't hesitate to insert the key. A brief brilliant flash of light emanated from the key before the door swung open.

The strong scent of pine was the first thing Peter noticed when he stepped through the doorway. Mosquitos buzzed around his head and the haunting sounds of the night serenaded him. He stood in a glade of knee-high grass, surrounded by pines and birches. The door began to fade, but this time, Peter reached back and locked it.

The house, no longer decrepit, stood along the shores of a picturesque pond. The green-eyed girl stood with her hands on her hips and a scowl etched across her face.

"Are you done playing God yet?" she asked.

"Where is she?"

"She's at the house with Elizabeth Bathory, her true mother."

Peter set off toward the house, surprised that the girl didn't try to stop him or follow.

Caw. Caw.

Two large blackbirds had landed in the nearest birch tree. Their dark beady eyes appeared to be appraising him. He ignored them, turning his back on their stares, and followed the shoreline until he stood in front of the house. The sudden silence unnerved him. He wasn't ready to confront whatever was inside, so he walked onto the dock and studied the entire scene.

The quaint landscape was too perfect. The calm waters of the pond were dark and deceitful. He dropped to his knees and splashed water on his face. When his vision cleared, hundreds of small ghost-white faces stared at him from the depths of the pond.

Peter hurried off the dock. Sensing he was being watched, he scanned his surroundings. A black blanket of night birds and cormorants covered the trees, their chorus discerning and troublesome. When he approached the house, the children stepped out of the trees' shadows, their fangs glistening. Naked fear cursed through Peter's body. He stepped onto the porch and knocked. A few moments later, he tried again. Nothing. He glanced over his shoulder. The trees were fuller, and the feral kids stepped closer. Peter opened the door and stuck his head inside.

"Hello. Is anyone home?"

Hearing no response, Peter entered. He locked the door and breathed a sigh of relief, happy to have a barrier between him and the children. With a general idea of the house's layout, he went in search of Trish. He wandered the first floor for several minutes, then headed to the basement.

As soon as he opened the door, he was hit with a wave of stench so fetid and nauseating he had to cover his face. But something far worse lingered at the back of his throat, something dark and diabolical. Black magic.

Evil wrapped the entire house. Creatures rose from the darkness and started for the stairs, their glowing eyes full of hellfire, their jaws snapping together. Peter wasn't going to explore the damp place, especially when creatures larger than rats scurried in the absolute blackness below. He locked the door and turned towards the kitchen. The sight of a dozen children's faces pressed up against the large window made him scream. The girl with the green eyes pounded on the porch door and laughed maniacally. Muffled footsteps sounded upstairs as a young girl stepped out of the shadows.

"Who are you?" Peter asked.

"I am Bernice and I'm here to warn you. She's coming. You better leave."

"I can't. I need to save Trish."

"They won't let you."

"I have to try."

"There's a door in the attic. When the time is right, grab Trish and run. Don't look back. I'll distract Elizabeth as long as I can."

"Do you want to come with me?"

Bernice's eyes saddened. "I can't. It's not my destiny."

An upstairs door opened, and a woman called down the stairs. "Bernice, who are you talking to?"

Elizabeth, the same stunning woman from the church, bounded down the stairs with a frightened Trish firmly in her grasp. "Ah Peter, welcome to my home. You've found Trish at last," she said, as she pushed Trish into the kitchen.

"I plan to leave with her too."

When Elizabeth laughed, the white worms circulating in Peter's body shuddered. A strange sensation overcame him. It was as if a dark foul wind blew away his words and thoughts. But just as suddenly, the invasive feelings receded, and Elizabeth's words came to him. "Fear us, for we are many." Elizabeth was darkness in human form.

Outside, the nightbirds' squawking made a terrible racket, as if they were warning or scolding someone. Peter glanced out the window just as all hell broke loose. The porch door exploded inward, and the green-eyed girl and the feral children stormed into the house. Two fireballs appeared in Bernice's hands, and she threw them at Elizabeth.

"Peter, run. Now!" Bernice screamed.

In the chaos, Peter experienced a moment of clarity. A sense of peace settled inside of him. He ran toward Trish, picked her up, and carried her up one flight of stairs. A door behind them rattled. He didn't dare glance back as they rushed up another set of stairs into the attic. The door that had frightened him before no longer appeared as frightening. He slipped the key into the lock.

"The Guardians are waiting for you," Peter said, placing the key around Trish's neck. "They'll protect you."

Peter tossed her through the entrance and closed the door. He had more innocent souls to save.

At a young age, CHRIS STENSON had success winning young author contests, and his love for writing continued throughout high school and into adulthood. He is the founder and leader of the Moorhead Friends Writing Group which has hosted nationally known authors as guest speakers. He has published nine short stories in various anthologies including the MFWG publications. In 2024, his debut novel, *Sins of the Mother*, was published. He is currently working on several short stories and the second book in the Maiden, Mother, and Crone Chronicles, *Sins of the Land*, will be published in 2025.

BROKEN WINGS

Sarah Adams

THE SUN-DAPPLED HALLWAYS HIGHLIGHTED the dust particles floating in the air. Books, paper, and silence permeated the open space. Doors facing the hall, and a small open area embraced a vivid, youthful spirit exuding from the space. The tired beige plaster walls brightened the hall above the darkly stained oak wainscoting. The brick multi-story building reflected modern updates while retaining its early 20th-century charm. Colorful posters advertising student activities and the promotion of an upcoming football game between Effham Falls High School and a nearby town hung on the wall. Muffled voices filtered into the space from behind closed wooden doors.

The colorful leaves and the bright blue sky offered an invitation to sit near the large glass windows. A tall, slightly built young girl, Elissa Pemberton, accepted the window's generous allure as the filtered sun bounced on her long black hair. The outside was filled with colorful leaves of red, yellow, and orange, precariously hanging on dark branches. The brilliant blue sky allowed the contemplation of one's fleeting thoughts. A murder of ravens roosted on the branches of a nearby naked tree. She absentmindedly fingered a book cover lying in her lap as she stared out the window. The outside world seemed infinitely more interesting and sane when compared to a well-worn copy of AP Western Civilization.

The classroom discussion failed to keep her interest. In her mind, the ancient battles in Greece and Persia did not echo in today's persistently violent climate. The brutality and incivility among humans made her miss the more simple aspects of being out in nature. She felt lost in the modern world and hunted. The attacks on her Native background wore her down mentally.

Elissa's thoughts flashed back to the classroom discussion relating to Greek philosophy and the sanctity of humanity.

She listened quietly while Charlie Talbott and his friends criticized the teacher's lesson that focused on the first Olympics and the Greek philosophers: Plato, Aristotle, and Socrates. She bit her tongue to keep from reacting to Charlie Talbot's comments about the Greek athletes' state of nudity along with his contrived version of ethics. Elissa innocently questioned if the philosophers' ideas were original thoughts or if they were taken from earlier peoples who resided in Greece or Asia Minor. She considered her Native ancestry and its appropriation by others. She questioned this in relation to the philosophers and asked herself why they didn't acknowledge this.

The teacher had flashed pictures of the philosophers on the screen. What did they really look like? The statutes and reliefs were often based on recollections or ideas of what a sculptor thought they looked like. Were the sculptures a realistic interpretation or a fanciful aberration of humanity? None of the philosophers were alive when the images were cast, nor were they alive to offer authenticity and testimony to its accuracy.

Poets, rulers, and power seekers interpreted and then reinterpreted ideas through the passage of history. Elissa viewed history as a way to hide past indiscretions in order to empower their interpretation over those they controlled. This action created a sense of brokenness among marginalized peoples, which perpetuated a cyclical sense of a broken soul by creating fear and allowing insecurity. This was the case for her Native ancestors whose stories and values were marginalized by colonials.

Her question regarding cultural appropriation in relation to the philosophical teachings was innocent, but it left her unprepared for classmates' reactions. She glared angrily at Charlie wrapping a bandanna around his head and sticking a paper feather in it. He proceeded with his tomahawk and war-whoop dance. His friends started giggling and egged him on as Charlie continued before joining him in their prance around the room. "Hey Elissa, I'm an Indian too, watch me dance to the Holy Spirit. Smile and come dance with us, happy little snowflakes and fruitcakes! It's a great way to pray to the Great Spirit."

"Charlie, you don't have any respect for others. You're insulting other cultures, and my question was appropriate. Your actions disgust me," Elissa grumbled, struggling to keep her anger in check. Charlie and his friends' actions left her blood boiling, and she wondered what propelled his behavior. "You're a jerk, Charlie, and besides you don't have any sense of rhythm or respect."

"Charlie, knock it off right now! Sit down now and take that bandanna off!" snarled Ms. Jacobssen. Charlie glared at the teacher but sat at his desk with his arms crossed.

"Hey, teach, just having a bit of fun. Indians are not that bright," retorted Charlie. "They're not on the same level as us. My dad even said so."

"You have a choice. Remove the bandanna or you will go to Principal Johnson's office. I will also be speaking with your parents and Coach Winslow," ordered Ms. Jacobssen. Elissa had enough. She got up and left the room.

Her classmate's positions and questionable ethics left Elissa wondering how they could identify as Christian. Christianity and the philosophers spoke of love and acceptance, so why did her classmates refuse to accept the differences? Philosophy offered a way to think. It raised you up but it crushed the soul if it proved contradictory to the dominant thoughts of society.

The idea that stated the essence of a true human being was an individual at peace with the natural world flooded her thoughts. The debate of the Greek philosophers made her question which belief system was truly accurate: the beliefs of the first peoples they encountered in Greece or the ideas that formed organized religion and society. The Greeks got it right, but Christianity went astray. The disconnect between the ideas left her lost and fragmented, making it difficult to spread her wings broken by the diatribes.

She realized that in ancient Greece the philosophers examined and debated different ideas. They contemplated the belief that humans originated from a single substance, which could be water, air, or an unlimited substance called Apeiron. In contrast, she understood that her people came from the earth and stardust. This idea led to the development of the universe and perhaps the philosophers recognized it also. She respected the mysteries of the world on a philosophical basis but also accepted the reality that science was present. The lack of ethos and compassion bothered her. The balance of science and the esoteric ideas were battling for control.

The thought led her down a long and dusty road of soul-searching to understand the relationship between logos and human ethos, while applying logic to questions and engaging in debate to better convey philosophical ideas. She found the idea fascinating yet confusing. Her soul and mind were at odds with her feelings as she struggled to calm the raging mental storm.

"Elissa, are you okay?" asked Ms. Jacobssen. She walked up and placed her hand on Elissa's shoulder. "I'm sorry, I let you down."

Elissa cringed at her teacher and considered her words before speaking. "Wounded and hurt. I can't believe you let them attack me like that. I asked an innocent question. Their behavior was unacceptable. War whoops and tomahawk chops? Really? Those comments hurt deep down. They injure one's soul and it manifests in unexpected ways. I dislike being used as an experiment for a human ethics discussion."

"The appropriation question was a good one," replied Ms. Jacobssen. "It would've been a good discussion, but the boys got out of control."

Elissa rolled her eyes. They were always out of control in class, courtesy of too much testosterone. Part of her regretted taking the class with Jacobssen and not Mr. Walters.

In relative silence, they looked at each other while questioning the others' motives. "Do you want to come back to class?" asked Ms. Jacobssen.

Elissa looked at her sternly and slowly shook her head. "I know I should go back with my head held high, but I need to get myself sorted out to do so. Their actions were crude and demeaning."

Ms. Jacobssen nodded solemnly and rose from a chair near the window. "I understand. I'll let you remain out here until the end of the period." She handed her a piece of paper. "It's an assignment on Greek philosophers and I gave you Aristotle. You mentioned that you found his work interesting."

Elissa nodded politely as she took the piece of paper. She waited until Ms. Jacobssen left the hallway and looked at the paper. She smiled when she saw the question and already knew what her answer would be concerning the wider world.

Elissa looked up and noticed her cousin, Kayleigh Berlin approaching her in the open area where she was sitting. Kayleigh had been on her way to the parking lot.

"Hey, cuz, why are you sitting out here?" asked Kayleigh.

Elissa and Kayleigh looked in the direction of the room as the argument between Charlie and Ms Jacobssen drifted into the open space. Swallowing her anger, Elissa calmly informed Kayleigh of Charlie's words and actions.

"Is that Charlie Talbott?" Kayleigh slowly shook her head. "Geez, I hate that jerk. Just because he's related to the mayor, he feels he can get away with things. All inflated ego and no brains."

"Yeah, He won't leave me alone. It's been two years since we moved to Effham Falls, and he won't let up." Elissa sighed as she leaned her head against the wall and closed her eyes.

"Where are you going?" She shifted her feet to the floor and stretched her arms.

"I need coffee and a snack. Looks like you could use one too," said Kayleigh. "You can also use a break from the privileged fools in there. Let's go to Wallflower."

Elissa nodded. Kayleigh struck her as wise beyond her seventeen years. She grabbed her bookbag and followed her cousin out of the building. It was near the end of the second, ninety-minute class block and the end of her school day. She only had two classes on B-days. The beautiful day mitigated some of her growing anger.

They left school together and she enjoyed the drive and the company of her cousin. Kayleigh motioned for Elissa to get out of the car and head into the restaurant. Noticing a group of their classmates when they came through the door, they chose a table out of their line of sight. Elissa and Kayleigh quietly watched the group sitting in a booth at Wallflower. It annoyed Elissa that they were present in the restaurant, but she decided to choose the high ground. A waitress approached and took their order of burgers and fries. The smell of sizzling grease from burger patties hitting the grill echoed in the seating area. Music from a bygone decade streamed from small jukeboxes sitting on the tables. The song playing seemed to echo her state of mind.

"Ignore them, cuz, they aren't worth it. Remember colonials don't always learn what they're taught, especially when it focuses on how they treat people. They see themselves as privileged and above the rules of common sense and decency.

Besides, they cut their fourth block classes, and that won't sit well with coach Winslow or their parents," stated Kayleigh. "Grandma Mae alluded to that many times."

"True, she did. I miss her wisdom," replied Elissa meekly as she drew lazy circles in ketchup with a french fry.

"So do I," replied Kayleigh wistfully. "She saw the world through different lenses and the spirit of the time. Remember, she is also German, and we learned from both cultures. There is wisdom and lessons in all cultures. Sometimes they are good lessons and other times they are not beneficial for our soul. The biggest challenge is keeping the ones that are meaningful."

"Hey, Injun snowflakes!" yelled Charlie from across the restaurant while hopping on one leg. His friends buoyed his actions with tomahawk chops and war whoops. "You aren't strong enough to be here and handle people like us. You're too smart to be an Indian and too sensitive. You should go back to the rez for a proper education." Charlie and his friends sniggered at the remark and pointed at them.

Kayleigh snorted and rolled her eyes. "I suggest keeping a few things in mind. First, Charlie Talbot is notorious for getting his foot stuck in a football helmet, both real and metaphorically speaking. Once it is stuck on his foot, he runs around crying like a little kid and throwing a temper tantrum because he can't get it off. He has failed that lesson more than once. Metaphorically speaking, he sticks his foot in his mouth on a regular basis."

"Three games this year and counting," snorted Elissa as the memory played in her head of Charlie running down the sideline with a helmet stuck on his foot. "Coach Winslow is not going to be pleased with a big football game coming up."

"Yes, my dear cuz. Keep that in mind!" added Kayleigh. "He can't see beyond himself. It's all about him. Others drink the Kool-Aid and follow him because they are scared. They can't think on their own and they need guidance.

"The Greeks, Romans, poets, and modern philosophers learned how to think. Thinking is important because it allows love, reason and compassion to grow in our soul," stated Elissa. "Philosophy also plays a role in music." She appreciated the older songs that carried soulful messages."

A waitress walked by, filled their glasses, and proceeded to check the status of the other diners in her section. The exasperated manager walked over and reprimanded Charlie's table for their behavior. The manager requested that Charlie and his friends stand up and follow him to his office until their parents arrive. Charlie's head lowered.

"Coyote has called," snorted Elissa. "He's a trickster who'll always call your folly."

"Don't look at them and don't react. It's a reckoning that they have to face. Their past behavior may break our wings, but we can still soar in the sky if we stay on the higher ground. Their souls need to grow and learn," stated Kayleigh.

Elissa nodded at her cousin and wondered how she grew to be so incredibly wise. She could feel Charlie's eyes boring into her soul as he walked by the table. His privilege led him to cause trouble without knowing the consequences. She refused to feel sorry for him. One's actions always speak louder than their words, an aspect of virtue and humility that he still needed to learn. "His mind is closed and not open to new things."

Elissa's attention was drawn to the jukebox. "This song says a lot. I like the old songs. I like the music from the 80's because it's fun, insightful, and you can hear the lyrics."

"So do I. I miss the language arts teacher I had in the Twin Cities. She challenged us to think about things rhetorically," replied Kayleigh. "We analyzed song lyrics for one assignment, and I learned how messages were perceived and inferred. It was an interesting journey through text and video."

"I remember you talking about this assignment. What were the two songs that you did? asked Elissa.

"I studied *Broken Wings* by Mr. Mister and *Who Wants to Live Forever* by Queen. Grandma Mae liked Queen, and she talked often about their music. It's surprising how deep songs can be. Sometimes it's the timbre of the voice. and sometimes it's a lyric, but it forces you to appreciate them in a different context. I find it interesting how music often echoes the poets and philosophers. Older pop and rock songs have a deeper meaning than the current ones."

"I also noticed that videos provide a visual context that can heighten the meaning of the lyrics or detract from them. I sometimes wonder if the music's message is even understood by Charlie and his merry band of fools. I highly doubt it. I like the song playing right now. It is one of the songs that I did."

"This song, *Broken Wings*, brings back memories of working on my assignment. It encourages the soul to take our broken wings and learn to fly again so the soul can heal and grow strong. We have freedom to fly by loving ourselves through second chances and we help each other by loving one another. Grandma liked this song also. Life and love will find us in many unexpected ways," stated Kayleigh. "Don't let the fools destroy your soul. You have a lot to offer the world, and I've learned from you, cuz. You're an old soul who is insightful and reflective about the world around you."

Elissa looked at her and slowly nodded. Perhaps that was the largest challenge to learn. Spreading one's proverbial broken wings to fly, as long as a person believes in themself. "I agree. Thanks, Kayleigh, I feel better. What about the Queen song?"

"For me, it talked about being in the here and now. Appreciate those people you love and celebrate the things that are around you like we are doing now. Celebrate your gifts and what you can offer the world. It could be taken away tomorrow. It's asking us to be present," Kayleigh added.

"I watched the music video for *Who Wants to Live Forever* after I listened to the soundtrack for the movie, *Bohemian Rhapsody*. I was curious about the song and wanted to learn more about it. I was surprised to see that both Freddie Mercury and Brian May were singing the song," stated Elissa. "I did some reading and found out that Brian wrote it but they both did vocals on it. Apparently, he was inspired by a scene in another movie they were writing music for."

"You're correct in your assessment. It was originally written for the movie, *Highlander*. It has taken on a different meaning over the years since Freddie's death. It's a powerful song," added Kayleigh. "Things will happen in our lives that will crush our souls but seek the light and spread your wings even if they are broken. Your soul will thank you. Love is sometimes the greatest cure. We have to remind ourselves of that, cuz."

Elissa nodded at Kayleigh's comment. "Perhaps the Greeks and the Ancient ones had it right after all, and we have forgotten how to love and be present."

The girls grew silent when the manager escorted parents to his office to pick up their errant children. Elissa glanced casually over the top of her glass and witnessed the anger etched in the parents' eyes. Maybe the parents were also lost souls trying to find their way and that may be the biggest lesson of the Greek philosophers on the topic of ethics and virtue. Perhaps in Charlie's case, he was being called out for his actions in both the restaurant and school.

The sense of brokenness invaded her being. Perhaps the idea of forgiveness eluded individuals around them who saw her background as a threat. Their fragmented selves denied them the ability to see the good in others. It echoed a dull ache from the collective pain she felt from society. This pain manifested itself in unexpected ways by enforcing the desire to cling to the fear that makes them feel secure. They felt safe when they marginalized those who were outside their perceived normalness. It is reflected in how we treat the world around us, in nature, and the cosmos.

Grappling with the broken pieces of her soul, Elissa continued to search for an adhesive to heal her own frame of mind. The pieces slowly joined together, but they did not fit neatly, and a few spots left open gaps. This allowed the pain of human existence to escape the confines of Elissa's mind.

Elissa finally began to understand the essence of Grandfather's teachings. When we harmed the earth and our relatives, we diminished ourselves. The karma that we unleash onto the world comes back to us. Our own inhumanity to our fellow creatures and our earthly mother, whether intended or not, was our greatest sin.

It better served humanity and was more worthy to do something that was positive to make the world a better place. It healed the soul in countless ways. Forgiveness and love were the keys to healing. The broken wings would grow stronger, and it would be a better world. The beauty of the physical world comes in many forms. Appreciation of the earthly beauty cannot be appreciated without humans. The proverbial rocks would long survive without us humans, but we couldn't exist without them or Mother Earth. Their souls need to make peace with their wounds. We need to make peace with the earth and sky.

SARAH ADAMS enjoys the music that inspires her muse. Music often plays a role in her stories whether directly or indirectly. This is her second story for Moorhead Friends Writing Group.

TALES FROM A SCHOOL BUS DRIVER

Barbara Bustamante

As Chris Adams, the bus driver, boarded Bus #2 for the afternoon route, he glanced at the sign that hung on the wall in the school bus garage. "The Most Important Mile is the One Before You Leave." Chris and his friend, Travis Johnson, finished inspecting their buses. Both men had become bus drivers for Effham Falls Public Schools while studying at Tree Branch Community College.

Travis boarded Bus #1 and both men drove to Washington Elementary School to assist the teachers with getting the children on the right buses. What a sight it was as the kids dashed through the doors of the school to their waiting buses. With their short legs, each student mounted the high stairs and grabbed the handrail to pull themselves up and, once inside, they scampered to their chosen seat. Within minutes, the bus was filled with rambunctious chatter.

When Chris and Travis returned to their bus, they quickly scanned the seats for unexpected surprises then slid into their seats before driving down the street to pick up students waiting at the high school. After that, Travis headed north, and Chris went south down Eagle Avenue past the Wayside Motel.

After crossing Main Street, the children on the bus abruptly stopped talking. From experience, anything could happen on this side of town, even in broad daylight. One time, the bus had to stop to let a row of antique dolls cross the street. Another time, some crows were dive-bombing the bus. But this time, when reached the Niijii River by the waterfall, the normal noisy chatter resumed.

The little kids adored Chris, and the older students gave him a hard time. They would beg him to pick up speed at the bump in the road that crossed the end of Harm's Way. They loved how it felt to become airborne.

Chris's last stop was near the Barfly about a mile from the airport, and he enjoyed the scenery and solitude on the drive back to the garage.

Missing But Not Lost

This year, the cool mornings and warm afternoons of fall grew colder as winter came early to Effham Falls. Normally, November didn't have much snow, but the Halloween blizzard had dumped over a foot that heaped the boulevards high with snow shoveled from the sidewalks.

On this cold overcast afternoon, Chris arrived in his school bus for the route to Washington Elementary School. Once the students were all on board he took a quick check of traffic, and the race was on to deliver them home safely. Each stop went as planned—he counted the ones getting off and he counted the ones down the driveway. Sometimes more than one family got off and split into different directions, requiring visual traffic control.

Chris approached his last stop. Janie, a little kindergartener, had to cross the driveway on the other side of the road. She bundled up, wearing her Pretty Little Pony backpack, and walked down the steps to the door. Chris checked all seven mirrors for oncoming traffic. When he looked back, Janie was gone, and he assumed that she was walking around the bus. Chris checked the mirrors again. No Janie.

He waited a moment then checked the mirrors a third time. Maybe she had walked around the back of the bus.

FIND HER!!!

He got up, walked down the front bus steps, and looked down the road on the right side of the bus. No Janie. He stepped onto a ridge of plowed snow and looked to his right. No Janie. He looked to his left. No Janie. He turned back facing the bus door and below the step, underneath the bus, he spotted the lavender-colored pom-pom of Janie's winter hat.

"What are you doing down there?" he yelled. "Get out of there!"

He got on his hands and knees, reached down, and pulled her up. "Are you OK?" he asked as he brushed the snow off her jacket and snowpants.

Smiling, she replied, "Yes, Mister Chris, I guess I slipped."

"Give me your hand to help you get across this road." He escorted her across the road and returned to his seat in the bus. Once he saw her safely walking down the driveway, he held his head in his hands and wept.

Lost In Forest

Later on, Chris and Travis decided to spend the four-day Veterans Day weekend together on a trip to the Misty Pine Forest, north of Effham Falls to do some hiking and fishing. Travis had been to the forest before, but this was Chris's first time. Travis had to return early for a family commitment, so Chris would finish the weekend solo.

They finished their routes on Friday and met at the forest parking lot. They took the mile-long path to the campsite while Travis showed Chris the reflective signs to help him find his way back.

They spent the next day hiking and caught some fish for supper before returning to their campsite. On Sunday morning, Travis packed up for the walk back to his truck.

While finishing his coffee, Chris relished the serenity of the beautiful sunrise and cherished his freedom to inhale the moment. He was glad that after the cold, freezing nights the sun was warm enough to hike up to Vampire Outlook. What an amazing day of hiking, but he had two more days and saved the best for the last.

On Monday. Chris planned a climb up to Misty Pine Peak. He needed an early start in order to be back before dark. At sunrise, he headed up the southeast face of the mountain. The early hours brought cold crisp air, and by midday, warmer rays peeked through the bare branches. Chris climbed higher and higher. He came around a clump of trees to a huge boulder next to a majestic pine tree. And there in the open sky, he viewed the grandeur of Effham Falls from a distance. It looked like a toy village. He pulled out his phone to take a few shots of this magnificent sight.

He hoped for a better time going downhill back to camp because he needed to get back before five pm. Stomp by stomp through the forest, he vigilantly sensed his surroundings. Some of the scenery was normal; some seemed a bit odd, but he kept moving. About an hour and a half later, the scent of a skunk filled his nostrils. He glanced around for either victim or predator. Neither in sight. As the scent subsided, he resumed his speed. He recalled rumors of Bigfoot in the forest, but no real proof was found.

When he reached halfway down the mountain, thoughts of sharing his view of the peak energized his body and cold breezes made time and steps fly by.

With the campsite and the sunset in view, he checked the time. 4:28 pm. After he arrived and took a quick break, he moved his supplies from the tent, packed the tent, and loaded it all in his backpack—all this while the sun set below the horizon and the Belt of Venus illuminated the sky.

Heading into the darkened path to the parking lot, he reached for his flashlight as the twilight was waning. He turned it on.

NOTHING! Dead as a doornail. Shocked, he stopped in his tracks.

Oh, my God! You've got to be kidding. This can't be happening to me.

He set his backpack down and walked around the dead flashlight.

How stupid of me! Why didn't I check it before we left?

He threw the flashlight on the ground and continued to walk around.

What do I do now? I'm totally out of food and water. I don't know my way back to the truck.

He glanced at the horizon and the waning twilight.

I'm doomed!

He walked back to pick up the flashlight and his backpack.

I hope Travis calls and reports me missing. I think I might make it one night.

He picked up his backpack.

I'm stuck here for now. I guess I better go start a fire.

Chris stumbled his way back to the abandoned campsite in the last bit of twilight in the sky. He felt around for some leaves and dry sticks and knelt to light a fire with the extra matches from his backpack. He cupped his hand around the leaves, lit the match to the leaves, and softly blew on the flame to add oxygen. Stick by stick, the fire grew until he was able to stop and find a log to sit on.

He gazed into the fire. As he contemplated his situation, the image of the sign in the bus garage came to mind. If only he had prepared ahead of time by packing extra batteries or even tested the batteries in the first place. The sign will be a greater reminder in the future.

His hand grazed the side of an extra side pocket on his jacket. It had something in it.

What's this bump? I don't remember using that pocket.

Anything of importance was in the backpack. He pulled his glove off to check the little pocket. He reached inside and felt a small chain.

That's odd!

His finger caught the chain and he pulled it out. To his surprise, it was a miniature LED flashlight with the words "Mike's Auto" written on the side. He forgot that Mike gave it to him when he picked up his truck for the oil change.

He quickly stomped out his campfire, grabbed his backpack, and headed down the trail. He was so grateful for this gift.

"Boy, wait 'til I see Mike again. I've got a story for him."

BARBARA BUSTAMANTE started writing poetry in high school. Her love for words inspired her to write poetry and stories for the Moorhead Friends Writing Group in *Tales from the Frozen North, Welcome to Effham Falls,* and *Tales from the Water's Edge.* She's retired, active in church, promotes mental health, and lives with her feline writing companion, Talon.

LOOSE CHANGE

Dan McKay

HARRY LUGGED THE OVERSIZED shopping bags towards his car. He silently prayed the paper wouldn't tear, sending his purchases into the dirty snow. The wine bottle would probably break, and he'd have to shell out another hundred bucks to replace it. Only the best for his in-laws, although he had sensed in the past everyone would be happy with beer and a more casual get-together.

"Psst! Hey, buddy! Got any spare change?"

Harry turned and saw a street bum shuffling his way. Not now! He would have to set his bags down to unlock the car. No way to get the bags into the car before the bum got there.

One more step and the bum would be uncomfortably close. "C'mon, man, it's Christmas," the bum said. The odor of lived-in clothing announced his imminent arrival.

"Yeah, I know," Harry said. "What do you want?"

"Got any loose change?" The bum held his hand out.

"Pretty sure I don't. I use a credit card for everything." Harry pulled the bags closer so he could get his hand into his coat pocket and retrieve his keys. Almost there, just a bit more. Why didn't the BMW have a proximity sensor like his mom's Impala? A Chevy, of all things!

A bag tore open, and items fell into the snow. Harry swore softly to himself. The bum leaned down. "Here, I'll help you."

Harry dropped the rest of the bags. "Get your hands off that!"

"You think because I live in the back of a parking garage, I'm going to take your stuff?" The bum straightened, and they locked eyes.

"Look, I'm sorry," Harry said, surprising himself. "It's been a rough day, and I have to spend the evening with my in-laws, listening to rants about politics." His cell phone buzzed, and he answered it. "Yes, dear?"

His head bobbed as he listened. He glanced at the bum and rolled his eyes. "Yeah, I got the wine. Yes, it's the Chateau—whatever you had on the list." He nodded. "Yes, the same vintage. I got the last bottle."

He crossed his arms and stared at the anemic fluorescent lights above him. "Yes, dear, no store brand. Your favorite crackers. Yes, in the blue and gold box." He held out his arms as if pleading. The bum tilted his head and watched.

"That's nice, dear," Harry said, "but I have to get to another store before it closes." Sighing deeply, he looked at the bum.

"Crackers?" the bum asked.

Harry stared at the red and green box of crackers and gritted his teeth. He reached down and tossed the box to the bum. "All yours."

The bum caught the box and examined it. "They any good?"

"For what they cost, they'd better be."

The bum laughed. "Perceived expectations of value can be fragile."

Harry stared, mouth open.

The bum put his hands on his hips. "Oh, so you think I'm stupid, along with being a thief."

"It's not that, so much—" Harry stammered.

The bum snorted. "Just messing with you! I'd react the same way in your position—which I was, some years ago." He raised his chin and cleared his throat. "Fate can be a stern taskmaster, doling out punishments or rewards as it sees fit."

Harry blinked. "Shakespeare?"

"Kowalski." The bum opened the box of crackers.

"Who's that?"

"That's me. Jackie Kowalski, in the flesh." He popped a cracker in his mouth and chewed. "Don't look at me like that."

A pang of guilt hit Harry. The poor guy was just trying to survive. "Sorry, it's hard to put all this together."

"Deal with it. Life ain't all roses." Kowalski took another. "Hey, these aren't half-bad. What else you got?"

"Yeah, well, it's been nice chatting with you, but I need to be going." He unlocked his car door.

"Yeah, back to the in-laws and the Chateau d'Same-o."

Harry bent and picked up the rest of the fallen items. "Braunschweiger?" He offered the package to Kowalski.

"Are you kidding? You know how much cholesterol is in that?"

Harry raised his eyebrows.

Kowalski sighed. "Okay, let's see if I got this right. Which I did, but I'm going to tell you anyway. Number one, you didn't realize how much cholesterol is in Braunschweiger. It's processed liver—of course, it's loaded with cholesterol and fat. Number two, you're surprised I know. I'm just a bum, and what do bums know? Number three, you're wondering why a homeless loser like me doesn't just grab the food and eat it, regardless." He pointed his finger at Harry. "Let me tell you. I don't plan to stay this way. This is just a temporary setback."

Harry reached into a bag on the back seat and pulled out a bottle. "Captain Morgan?"

Kowalski brightened. "Now you're talking! Of course, it's a cliché, bums drinking booze, but hey, I'm not one to turn down a drink." He paused. "Got some glasses for it?"

"I was just going to give you the bottle."

"No way! We have to do a toast."

"Fine," Harry said. "A toast. It just so happens I got a set of tumblers with the Morgan. Thought I'd keep them in the office." He opened the bottle and poured a generous amount into each glass. The aroma wafted into his face.

Kowalski took the offered glass and sniffed. "Yeah, nothing like the Captain!" He raised his glass. "To success!"

"Success," Harry said and clinked glasses.

After they each drank some of the rum, Kowalski raised his glass again. "Don't forget, the ever-fickle Lady Luck."

"To Lady Luck," Harry said, raising his glass.

"I think I read somewhere that alcohol can neutralize certain cholesterols," Kowalski said. He scratched his scraggly beard. "Maybe in the Wall Street Journal or an old issue of People."

"Changed your mind on the braunschweiger?" Harry asked.

Kowalski held up the box of crackers. "Yeah, let's make us some hors d'oeuvres."

Harry retrieved the tube and dug in another bag for some plastic utensils and upscale paper plates. He placed a plate on the trunk and sliced the Braunschweiger. "Hold on, I've got some olives, too." He opened the jar and dribbled the juice into the snow. With an olive on top of the liver pate, the crackers looked almost festive.

"To man's ingenuity," Kowalski said through a mouthful of make-shift hors d'oeuvre. He clinked his glass with Harry's and downed the rest of the rum. Harry filled Kowalski's glass and topped off his own.

Harry's stomach rumbled. He'd skipped breakfast and had been on his feet all day. "Say, these are pretty good," he said through a mouthful of appetizer. His wife would not approve, but she wasn't there, was she?

The rum sent a warm sensation coursing through his veins, and he drank some more while Kowalski described the Porsche he'd owned before his luck had run out at Tri-State. "I still have my business cards." He dug in his field coat, pulled out a brass card holder, and handed a card to Harry.

Harry choked on his rum. "Wait, you were a senior sales rep for Tri-State?"

Kowalski puffed out his chest. "Salesman of the year, two years running. We were printing our own money before the sector took it in the shorts. No one saw it coming." He raised his glass over his head. "I went from here,"—he lowered the glass below his knees—"to here. Now I'm just another lost soul." He shook his head. "Don't get me wrong, I'm not bitter. I'm looking for my next big opportunity."

"There, but for God's grace goes me. Or I. Er, myself? However, that goes." He squinted at Kowalski. "What brought you to Effham Falls?"

"A cheap bus ticket, that's all. Had never been here before, thought I'd get a fresh start." He hiccupped. "'Cept no one was hiring anyone like me."

Harry topped off Kowalski's glass and his own. "You know," he slurred, "I'm an accountant for Fredrickson Mining. I'll check and see what we have for job openings in the office."

"You'd do that for me? Thanks, buddy!" Kowalski held up his glass, and they made it a toast.

"Say, do you play poker?" Harry asked.

"Haven't in a long time. Why?"

"Well, there was this one guy, Dave, who was like a pro-level player. Cleaned us out every game." Harry thought for a moment. "Time flies! He's been gone now for over a year now."

Kowalski furrowed his brow. "What happened to him?"

"I don't know," Harry said. "He was playing in some illicit backroom games. He just disappeared one day. Probably lost everything and went underground or something."

"You don't know what it's like, living like this. You feel your identity as a person slipping away with each interaction with the public. I can't blame them; that's what I did when I was in their position. Death by a thousand sneers."

"Well, look, I feel bad about that." Harry shifted uncomfortably. "A guy hears things in the news and thinks the world is a dangerous place."

"You're not wrong," Kowalski said. "You might think Effham Falls is small enough to not have big-city problems, but there are parts of town that change into something dark and evil at night. I've seen things you wouldn't believe. People who aren't really human anymore." He shuddered and emptied his glass. "Besides, who cares if some bum disappears? It's a quiet solution where good, tax-paying citizens don't have to get their hands dirty."

Harry's cell phone beeped several times. Kowalski elbowed him from the passenger seat. Harry shook his head to clear it. He pressed a button on the dash.

"Harry?" a voice came over the car's speakers. "Harry, where are you? Why aren't you home yet?"

"I'm right here," Harry said.

"Where is *here*?" she asked. "Harry, we're ready for the wine now. You know my family. They don't drink just any wine, it has to be—"

"Chateau d'Same-o," Kowalski said. "Oh, wait, I already made that joke. Did we open that bottle, too? I can't remember."

"Oh! You're not alone? Harry, who was *that*?"

"Just Kowalski," Harry said. "Don't mind him, he's har—harm—less."

"You're drunk! Harry, what are you doing? You get home right now!"

Harry belched. "Can't. Too drunk to drive."

The speakers crackled. "I'll call a cab. What bar are you in? The Rusty Nail? Please tell me you didn't drive out to the Wet Whistle. I've heard what kind of debauchery goes on out there."

Kowalski raised his eyebrows and pointed to the logo on the steering wheel. "The BMW bar. Stands for, uh, booze, and merriment, and—hic—women."

Her voice came through distorted. "Women? I knew it. You're in the Wet Whistle. I bet it's one of their low-brow exotic dance shows." He could picture her air quotes around "dance shows." She sobbed. "How *could* you?"

"Nah, I'm in my car. Front seat. Driver's side. Got crackers and braun-schtuff and olives. Oh, don't forget the Captain."

"Captain Morgan!" Kowalski sang in a rich baritone. "He's my captain! I'd follow him—anywhere!"

"Where are you?" she demanded. "Harry, I'm serious! I'll send Bob over to get you."

"Bob? I bet Bob's in no shape to drive," Harry said. "Annie always drives him home."

Kowalski tapped Harry's shoulder. "Hey, buddy, the cops are going to come through soon. We'd better get moving."

Harry searched his coat pockets for his keys before spotting them hanging in the ignition. In January, he'd get his annual bonus. Maybe he could trade up to a new BMW. One without the hassle of keys. "Dear? I have to go now."

The screen flashed black and then 'Call Disconnected' appeared. Kowalski shrugged. "She hang up?"

"I guess so," Harry backed out of his parking spot. "Man, I'm way too drunk to drive."

"Let me drive," Kowalski said. "I don't have a license. What can the cops do to me?"

Kowalski whistled. "Whoa! Nice house, buddy!"

Harry put his finger to his lips. "Shhhh! They'll hear you."

"Put it in the garage?"

"No, they'll hear that, too." Harry pointed to an empty spot on the street. "Over there."

Kowalski made a U-turn and parked. Harry opened a bag and pulled out a Vikings hoodie and a pair of jeans. "Here, these are yours. You can wear them inside. Happy birthday, Merry Christmas, whatever."

Kowalski wriggled out of his field coat. "Hey, thanks, buddy. That's rather kind of you."

They split up the paper shopping totes and plastic bags and walked towards the house. "This way," Harry called and opened the gate. He pointed to the patio door. "That's Bob on the left, Mike in the middle, and Joey over there."

Kowalski paused. "You sure this is okay?"

Harry nodded emphatically. "It's my house, and it's about time I wear the pants around here."

He tapped on the glass door. The men inside looked up. Harry held up a six-pack of beer.

Bob fumbled with the latch and slid the door open. "What are you doing?"

"Got to have beer to watch football." Harry handed the six-pack to Bob and tilted his head towards his new guest. "This here's Kowalski. Hell of a guy."

Harry offered his recliner to Kowalski and took a seat on the couch. "Where are the ladies?"

"They just left," Joey said. "Went looking for you."

"Hey, I get to watch the game in peace!" Harry opened a beer. "Pass interference? Are you kidding me? I swear the refs are blind."

Harry woke up to Karen nudging his ribs. "Harry, wake up!"

He peeled one eye open. "My head hurts."

"I'm sure it does, Mr. Drink-to-Excess," she whispered. "That guy is still here. Did he sleep on the couch in the den?"

"Yeah, in the den," he groaned.

"What are we going to do with him?"

"Oh, geez, I don't know. Feed him breakfast, I guess."

She leaned back and crossed her arms. "Well, you can just get yourself up and make ol'-what's-his-name some pancakes."

Harry moaned and stuck his foot out of the blankets. He swung his legs out and arrived in a seated position. "Kowalski."

"Is that his name?" Karen asked.

"Yeah. Can't remember his first name."

"Where does he live? Can't you take him home?"

Harry shook his head. "Doesn't have a home. Lives in the parking garage downtown."

She scoffed. "No one lives in the parking garage."

"Kowalski does."

Harry found Kowalski sitting at the family computer in the den.

"Hope you don't mind," Kowalski said over his shoulder. "I lost computer access after the library required a library card to use them. Can't prove I'm a resident without an address. No address, no card. No card, no computer. That's why I'm using yours."

"I don't mind at all," Harry said, making a mental note to run a virus scanner later.

"I've been in the dark since last year and lost contact with my former Tri-State crew. Best bunch of guys anyone could ask for."

"Did you find them?"

Kowalski nodded while he typed. "Got a hold of Jack. His company in Chicago is hiring and he'll give me a good reference. He thinks I'm a shoo-in. I just need to get there." He scratched his beard. "And I also have to get cleaned up, get a suit, book a hotel room, pay for a few meals..." His voice trailed off.

"Speaking of meals," Harry said, "I'm making pancakes for breakfast. All you can eat."

"I'll take you up on that." He closed his Facebook page. "After today, it's back to the soup kitchen for me."

"What about the job?"

"That's the thing about being down and out like this. Got nothing to pull myself up out of this hole." He offered a thin smile. "Need any help? I can run a mean spatula."

Harry stood in the BMW dealership while Karen joined the Christmas hustle and bustle at the mega-mall. As far as she knew, he was also at the mall, but the siren call of the shiny new BMWs at a dealership he saw on the drive from their hotel proved too much to resist.

Before their trip to the Twin Cities, he'd told Karen he wanted to do something special with his bonus. He stared wistfully at a car on the showroom floor. Its windows were open, and the new car smell had an almost narcotic effect. He inhaled deeply, savoring the aroma. That, along with the keyless entry and push-button start, could make a sale.

His phone beeped with a new message from a number he didn't recognize. Just a selfie picture of a grinning man standing in front of an office desk. At first, he didn't recognize him. Without a beard, he looked ten years younger. Harry looked closer. Next to a nameplate on the desk that read "J. Kowalski" were a box of fancy crackers, a jar of olives, and a tube of braunschweiger.

His laughter attracted the attention of a salesman.

"Looking for something special for Christmas?"

Harry wiped tears from his eyes. "Already got it." He looked at the car one last time. "Maybe next year."

DAN MCKAY has had several short stories published in anthologies since 2016, including the Fark Fiction Anthology, the Talking Stick, the Fargo Library's *Northern Narratives*, the Lowestoft Chronicles, and the Moorhead Friends Writer Group. He is the winner of the 2005 Bulwer-Lytton contest, and his winning entry was featured on Car Talk. He is active in local writing groups and lives with his family in Fargo, ND.

UNINVITED GUESTS

Sadie Mendenhall

ANDREW STOOD WAVING ON the porch of his grandparents' house as his parents drove off. The one civil thing they had managed to do was to drop him off with his grandfather. He was sure an argument would ensue as soon as they were far enough down the street. He faced his grandfather and smiled a bit then walked into the house behind him and sat on the couch. His bags had already been dropped upstairs and he was waiting for the rules on how the summer was going to work.

The place seemed different than the last time he was there. It had been a couple years since he'd been to Effham Falls. The last time he was there his grandmother had greeted him with cookies, freshly baked and served with a smile. This time he was greeted by chips and dip served with an awkward glance by his grandfather. His grandmother had been in the nursing home for a year now after having a nervous breakdown they believed was caused by the early onset of dementia. He wasn't thrilled about it, but she was in the best of care—at least that was what he had been told by his parents. Now all that was left was clearing out the house some so that his grandfather wasn't constantly reminded of what he lost. Perhaps to also make the pain of returning home after visits easier, but Andrew wasn't sure if it would work. He felt that it was wrong to erase her from the one place where she had chosen everything, from the paint and plants outside to the throw pillows and dishes inside. For Andrew, it was like everyone was treating his grandmother as though she'd passed away. Yet, she was very real and very alive.

"So, it's just us guys now, Pops." Andrew shrugged as he slumped onto the couch, reaching for the chips. The dip wasn't bad, but it wasn't particularly good. He had a hunch it was scooped from a jar and not made fresh. "Anything planned?" Man, he missed the freshly baked cookies.

"Well, Andy, now that you mention it. This is how it's going to be for the summer. You are going to help me clear out a lot of the junk around this house so that it's easier to live in. There is just too much stuff for one person. It's about time I cleaned up, and well..." His grandpa paused, leaned forward with his hands on his knees, and rubbed his face, hard. "Anyway, where was I? Photos and important keepsakes will be packed up for your momma, you and your kids when you have 'em. We're going to donate what we can to Goodwill, and the rest will be tossed with rubbish. It's going to be your job to do most of the lifting since I can't do it with my back. Sound fair enough?" His grandfather leaned back on the floral print sofa and nodded his head at him, waiting for an answer.

"Sure thing, Grandpa." Andrew looked around the living room, wondering just what they would be de-junking first. It was so full of his grandmother's things. Her collection of angels in the china cabinet, her bird plates on the walls, and her flower statues all over the tables. It was as though she wasn't gone. He chuckled inside as he noted the doilies on the coffee table that were made in the same colors as the awful blue, pink, and white flowered sofa he was sitting on. He loved his grandparents, but they really lacked sense and taste. Everything was dated by its appearance. Of course, there was no denying that his grandmother was the one who had placed everything where she felt it belonged. He sighed. He wanted to ask if they would be doing anything else over the summer but decided it was best not to. "So, when's dinner and what are we eating?"

"Well, I have some hotdogs with cheese in the oven with some tater tots, just the way your grandma makes them. I have some corn on the stove ready to be turned on too. So, get in the washroom and clean up and we'll eat in five minutes. You'll have time to unpack and get settled before bed. Tomorrow is a long day ahead of us." His grandfather turned and went to the kitchen when Andrew headed to wash up.

Andrew stared in the mirror after he washed up. This was going to be the oddest visit. He placed the small sea horse-shaped soap on the dish, smoothed the small lace knit doily, and hung up the hand towel. The sweet floral scent still hung in the air from all the different soaps that were finally being used. It made him think about his grandmother scolding him for using her decorative soaps when he was younger, and he smiled.

But realization hit him hard when he heard his grandpa calling up the stairs to come eat.

The night passed quietly, with little conversation between Andrew and his grandfather. He went to bed feeling lost and bored and passed time playing his Nintendo DS until he fell asleep. He slept soundly until his grandfather banged on the door at seven in the morning.

"Grandpa! Why are you banging? I'm tired, man!"

"C'mon, boy! It's time to get up. There is lots of work to be done today. Come downstairs and eat so we can get started." His grandfather's voice trailed a bit as he walked off down the hallway.

Andrew groaned in the bed and pulled the pillow over his face for a moment. It was only seven in the morning, and it was summer! Why should he have to get up so early in the summer? It wasn't like the junk was going anywhere. He slammed the pillow to his lap, then sat up and threw his feet over the side of the bed to the floor. He looked around the room and shook his head before getting up and getting dressed. Today was going to be a long day.

Breakfast was uneventful. His grandfather gave him a list of chores to do in the basement, everything written down on a tablet of paper. He would be working in one of the other bedrooms upstairs, gathering old clothes and boxing them up. They weren't going to see each other until lunch unless there was a problem. Andrew nodded through the conversation, placed his iPod headphones into his ears, and made his way to the basement with his list after scuttling his dishes into the sink.

If Andrew was asked how to describe the basement in one word it would be unremarkable. It was overcrowded with boxes and junk. There was a little of everything scattered about, from statues to old clothes on racks and furniture. There were stacks of newspapers at the base of the stairs, a rolled-up rug in the corner, an ice skate hanging on the wall with a shelf of paints and cleaners. He turned his music up and began moving boxes. Instead of traipsing up through the house, he used an old storm door on the other side of the room to go outside. Having the door open made it a little easier to breathe in the dusty room. It didn't take long to clear out the space at the base of the stairs. Most everything in that area was trash, which he left by the bins on the road, then he went back for more. Needing a quick drink, he went through the house and grabbed a bottle of water from the fridge. As he came down the stairs he noticed a small door. It was set into the wall, rounded on the top and so small that a child would have to crawl into it. In his rush to get the boxes out in hopes of free time, he hadn't noticed it before. Gooseflesh pricked his arms and the back of his neck.

Staring at the door, Andrew made his way slowly down the steps. He was sure he had seen the doorknob turn. His heart was pounding. He stepped closer but more slowly until he reached the third step from the bottom. Had he really seen what he thought he had? He pulled his headphones from his ears and knelt in front of the door, watching it with his breath caught in his throat. The knob turned again. He didn't stay to confirm anything. He raced up the stairs and ran to his grandfather."Grandpa! Grandpa!" he called out as he ran through the house, up the stairs, and to a spare bedroom. "There's a door in the basement. The handle! It turned. I saw it turn! Twice!"

"Calm down, boy." He shook his head. "There is nothing to that door. There is no way that knob turned. It's been stuck tight for years, never got to use it." His grandfather just kept piling things into donation bins. When Andrew didn't move, he placed his hands on the sides and finally faced him. "It's just an old crawl space, been here since we got the place. Now get on down there and finish up. We'll have lunch in an hour and then we'll go to Blakewood to visit your grandma. She'll be mighty happy to see you, Andy. Now go on, get."

Andrew knew what he had seen. He slowly made his way back down to the basement and crept down the stairs very slowly. He stood on the third to last step once more and watched the door. Nothing happened. He took another step and still nothing happened. He shrugged, thinking perhaps he had been seeing things, and walked down the rest of the stairs. He grabbed the old skates and made his way over to a box of junk and rifled through it. Seeing that there was nothing to save, he took the box to the curb and stood there a moment. Had he really seen the doorknob turn or had it all been in his mind? He couldn't tell, but the uneasy feeling was staying with him.

Andrew placed his headphones back onto his ears, keeping the music low, and went back to the basement. He grabbed a bunch of the clothes from the rack and started to shove them into bags for Goodwill. Every so often he looked back to the door and looked at the knob. He turned his back on it and went back to working. He found a box of old journals and albums that caught his attention on a shelf. Some of the photos were of his great grandparents, various aunts, and uncles, some he met, some he hadn't. They were mostly covered in dust and some of the photos had slid from their spaces. "Well, these we can't throw away," he muttered. He was busy flipping through an old book, trying to figure out what it said after seeing an old family tree in the front with dates and years when his grandfather came to get him.

Andrew jumped at the touch of his grandfather. "Whoa, holy shit!" He scooted, spun around, and scrambled away. He gripped his chest as he looked up to his chuckling grandfather.

"You look as though you've seen a ghost. C'mon now, let's have lunch and go visit your grandma. We can drop off the clothes you have there and the boxes I put in the truck on the way." He turned and left, not even glancing at the door. He was still laughing as he went upstairs. "Oh man, if you could have seen your face, kiddo."

Once he was alone again, Andrew stood up and grabbed the bags of clothes, two at a time, and made his way to the truck. "Crazy old man half scared me to death," he muttered as he went into the basement and closed the outer door behind him. He half chuckled until he came to the little door. He stopped and knelt, listening to see if he could hear anything. Again, nothing happened. He started up the stairs. As his foot hit the third step, he turned to look over his shoulder. The door handle was turning, and he heard a definitive click and moan. This time, the door had opened slightly. Without hesitation, he ran upstairs crying out for his grandfather again.

"Grandpa! It opened. The little door! It just opened all on its own. I saw it!" He was standing in the kitchen, pale and trembling.

His grandfather turned around from making the sandwiches and shook his head."Again? You're screaming about that danged door again? I told you it's been stuck since we moved in." He set the plates down on the table and moved to the basement steps, dragging Andrew along with him. "C'mon Andy, we'll look. I swear, you're starting to sound as crazy as your grandma did." He grumbled something about the door under his breath and pointed to it as they reached the landing at the base of the stairs. "See it's shut." He rolled his eyes when Andrew shook his head, then paused and moved closer. "Well, I'll be, you're right. It's open a bit. You must have jarred it somehow while you were cleaning."

"No, Grandpa, it opened on its own. I was just standing here, right here where I'm at now, and it opened. I didn't touch it. I swear, Grandpa." Andy was almost in tears. Why wouldn't his grandfather believe him? He had never lied to him before. What would make him think he was lying now?

"Ok, Andy, if you say so." He threw his hands up "Let's just go on upstairs and eat lunch. We can take a better look inside after we get back from visiting your grandma and dropping off those donations. There's still a lot to be done around here." He moved past Andrew, shaking his head. "First, she goes on about that danged door, now the kid. It must be on her side of the family." He chuckled and looked over his shoulder. "You coming up, or are you going to guard that door the entire time, Andy?"

"Yes, Grandpa, I'm coming." Andrew raced back up the stairs and ate his lunch in silence. He heard what his grandfather had said. He was going to ask his grandmother when he saw her. Maybe she could tell him about the door. Surely, she would believe him.

They dropped off the donations and collected receipts as proof. Andrew's grandfather was always a stickler for paperwork. When they pulled up to Blakewood Assisted Living Center Andrew watched him. He knew it was hard for him to visit his grandmother here. He didn't know what had happened exactly, but she belonged at home.

"Grandpa? Can I visit with Grandma alone for a little while?" Andrew asked as politely as he could. "After you do, that is." He hadn't seen her since she was admitted. It didn't feel right to talk with her in front of others. Plus, he knew his grandfather would just laugh at him some more if he decided to talk about the door.

"Sure, Andy. I'll just wait out here when it's your turn." His grandfather slid out of the truck and led the way to the doors. When they entered, he nodded to the receptionist and smiled politely as he signed them in. Andrew followed him all the way down the corridor to his grandmother's room.

She was sitting by the window, staring out to the courtyard when his grandfather went in. Andrew smiled and then moved to sit outside the room to wait his turn. He didn't want to infringe on their privacy. It wasn't long before his grandfather came and stood at the door, exasperated. "I told you, Edwina, the house is getting cleaned out so that you might be able to come home. That means the basement too. There's nothing down there but junk, and that's it. Nothing else."

Andrew stood up when his grandfather walked by. He looked at Andrew with a roll of his eyes and nodded. "She's all yours, kiddo. I'll be in the truck." He slapped his hand on the reception counter lightly and let them know Andrew would be in there a bit longer.

Before going in, Andrew waited to make sure his grandfather left the building. He nodded to the nurse walking by. Wanting to avoid startling his grandma, he gently tapped on the doorframe and walked in. Everything was so sterile and minimalistic, not something he ever pictured for her. She was always a cozy and comfortable person. Always inviting, even if she was eccentric at times.

"Hey, Grandma."

"You have grown up so much." She embraced him in a tight hug. He welcomed the squeeze to his hands as he stepped back from the hug.

"Not that much." There was a pause as he sat across from her. "How have you been?"

"I'm doing okay. I'm safe here." She smiled when she patted the back of his hand in hers. "What have you been up to? Any girls back home?"

"Eh, you know how it is. A little of this, a little of that. I have a girl I like if that counts, but she doesn't know I'm alive."

"You'll be beating them off with a stick when you get back. You'll see." She looked forlorn. "Are you having fun here? Enjoying your time with your grandpa?"

"Well, I miss your cookies, I miss your fresh breakfasts, and I would love to hear you sing while doing laundry. He pranked me though, got me good while I was cleaning the basement. Came up behind me while I was going through an old book I found. It was the first time I've seen him laugh since getting here yesterday afternoon."

"He said he had you down there to clean. Lots of memories down there in those boxes. You be careful though. Be careful in that basement."

"Actually, Grandma, that's something I wanted to ask about. Did you know there's a door down there? I uncovered it when I was coming back from clearing out the boxes of recycling and trash. I saw the handle turn and later the door opened." Andrew frowned when she withdrew her hands from his.

"You stay away from that door. Do you hear me? It's dangerous. They'll get you if you mess with it like they almost got me."

"They?"

"The Red Caps. They're nasty little creatures. They don't like our kind. They don't like us at all. There's a way to get rid of them, though I just can't remember how. All these danged pills they have me on. They think I'm crazy here. They think it was delusions, that I have dementia and it's causing me to see things that aren't there, but I don't. I didn't. It's those nasty little creatures."

Andrew listened, wide-eyed, to his grandmother. Red Caps? What were Red Caps? He shook his head. He knew she was telling the truth. He could see it. Why wouldn't anyone believe her about what she saw? "Grandma? I believe you, but I haven't seen any little creatures. Can't I just close the door?"

"It's in my diary, Andy. I don't have it here though. I left it at home. It's in my nightstand in my sewing room, with all my others. Just be careful of the Red Caps. Don't let them get you, Andy. Don't let them get your grandpa."

"Grandma, I don't understand."

"Listen to me, Andy. You need to find the journal. You must stop them before it's too late."

As she was talking, the nurse came in and ushered Andrew out of the room. "You really shouldn't be getting her so excited, young man. She needs her rest. You can come back tomorrow and mind your manners."

Andrew turned to wave at his grandmother then dashed down the corridor and out the doors to the truck. "Grandpa!" He smacked into the side and leaned into the window. "Are we going home now? Like, straight home? Grandma asked me to bring her some of her journals and some sewing things tomorrow. Can I do that?"

"I don't know right now, Andy. I have things to do. We have things to get done."

"I can't walk it up here. That's not a problem. It's not that far, really. I can spend some more time with her, maybe draw something to cheer her up." He clambered into the seat and buckled up. "Plus, it doesn't feel right without her at the house, and her room is so blah."

"Ok, Andy, you can do that, but let's get home so we can get more work done. That basement isn't going to clean itself. I want your grandma to be able to come home as much as you do." With that, they pulled out of the parking lot and headed back to the house. "Let's just take it one step at a time."

When they pulled into the drive, his grandfather sent him inside while he checked the driplines and the mail. Andrew skipped steps when he heard the phone ring from inside. Leaving the door open, he barely made it to the phone table in the hall. "Hello?"

"Hello, yes, this is Nurse Walters from the Blakewood Assisted Living Center. Is Mr. Fuller available?" The voice sounded familiar, and Andrew realized it must be the nurse from earlier."He's outside. This is his grandson, Andy." He waited for her to speak, fearing that something had happened. "Can I take a message?"

"Could you please inform him that Edwina has left the nursing home again? It's very important. If she shows up there, please call us as soon as you see her, for her safety."

"Yeah, yeah, I'll let you know if she shows up here." He didn't wait for a response before he hung up. He raced upstairs to find his grandmother's diary. He then sat in the basement by the outer door and read it. There were pages and pages of drawings of little creatures with their skulls colored red. It looked like the ramblings of a madman to him, but he had to trust her. He read until he got to the part about stopping them. "'Red Caps are homicidal fairies that soak their caps in blood to stay alive. To stop the Red Caps, a sacrifice must be made to them regularly or their caps must be dried completely.'"

Andrew looked back at the door and shuddered. A sacrifice was out of the question. He shoved the diary into his pocket and walked over to the open door. He thought of getting his grandfather. Maybe he would help if he could see one of the Red Caps, then he would have to believe. Don't let them get you. His grandmother's words throbbed in his ears. He had no choice.

He grabbed the flashlight and pushed open the little door. It was so dark, and it smelled of something rotting. He shined the light in. There was a narrow corridor with three hollows. He crawled a little closer and stuck his face in. His racing heart felt like it would come out of his chest. Nothing was behind the door. He moved back and turned to look up the stairs, resting his hand on the door. Sharp pain ran through his arm, and he jerked it away and jumped back. He screamed out as a toddler-sized, hunchbacked creature with a long nose and red cap on his head came out. His little claws slashed at Andrew.

"Grandpa! Grandpa, help me!" He climbed up the stairs, not daring to take his eyes off the creature that had just clawed open his arms. "Grandpa!"

Andrew's grandfather came rushing down the stairs just in time to see the creature, and two more coming out of the doorway. "What in the world?" He grabbed a broom and swatted at them, keeping them away from Andrew as he launched himself up the stairs.

"Grandpa, Grandma was telling the truth. They're Red Caps. They came from the door! We must stop them! They'll kill us if we don't!"

The little creatures chanted repeatedly. "Blood is life. Blood is night. Blood is for you and blood is for I." They crawled up the steps only to be pushed down again.

"Alright Mr. Wizard, go upstairs and get my gun. It's under the bed. Hurry!"

"No, that won't work. Grandma's diary says we must either sacrifice something to them or we must dry their caps completely."

"So, are you volunteering to be sacrificed to get out of cleaning this basement?"

"Thanks a lot, Grandpa."

Andrew's grandfather continued to swat the creatures from the stairs, but the three kept coming up again, and he looked like he was getting tired. Andrew tried to think of something, but how could he dry the caps? There was nothing down here to do that and he wasn't going to let them kill his grandfather. He turned to go upstairs and bumped straight into his grandmother.

She was standing there in the doorway with her hairdryer attached to an extension cord.

"Grandma? What are you doing here?"

"Edwina, you're supposed to be in that nursing home, how in tarnation did you get out of there?" Andrew's grandfather kept swatting at the Red Caps until he slipped and slid down a bit. Readjusting, he began to push at them to keep them off him.

"Oh heck, never mind that. I tried to warn you. I told you they were here. I even blocked the door so they couldn't get out. You just couldn't listen to me, could you? Then Andy tells you about the door, and don't you tell me he didn't. But you just go on and ignore him too. Now both of you get out of my way. I got this." With that, Andrew's grandmother pushed past with her hair dryer on high speed and high heat and aimed at the creatures. They backed into the corner by the door but because of the heat from the dryer they couldn't get to their escape route.

The basement filled with shrill shrieks and cackles as the creatures cowered in the corner. The smell of drying blood and rot filled the air, making them all queasy. Andrew plugged his ears to try and make the sounds stop, moving closer to his grandmother to close the little door in case more should come out. Finally, after what seemed like forever, the creatures collapsed, their caps a crusty brown, flaking with who knew whose blood dried on them. The three of them stood at the base of the stairs as Andrew's grandmother kept using the hair dryer on the creatures. They exchanged glances and shook their heads.

"The next time someone tells you a door opens by itself you think you'll listen to them, Robert?" Andrew's grandmother shook her head and turned off the dryer. She put her arm around Andrew and smiled. "They're gone, at least for now."

"Grandma, what do you mean 'for now'?"

"If any blood gets on their caps, they'll be back. We need to get rid of their bodies somewhere that can't happen. Even a drop can bring them back."

"When did you get so knowledgeable on them, Edwina?" Andrew's grandfather asked, running his hand through his thinning hair as he nudged the creatures with his toe.

"I read about them in the library when I saw one down here last year. My grandmother had told me stories about them from when she was a child. She used to tell me all about fairies. I remembered what she said, and I looked them up at the library to find out what to do."

Andrew looked around and shrugged. "I'm bleeding still so I can't help."

"It's ok, Andy, you go wash up. We'll do this." His grandfather shook his head and began dragging the creatures outside to the back yard. Moments later, he returned for the shovel.

Andrew went outside, holding a towel over his arm, and watched as they buried the Red Caps in deep graves. His grandmother placed rocks over them before covering them with the dirt. He couldn't shake the feeling that they would be back, but he hoped that it wouldn't be anytime soon.

When the creatures were buried securely, they went back inside. His grandfather placed a hasp on the door and locked it tight with a padlock so that nothing would ever be able to open it, at least not from the inside. Andrew slowly went upstairs with his grandmother, and they cleaned up his arm. They didn't talk much while she did it, just smiled easily at one another."Grandma? Do you think you'll come back now?"

"I think I just might, Andy, I think I just might."

Andrew smiled and walked out of the bathroom, leaving the diary on the counter. He went to his room and lay on the bed. Everything came crashing upon him and he just cried for a while. He had come so close to losing his grandfather, on his first real day of summer vacation. It was something too that he would never be able to tell anyone about, but somehow, he had to chronicle everything and leave it somewhere so that someone would know what had happened and what to do should anything like this happen again.

"Andy?" His grandfather called into the room. "I'm going to take your grandma back to the nursing home to get her things and get her discharged. We'll be home in a bit. There are leftovers in the fridge."

"Ok, Grandpa." Andrew wiped his eyes and moved to the window to look at where the creatures were buried for a few moments. When he was sure nothing was happening, he went to the bathroom, grabbed his grandmother's diary and wrote what had happened that day. He then went downstairs and placed the diary behind a loose brick by the little door. Hopefully, should the creatures ever return one day, someone would find the diary and be saved.

Since she was a child, SADIE MENDENHALL has had a passion for writing and remembers telling teachers and family members that she wanted to be a writer. She has won awards, certificates, and scholarships for her essays, short stories, and poetry since sixth grade. Sadie became more inspired and determined to see her dreams come to fruition while serving in the United States Air Force and began participating in workshops and pursuing degrees in Creative Writing. Drawing inspiration from her own life and everything she feels affected by. Her writing has been published in both online and in-print journals as well as the anthologies *Tales from the Frozen North*, *Welcome to Effham Falls*, and *Tales from the Water's Edge*. Sadie's goal is to complete her poetry collection and her book and to never stop writing.

VENGEFUL SOULS

Scott Dyson

I WASN'T REALLY UP for the gig our manager had booked for us, but at least the pay was good. We'd been 'touring' the Midwest for seven months but hadn't played a date farther north than Minneapolis yet. It was a new town, a new area for us, and a whole new set of experiences.

At least that's what we told each other when we were trying to convince ourselves to make the drive to the Arrowhead region of northeastern Minnesota, to some little town we'd never heard of called Effham Falls. We never asked ourselves how it was that they'd heard of us. After all, we weren't exactly famous. We played classic metal covers and a smattering of our original tunes at our gigs. We sold our CDs and plugged our songs on music streaming services. We sold some merch, met some new people, and banged some hot (and sometimes not so hot) chicks while drinking and getting high on whatever illegal substances we could find. We made a living.

Barely. But we did.

We were in Eau Claire, Wisconsin, when our manager called to tell us of the gig in Effham Falls. Last night of an appearance at a local club. Our style didn't play great in the middle of nowhere, so my first inclination was to decline the booking in another out-of-the-way small town in the middle of nowhere.

Then he told us the pay. On speakerphone. It was significantly larger than what this place was giving us. And it wasn't that far. Only what? About a four-hour drive? We'd done worse.

We could play for a few new people, sell a few CDs and tee shirts, maybe meet some Nordic goddesses. That's what the guys said as we discussed it with our manager.

I shut up. Something felt wrong.

I guess I should introduce myself. I'm Penn Patterson, drummer for Vengeful Souls. Dumb name, I know, but we had three CDs out under that name, and we were supposed to make a fourth after this 'tour.' Jerry (that's our manager) told us that they'd fifty/fifty the sessions, meaning they'd pay half for the studio time and we'd pay the other half. We'd been writing and breaking in some new material on this tour, and it seemed to get a positive reception so far.

Jig Masters was our lead guitarist. I don't know how he got the nickname "Jig" out of his real name, which was Nathan, but that's what everyone called him. He was talking about getting his name legally changed, but I was always like, why? Who cares? Everyone already calls you Jig. That would usually shut him up.

Jig was truly a master when it came to the guitar. He could copy just about anyone, and he swore he'd never heard a lead that he couldn't do himself. If one of us was a potential star, it was probably Jig.

Dubya Perks was our lead singer (his real first name starts with a 'W'— Walter). He had a good voice, but he wasn't no Dio. Personally, I didn't think he was the guy who was gonna get us to the big time. But what do I know?

Our bass player's name was Curt Farris. He was just a normal dude, one firm hand on the underlying rhythm and the other on his beer, and he was a big guy, in more ways than one. A chick once told me that she'd never hook up with him again because of his size. You mean, because he's like six foot six? I asked. Nope, she said. Then she winked.

The last passenger in the van was our sole crewman, Jeff Rauch, who hardly ever talked, but he was a truly diligent worker. He did half the loading and unloading by himself, arranged our gear, ran the cables, made sure everything was working, and then ran our sound during our performances. Jeff never hung with us too much. Our manager paid for him to get his own room, and I suppose he deserved it.

Besides, none of us particularly wanted to hang with Jeff anyway. He was a nerdy looking guy and didn't really fit with our metal aesthetic. Jig and Dubya always said he cramped their style, which was hogwash, and I didn't care much either way. I could take him or leave him – except before and after our gigs. He was damn near indispensable then.

So there we all were, in our van, riding along some little highway in the middle of nowhere. It was late afternoon, and according to the Google, we still had about three hours to go before we pulled into Effham Falls.

Once again, something told me we should just turn around.

As we approached the town, we started to see signs of human existence. A house here. A gas station there. The buildings became denser and more frequent; lighted intersections popped up in the middle of the forested nowhere. It was approaching night when we passed the sign for Effham Falls. 'A Nice Little Town,' I think the sign said, but we passed quickly and no one else seemed to notice.

I checked the email our manager sent us and tapped the name of the motel where we were booked into the Maps app, then waited for directions. "Google says to go a half mile and turn left." We were on Main Street and were going to turn on Landers Avenue. A few more zigs and zags and we'd arrive at our lodgings for the duration of our stay.

I didn't much care how bedbug-infested the mattresses were at that point. I just wanted to collapse as soon as we got into our rooms. It had been a long week. And a long drive.

Dubya followed my instructions as he piloted us through the unfamiliar streets. The town was dead at that hour, just before dusk. Idly, I wondered if anyone worked in that godforsaken corner of the world. It was past five and I don't know, I guess I expected that people in these types of towns should be coming home from their farm jobs or whatever.

I googled Eau Claire, Wisconsin on my phone. Service was better now that we were in the heart of Effham Falls, so I saw it right away. Top story. "Girl Found Murdered in Home."

Shit like that seemed to follow us around. I made a habit of checking on places we'd just played specifically to see if the bad karma kept following us.

I clicked off the story; I didn't want the other guys to see it because I wondered about them sometimes. I had periods of time where I didn't know where one or the other one of them was, especially after a weekend gig. I suspected they were doing just what I was doing—hooking up with some wannabe groupie type and, well, ya know.

As I climbed out of the van, I felt that sense of dread again. Of wrongness. I looked behind me, feeling like someone was watching me. But no one was there.

Jig called over to me, "Hey, Penn, what about the stuff?" I understood that 'stuff' meant our musical equipment. Jig was insanely protective of his guitars.

"It's cool out. They should be fine in the van, right?"

Jig shrugged, opened the rear doors, and removed two guitar cases. I knew they held his prized Flying V and his favorite Strat. "I'm takin' my babies in," he said. "No sense in takin' a chance someone steals 'em." I just nodded.

"Hey, Jig."

He turned toward me, continuing to slide the hard case of his Strat out from under some bags of cables.

"They found another one."

"Another what?"

"Another girl."

"Where?"

"Eau Claire. Right after we left."

Jig looked away. "What? You thinkin' this has something to do with us?"

I sighed. "I dunno. Seems kinda coincidental, doesn't it? What's that? Four of them now?"

"Five, 'less I counted wrong." Jig ticked his fingers but didn't say anything until he got to five. "Out of eight stops on this little tour."

"Nine stops."

"Maybe some guy following us from city to city?"

I laughed. "Hard to call our gig locations 'cities.'"

"Yeah, you know, this is getting to be a bit of a slog. Playing gigs in the ass-end of nowhere. This ain't the road to success."

I shrugged. I didn't disagree with him, but this seemed to be our lot in life. The toll we must pay for a shot at stardom.

"And Dubya ain't it either," Jig said the quiet part aloud. Again, I didn't disagree.

But I did want to get back to the subject. "I haven't noticed anyone being at multiple gigs. Have you?"

"One chick came to see us twice. I think she lived between the two bars."

"That was because she wanted to get some Dubya again."

"Yeah, but would we notice a repeat customer?"

I shrugged again, then turned away and yawned. "I'm beat. Gonna call it a night as soon as we get in our rooms."

Jeff returned from the office with our keys. I hadn't even seen him leave the van. But he was like that. Quiet. Mysterious. He handed Dubya and me our keycards, and then gave Curt and Jig theirs.

"Thanks, Jeff," I said.

He looked at me, then made that "huh" sound that some people make when they're amused by something. He nodded and moved away from us.

We located our rooms and unlocked the doors. Before I entered, I saw Jeff standing outside the motel's office, cell phone to his ear. I wondered who he had called. But when I shut the door and flopped down on one of the beds, I never thought about it again.

We slept really late the next day. The previous few days had taken a toll on us, and the opportunity to catch up on some of our lack of sleep was welcomed by all four of us. When I woke up, Dubya was already out of the shower. He tossed his long blond curls off his face with a snap of his head and looked out of the bathroom at me.

My own sleep had been restless. I seemed to have more dreams than I usually had. I couldn't recall much, just faces. An endless parade of unfamiliar female faces. As far as I could recall, none of them were happy or smiling.

None of them seemed significant to me. They seemed random, like people one might encounter in a crowd. But one seemed to stand out. I figured that it was the last face that my mind had conjured.

I didn't say anything to Dubya, or to either of the others when we climbed into the van. "You drive," Dubya said, tossing me the keys. "I drove a lot yesterday."

I nodded, went around to the driver's side and climbed in. "Where are we going?" I turned around and looked at the band. "And where's Jeff?"

"Check your phone," Dubya said. "But start the friggin' van already. Crank the heat. It's cold in this friggin' town."

"It's cold in the north," Curt said. "I spent some time up here when I was a kid."

"Really?" I hadn't known that. It made me think of how little I knew about my bandmates, aside from their musical inclinations. For example, I knew that Curt loved The Who and copied his look from their bass player. I knew that Jig was an Eddie Van Halen fan, and loved those speedsters who played leads at a million notes a minute. And I knew that Dubya loved Chris Cornell, who had sung for Soundgarden before he had died in 2017.

But I didn't know much else about them.

I started the van, then checked my phone. Jeff had texted that he'd gone to the gig location. The venue was marked by a pin in the text so our GPS would tell me where to go. 'Falls Midtown Theater' was its name.

"I thought we were playing at a club," I said to no one specifically.

"I remember a theater in some little town outside of Chicago that they turned into a music club. Maybe this is like that one," Jig said.

"Did you play there?"

"Years ago. When I was just out of high school."

I knew Jig was from the Chicago area, but like Curt, I really knew nothing else about his history. "What was the name of the band?"

"Called ourselves 'Blue Collar' and we did a lot of Styx, Kansas and Journey – that sort of music."

"With your mates from high school?" Dubya asked.

"Some of them. Some guys from Chicago. We were a five piece. Me and two guys from high school. A keyboard player and a singer from Chicago. We were good, but I hated playing that fucking music night after night."

I laughed. "I know the feeling. My first band was a cover band, too. We played Mellencamp and Seger. We sucked, but we played a lot."

No one else volunteered much. After following the GPS for a while, I pulled up in front of a marquee jutting over the sidewalk. "Guess we're here."

"One good thing. They probably have a nice stage," Jig said.

"Jeff says pull around the back," Dubya said. "There's a loading dock in the alley."

I nodded and found a way into the alley. Soon we were unloading our equipment. Once the guitars were safely out, Jig disappeared with Dubya, leaving me and Curt to unload my drums onto the platform. Jeff piled the gear onto a flatbed cart and wheeled it all off.

After the van was emptied, I made my way into the back of the theater. The place was a maze. So, of course, I promptly got lost.

Sometimes you have to go down to come back up...

"Who said that?" I demanded. I turned around, but there was no one present. Still, it felt like I'd been spoken to. And it seemed like the answer to a question I hadn't even asked yet. Go down to get up to the stage.

I used the flashlight function on my phone to see what was in front of me and, indeed, there was a concrete stairway leading...down.

"No friggin' way," I said aloud, and turned around, weaving my way back through the maze of halls and narrow passageways until I found myself back at the loading dock.

Alone.

I climbed down the short stairs and walked around the buildings until I got to the front of the theater.

Something about this didn't feel right.

I avoided the backstage area as much as I could for the rest of the afternoon, and was ready to go, primed up with a few drinks and just a touch of blow to give me some extra energy. When I moved behind the set for soundcheck, I was feeling great. Strong. Powerful. The way I always felt before, during, and after a performance.

The blow helped me maintain that feeling.

The evening flew by as we sat around in a backstage area, sipping on our drinks and bullshitting about anything that crossed our minds. I twirled my drumsticks without any conscious thought about the action. Having the sticks in my hands was as natural as taking a piss or breathing. They became almost part of me.

Jeff reappeared. "They're starting to come in. Half an hour until curtain."

That sounded funny. We usually just pushed through the bar crowds, making our way to whatever corner or tiny elevation they called a stage, but this place was the real deal. The stage was about three feet off the ground. Underneath the floor in the front of the stage was a pit where an orchestra would be placed if they were staging a musical in this venue. An unused remnant from the past history of the theater.

It felt like we were playing Carnegie Hall. It felt amazing.

I led us onto the stage when it was time. As I settled behind my kit, Jeff's voice sounded through the PA system. "In their first ever appearance at the Falls Midtown Theater, please welcome...Vengeful Souls!"

The curtains parted and Jig's opening riff cut through the club. I came in after a four count and we launched into our first song, an original penned by Dubya that was on our first CD.

The lights on the stage and the darkness in the theater made it hard to make out what kind of crowd we had. But I could see two young ladies standing there, right up in front. One stared up at Jig as he rocked out on his crazed lead.

The other stared directly at me.

And I knew her. She was the final face in my dream from the previous night.

I missed a beat. Came in late, something I never do.

The others looked back at me as I scrambled to cover up my obvious error. Dubya let out a rock and roll scream, and I did a fill before clicking out a four-count to resume the song. I stole a glance at the woman. Still there. Still staring at me.

"Hey, Penn, that chick is still here. I think she's waiting for me."

I didn't answer.

"You still sulking over missing that beat? Hey man, it happens to the best of us. Just more obvious when it happens to the drummer. Shake it off. We have two more shows here before we move on."

"Is her friend still here, too?"

"What friend?" Jig asked, giving me a perplexed look.

"The chick with her at the front of the stage."

Jig shook his head. "You must be hallucinating, dude. There was only one chick standing there."

"I know what I saw, man. She's the reason I missed that beat. I, uh..." I hated to even tell him about my reasons. "I fuckin' dreamed about her last night."

Jig nodded. "Someone musta laced your blow with something weird. There was only the one chick standing there. And she's mine."

I didn't want to argue with him. I also didn't want to see the woman who'd been staring at me. Ever again.

"Least we don't have to tear down," I said. Jig just nodded and moved away out into the club, I assumed, to find the woman he'd be trying to bed tonight.

I sat alone backstage. There was another line of blow in a little foil in my pocket, but I didn't feel like doing it. I sipped my beer and mulled over that girl. Who was she?

"Fuck it," I said, rising from my chair and making to follow Jig.

Psst!

The noise came from the dark section of the stage right area.

"Somebody back there?"

Come find me!

"Who's there?" It felt like a repeat of earlier. Someone was fucking with me. Nevertheless, I made my way toward the source of the voice.

It was her. The woman from the front of the stage. "I knew you were real!" I exclaimed. "How could Jig have missed you?"

The woman was beautiful. She wore short cutoff Daisy Dukes and a shirt tied off, exposing a pale midriff. Her hair was blond, long and straight. And her face — it was a face to launch a thousand ships. She turned and moved deeper into the darkness.

I followed. Damn right I did.

"Wait for me!" I said. I could see a subtle glow in front of me, and I got glimpses of her off and on, until I found myself standing in front of a stairwell.

The same stairwell I'd been standing in front of earlier.

There's a place down here! Her voice floated up the stairs.

I went down. "Place for what?"

For what you enjoy most about girls like me!

I knew what that was. I grinned like an idiot, rubbed my hands together, and descended the stairs, again using my phone as my light source.

There she was. About five feet in front of me.

She smiled and motioned with her finger for me to follow her. The hall turned one way, then the other, and I found myself once again at the top of another concrete stairwell. She stood halfway down, still smiling.

"What's your name?" I asked.

Heather.

I could have sworn that her lips didn't move. "Are you from here?"

She nodded. Then she disappeared farther down the stairs and into the passageway.

"Heather? I don't want to go any farther." That bad feeling was overcoming me again.

She reappeared at the bottom of the stairwell and grinned. Her right hand reached for the knotted shirt above her bare stomach and tugged until it came loose. My eyes widened, then she disappeared again.

I ran down the stairs as fast as I could and chased after her through a long corridor, eventually reaching another bend. As I turned, I noticed the smell for the first time. It smelled like I was in a sewer.

Or worse.

My libido subsided along with my erection, and I looked behind me. It wasn't a hallway at all. It was a tunnel. And I'd come to a junction.

As I turned around, my phone's flashlight went out. Shit! I knew I'd never find my way without some light. I sighed and moved forward.

The light came back on.

"Great! Not dead yet!" I turned and hurried back into the tunnel.

The light went out.

Penn...find me!

The light came back on. If I hadn't been scared before, I was then.

I moved forward, following the passageway until I saw the glow in front of me. Shutting off my phone's light to save battery, I hurried toward the source of the illumination.

And came out in a basement.

Heather stood, blouse hanging open and Daisy Dukes unbuttoned. *Do you remember me now?*

I did.

God forgive me, I recognized her. A heavy wooden door opened, and five more women entered the room.

Hello, Penn! They all spoke at the same time. All those voices talking at the same time, different pitches, an out-of-tune chord that sounded really strange.

Welcome to the Well, Heather said. *Join us, won't you?*

Did I have a choice? No. No, I did not have a choice. No more choice than I'd given these five girls, and countless others. I hung my head. I remember now...

I looked back at Heather, pleading. "I didn't know..." I whined.

It doesn't matter. Heather was blue now, and I could see the finger marks on her neck. They were all blue. They all had the same finger marks. My finger marks.

They converged on me, and I was dragged through the door marked 'Effham Falls Mine #1.' There were others here. I could feel their presence as these five of my victims tore at my soul. And I knew they would shred it until I was no more.

I shed a single tear for myself before I could no longer shed tears.

"It had to be done," Curt said to Jeff. Jig and Dubya lounged on the floor, Jig smoking a cigarette against the theater's rules, and Dubya sucking brew from a long neck bottle.

"Yes. But how did you know it would work?"

"Because I grew up very close to here. I heard the stories. I knew of Agnes Bagman and heard about the tunnels and the mines."

"I followed him through the tunnels," Jeff said. "I thought for a minute there, he was going to turn back. But then his light went out. I guess they kept him moving toward the end."

"What did you see?" Dubya asked.

"Nothing much. He was talking, but there wasn't anyone in the room. Then the door opened..."

"By itself?"

Jeff shrugged. "Looked like it. And he went through it. Looked like he was being dragged."

"And you were watching?"

"I stayed until it closed."

Curt held up an enormous hand to silence Jeff. "We had to stop him. We all knew what Penn was doing, but we also knew that it wasn't our Penn."

"Did he do it last night?" Jig asked.

"Yes," Jeff answered. "I had someone watch him. Called the guy right after you all went into your rooms. But he was too late to stop Penn."

"Who was she?"

"A young woman from Effham Falls named Heather Priestly. He met her at an all-night gas station just down the street"

"Will there be any blowback on us?" Jig asked.

Curt answered. "Shouldn't be. Of course, we have two more gigs here, and we don't have a drummer."

"I isolated the drum track from last night's gig. You can play to it. We'll just stick some kid back behind the kit. Meanwhile, management already has a replacement who will meet us at your next stop." Jeff had their bases covered.

"Where to next?"

"The studio."

Curt smiled and nodded, and Jig and Dubya bumped fists.

Jig rose. "I got a date," he said, and hurried out.

Jeff stood up. "I have some plans of my own." He rubbed his hands together. "Cute little thing who likes sound guys." He laughed and walked away.

Curt watched. Something Jeff said...

"I stayed until it closed." 'It.' The door. Could a soul have escaped? Could it have 'hopped a ride' with Jeff?

Curt shook his head. "I'm never coming to this town again after this," he said, forgetting that Dubya was still in the room.

"Why not?"

"Too dangerous."

"This town?"

"You just don't know," Curt said.

No one does...

By day, SCOTT DYSON works as a healthcare professional. He is a husband and a father to two young men. In his spare time, he writes and self-publishes his tales of horror, mystery and science fiction/fantasy. He has been writing since grade school, but it wasn't until the mid-1990's, when he was helping to host a book and writing forum on Delphi Internet Services called "The Book and Candle Pub," that he got more serious about creating works of fiction.

Besides writing, his passions in life are his family, making music, reading and watching movies, and following Chicago sports, especially the Cubs and the Bulls. He plays keyboards and enough guitar and drums to get by. He is a big fan of Disney films and theme parks as well!

MIDNIGHT CAFÉ

Tristan Belmont

I LOVE MY JOB as much as I love the setting sun casting its golden glow over the horizon. I own a small cafe in the even smaller town of Effam Falls, having moved here from somewhere some would consider far away, and others would consider right next door. It was a matter of perspective. But I digress. My job is truly glorious.

The smell of coffee, the grinding of espresso beans, milk steaming in a sound almost like paper being gently pulled apart, and watching all these intricate moving pieces moving in a certain order to create one simple beverage that help people get through their hard days. Speaking of the people, that's arguably the best part. You get all kinds of folks working at a place like this: blue-collar workers heading off to their shifts, rich businessmen on a call with a client, high schoolers typing on their laptops to get their papers in on time, and parents getting their caffeine kicks as they get their kids a treat for being good, or to simply make them quiet for a few minutes. No matter who they were, they were always fascinating.

"Lovely, isn't it?"

"Sorry?" A barista friend of mine named Jenna asked.

"Oh, sorry, Jenna. Just thinking out loud." I smiled, wiping down the counter.

Jenna immediately went back to rapidly making a drink without a second thought, causing her to accidentally pull the steam wand too far down on the milk, splashing it out of the cup slightly before she got it under control.

Jenna was nervous, terribly so from the look of it. I knew why all too well but decided to ask regardless. "Something troubling you, Jenna?"

She turned off the steam wand, sighing almost longer than the sound of the steam decompressing. "It's that test I have coming up, the college entrance one."

Jenna had taken two years off from school since graduating high school to save money before diving in. However, the college where she was applying had her take an entrance exam because her SAT score was not the best when she graduated. Technically, it was too low to be accepted but since she'd had such good grades, they decided to give her an entrance exam to determine if she would be accepted.

"Oh I wouldn't worry so much, Jenna," I said, wiping up the few tiny puddles of milk. "You're smart, I'm sure you'll pass easily."

"Thank you." She set the latte on the counter. "Large Latte for a Jane."

A woman soon came out, thanking Jenna before exiting the cafe.

"I'm just worried I will forget things I've learned from studying at the last minute. I was never good at taking tests. I got so flustered during my SATs that my score was terrible even though I was more than prepared."

I looked at the clock then back to Jenna. Her mind was only half present and her hand occasionally twitched.

"Why don't you go home for the night, Jenna?"

This snapped her out of her trance. "No, it's okay I'm fine." She said, getting more nervous for a moment.

"It's quite alright, Jenna. I'm not doing this because your work is bad or you're in trouble. You just look like you could use some needed rest is all."

Jenna said nothing for a moment. "Are you sure you won't get too busy?"

I smiled at that remark. She was always full of kindness. Even when her mind was tearing itself apart with paranoia, she was still worrying about me being too busy without her help.

"Not at all. There was only an hour left of your shift anyway and it's a slower night. I'll be just fine."

Jenna nodded, which was soon followed by a relieved smile. "Thank you, Jacob. I can make it up on another shift."

"Don't even worry about it. Just go home and rest now."

Jenna gave a parting wave after packing her things and leaving the cafe. She had a lost look on her face, full of uncertainty and fear. Fear of disappointing herself and her parents, fear of not getting in after advocating so hard for her plan to take a break from school to save money. The turmoil of the human mind was often mightier than any storm in my experience, one of humanity's greatest blessings and yet also one of its most horrid curses.

There was only one customer in the cafe who had already gotten their drink. Seeing as no other tasks needed to be done, I took the opportunity to partake in a little hobby of mine: weaving. Much like coffee, weaving is about taking a singular variable, in this case thread, and turning it into something more. Espresso is fine on its own, yet add milk and maybe a flavoring, and you get a latte. A single thread on its own has its uses, but weave it in a certain pattern, combining other threads with multiple colors, and you get a necklace, a tapestry, and unlimited possibilities— much like coffee, much like people.

The last customer packed up their things and left just as I was finishing a necklace made up of a black cloth band with a design in the light blue of the *Tiwaz* rune.

"Have a good night," the customer said as he was leaving the cafe.

I looked at the clock. ten pm.

"Suppose I should get ready for the night crowd. Something tells me they're gonna be riled up tonight."

11:50 pm. Incense sticks burned gently, their dim lights like distant stars in the night sky. The lights had been dimmed for it tended to be darker on the other side and I didn't want to startle any wayward soul. I enjoyed the peaceful chats as opposed to the incoherent rants that frustrated souls tended to spiral into. Much like with the living, a welcoming atmosphere tended to aid in striking up an interesting conversation.

11:55 pm. I grabbed the ground cinnamon and ginger we kept for people to add to their drink and sprinkled it at the entrances to the cafe. Baneful spirits and wights tended to despise such substances, which allowed it to work wonders at keeping myself, my establishment, and, most importantly, the peaceful spirits themselves safe. The final touch: a small pendant of Mjolnir placed gently on the table. No less than a second after I'd placed the small piece of hand-forged steel on the counter, the front door of my cafe opened.

"Ah. Welcome in. You're much earlier than usual."

It had just reached midnight, and while that was technically when I opened my doors to them, they usually arrived about five minutes or so later.

"Am I? Time works strangely between *Midgard* and *Hel*."

The man's voice was low and raspy, like sandpaper grinding against a rock. His soul was an old one, a tired one.

"It is no trouble, Sigurd. I had just finished my preparations. Please have a seat and let me get you something."

Sigurd gave a puzzled look when I said his name, just like all the others had, yet he approached one of the chairs and took a seat.

Sigurd adjusted himself in the comfortable seat. I could tell by his clothing he wasn't from this time or place, which explained his soul age. His skin was as pale as freshly set snow, and his hair and beard were long and blonde, but unlike the rest of the man, looked well-kept and healthy. His eyes had deep, dark black circles. He hadn't rested, not in a long time.

"Comfortable?" I asked.

Sigurd took in his surroundings for a moment. "I feel..." He paused as if he hadn't said the words in a long time. "Warm."

I smiled and handed him a hot chocolate and a scone with honey drizzled on the top. "Good. Here, let these warm you further, friend."

Sigurd stared at the white ceramic cup with a slight moniker of confusion before taking a sip. His eyes lit up with a sparkly joy that had not graced the man's eyes in quite some time. "Thank you, my friend."

"It's no trouble, Sigurd. Now tell me, what brings you to my establishment on this wondrous evening?"

The glimmer in Sigurd's eyes faded like snow being gently carried away by the wind, being whisked off to be later seen by another. I hoped his joy could be blown into the eyes of someone else who needed it, as so many seemed to nowadays. Perhaps a bit of that glimmer would make its way to Jenna. The thought of it made me smile.

"I'm trapped," Sigurd said, defeated and downtrodden. "It's cold there. Not torturously so, but enough to where no matter the thickness of my coat, or the height of a roaring flame, it cannot quite warm me. It's like small daggers constantly poking into my skin."

I nodded in understanding, knowing the place all too well. It was often confused for another, far more fowl realm whose name I wish to not utter here. But given the description of the realm and the fact that Sigurd could pass my protective precautions, I knew he wasn't from that place of cold-hearted Jotun.

"I understand all too well, Sigurd. Your soul, beautiful as it may be and as all human souls are in their ways, save for a few unsavory ones, is caught in turmoil."

Sigurd's thin lips tightened against his teeth in a twisted frustration that had had time to fester for over a thousand years. "I'm dead. I know that I am dead and have come to peace with that fact," he said in a tone that was a cocktail of anger and sorrow. This made a flavor profile that exposed a man who was in a type of pain that human language would have trouble describing. It was a pain I had felt when I was young, and I saw the hairs of creation form into the very first trees.

"I died bravely in a battle of great struggle. Even when my punctured lungs drew in a final breath, I still clutched my sword and shield with the same strength as a berserker. What turmoil is there to be inside of me or with God's judgment?"

"The turmoil does not lie with the gods," I said blatantly as I stood. Then I walked back to the bar to make myself three shots of espresso. It was going to be a very long night. "It does not lie with the Valkyries, it does not lie with your Jarl who sent you to fight, and it does lie with any supposed lack of courage."

The beans made a satisfying crackle as they were ground, like a roaring bonfire that snapped logs of wood every second it raged. They then transformed into a gentle flow of liquid, like a small creak bringing water to a soil that would soon bloom into a self-sustaining ecosystem. I turned off the machine and threw the puck of ground coffee into the garbage at my feet.

"It lies within yourself, Sigurd." I took a sip from my espresso.

Sigurd gave me a baffled look. "What possible turmoil could lie within me?" he asked through a half-frustrated, half-amused chuckle.

"That is what we're here to figure out." I set down the small espresso cup. The ceramic gently clicked against the wooden counter. "Souls that end up in Hel, or at least our version of it, aren't there for punishment. It's rather a sort of in-between, a place where a soul gets stuck so to speak when they're caught on something that happened in life. I believe the Christian version of such a place is called Purgatory, if that helps describe it."

I didn't know if the conflict within him was one of faith, so I described the comparison in case that was the issue. However, given his bewildered look at the remark, I could tell that this wasn't the case.

"Regardless, I would appreciate it if you would tell me a little about yourself, Sigurd. I unfortunately didn't have the pleasure of knowing you when you were alive."

Sigurd pondered the statement but didn't follow his curiosity. He answered the question instead.

"As I said before, I was a Viking for my Jarl."

"Deeper than that?"

"How do you mean?"

"What did you like to do beyond that? Was there anything else that you partook in? You don't come off as a berserker, so I assume you participated in your village in other ways besides warfare. Am I correct?"

Sigurd nodded as he took a bite of his scone. "I was a farmer. It was, in part, why I joined the raids." He took another bite, his speech muffled as he chewed the sweet pastry. "To find better land for me to farm."

"A provider."

"I liked to fancy envision myself as one, yes. I loved seeing crops slowly grow after putting so much work into them, seeing how it provided for people."

His eyes seemed to shimmer a little, in wonder.

"I heard other farmers sometimes complain about the work, the dirt, the time needed to do the work, groaning on and on about how sore their legs got. But for reasons even unknown to me, it never seemed to bother me."

"You were quite skilled at the craft too from what I recall. Your village got through many hard winters because of your help."

Nothing else was said for a moment. I let Sigurd hold his memories for a moment. He deserved a happy moment. He'd spent most likely over a thousand years trapped in the realm of Hel, so turmoiled in his own inner conflict that I sincerely doubted he had hardly, if ever given himself a positive thought, especially about himself.

In the old Norse cultures, society placed a heavy emphasis on a sort of honor. Honor in battle, honor in professions, honor in leadership, the definition could vary depending on the village or profession, but largely, honor among the Vikings was Valhalla. Sigurd had died in battle, weapon in hand by all accounts. An honorable death for a warrior, and yet, he wasn't in Valhalla.

I could only imagine the sheer shock of what such a revelation would've brought to such a man. For the last thousand years, he would've sat, cold, alone, wondering what he could've possibly done wrong, throwing around millions of ways he could've dishonored himself, his village, his Jarl, and many others.

"I think the Gods have forgotten me."

My head snapped to face him in surprise at such a statement. I saw his eyes shimmer more, and tears streamed down his cheeks like the mighty fjords that flowed through his homeland. I wondered if he felt ashamed for showing such emotions the way humans often showed shame for these more vulnerable emotions. It was one of the many things about them that had always perplexed me. Their emotions, especially these vulnerable ones, were never meant to be a curse. These emotions were the very thing that tied them so closely to the Gods.

"I'm sorry," Sigurd said, quickly wiping away his tears and clearing his worn throat with a raspy cough.

"Would you fault Freya for weeping if the story of her son, Baldur, passing came to pass?"

Sigurd said nothing before slowly shaking his head.

"Then do not fault yourself, for tears are not a weakness. They are what separate you from the baneful creatures of the realms."

"What must I do? What must I do to please them?" Sigurd asked, looking at me in desperation.

"As I said, your situation has only to do with yourself. You cannot find your destination because you were looking in the wrong place."

"Why must you speak to me in such infuriating riddles?" Sigurd had a bit of anger in his tone.

"I am simply a guide. I can show you a path, but I cannot force you down it. It is up to you to take the steps."

"Perhaps this is some trick of Loki, aligning with his daughter to torment me, luring me in with these sweet foods only to give false hope."

I faced Sigurd with a small inferno in my eyes. *"Sigurd Bjornson! Do not sully the name of Loki or Hel in my presence.*

This is no cheap trick, or curse of the runes. Had I had control of your fate, you would have not needed such aid."

Sigurd's eyes widened, showing his instantaneous regret. "You are...a Norn, a fate weaver, aren't you?"

I calmed myself, realizing I had allowed my passions to get the best of me. "Yes. But I wasn't the one who weaved your fate."

"Then why are you here with me now?"

"Tyr. The mighty god of justice and many other things under the heavens works with Hel, Goddess of the Dead, to work with souls who are trapped in her realm. It is seen as a cosmic injustice when a soul is unable to fully move on."

"I understand."

"You see, the gods have not cursed you. They wish to aid you." I placed my hand on his shoulder. "Sigurd, let me ask you this so that you may become wiser. Was the time spent fighting and raiding more fulfilling to you than the time spent in your fields?"

Sigurd pondered the question for a moment before answering confidently. "No."

"Let me ask you a second question so that you may become wiser still. Did you enjoy the faces of your enemies cast with fear, hatred, and rage at your charge, or did you enjoy the faces of those you provided for, the smiles, the laughs, and the talks amongst friends by the hearth of the halls in your village?"

Sigurd straightened his posture. "The smiles. I always preferred wiping away food crumbs out of my beard than blood."

"Then it sounds to me, Sigurd Bjornson, that Valhalla isn't the realm that you would be happy in."

"No, I suppose it doesn't."

"Find yourself, Sigurd, then you will find yourself in Gimli, the highest of all the halls."

Sigurd's body seemed to get less thin, his eyes less sunken and tired. The front door of the cafe opened once again, and a small, warm light filled the room.

"I'm....awaited?"

"With open arms, friend."

"What if I get lost again?" Sigurd asked with a whisper of fear in his tone.

"Then I will be here for you again until you find your way. Should you ever need a place to warm yourself, you are always welcome here."

Sigurd gave a smile and walked confidently out the door. I looked at the clock and saw that it read 12:02 am. "A long night indeed."

A few days passed, and I was sitting behind the coffee bar, finishing the weaving project I had started the day Sigurd walked into my cafe. I put in the final touches and admired the work. "Nothing more than what is deserved," I said proudly as Jenna burst through the door.

"I PASSED!" She screamed out in joyous hysteria "I PASSED MY ENTRANCE TEST!"

I smiled warmly. "I told you you'd do well!" I patted her on the back.

"I'm not sure what happened. I was so nervous but as soon as I started everything just seemed to click together. Throughout the test, I couldn't stop thinking about the reassurance you gave me, and I just felt so confident in myself."

I looked at my weaving project and then back to Jenna. "Perhaps all you needed was a guide in the right direction."

TRISTAN BELMONT has always been fascinated with arts of many kinds and tries to apply himself to as many as he can. From writing stories to acting on stage in local theater productions, he loves bringing stories and art as a whole to life. Whenever he's not doing so, you can find him at your local coffee house, thinking about the next tale he wishes to bring to life.

Letter to our Readers

Dear Readers,

Thanks for purchasing this book. We hope you enjoyed, *Return to Effham Falls: Tales of Lost Souls*.   You can learn more about Moorhead Friends Writing Group on their website. https://moorheadfriendswritinggroup.com/

Please leave a review wherever you purchased this title. It will help other readers find us.

You can find our other Anthologies; *Tales from the Frozen North, Welcome to Effham Falls: Tales of a Small Town,* and *Tales from the Water's Edge* wherever you purchase your books.